The Diamond Bearers' Rising

The Unaltered Series: Book Six

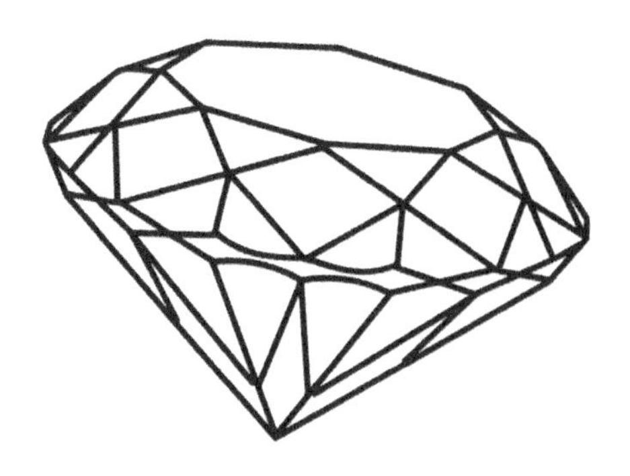

Lorena Angell

Lorena@lorenaangell.com

or

Fantasy Books Publishing, LLC
3242 NE 3rd Ave. #116
Camas, WA 98607

ISBN 10: 0-9989731-2-2
ISBN 13: 978-0-9989731-2-8

Cover art by Creative Alchemy Inc. and CC Covers

License Notes

For more titles by Lorena Angell visit
LorenaAngell.com

SPECIAL THANKS

To Mom and Dad, for sharing your creativity and for teaching me how to persevere. Oh, and sorry for blowing up the microwave when I was eight.

Thank You to my Patreon supporters:

Richard Baxter, Linda Baxter, Jeremy Baxter, Carolyn Collette, Jeanie Filter, Tiffany McClaskey, Kim Snyder, and Manuel Villaveces.

Contents

Chapter One - New Year's Resolutions 1
Chapter Two - The Gathering 21
Chapter Three - Repeating With Police 44
Chapter Four – China 68
Chapter Five – Confusion 96
Chapter Six - Clara's Apprentice 115
Chapter Seven - The Surrendering 132
Chapter Eight - Changing of the Guard 155
Chapter Nine - Brand on a Mission 171
Chapter Ten – Norway 193
Chapter Eleven - Clan Meeting Woes 214
Chapter Twelve - Bullseye on his Back 235
Chapter Thirteen - Birthday Surprises 255
Chapter Fourteen - The Backup Guy 279
Chapter Fifteen - The Bureau 297

Chapter One - New Year's Resolutions

Am I really virtually indestructible as Crimson and Maetha said? Is that even possible?

The revelation Maetha and Crimson gave me earlier tonight has dug a deep hole in my mind, swallowing everything else. Well, almost. Nothing can overpower the irrepressible memory of being in Chris's arms just a little while ago. Once my body healed, I healed his—an intimate, all-consuming process. A warm flutter fills my stomach followed by a quick shiver as I remember his exciting touch.

"Are you cold?" Chris asks, walking into the living room from the kitchen with two mugs of cocoa.

"A little." I don't want to admit what really caused my shiver.

He sets the mugs down on the coffee table in front of me and walks over to the fireplace. I admire his shape and the perfect way his body fills out his relaxed jeans. As he pulls the screen away and checks the flue, I observe his strong back and well-defined trapezius and lattisimus dorsi muscles through his snug-fitting tee shirt. I smile at my knowledge of the muscles' names, something I learned in one of my college anatomy classes.

"I'm going to build a fire for us."

"Is there any wood?" I ask.

"My dad always stocked more wood than he could burn in one winter. I'm sure there's a pile out back. This is Denver, you know."

"Yeah, I know. The run here from the mall was freezing." A sudden realization hits me and I become a little distressed. "Chris, Marketa drove your car to the mall. It's still there. I think she had the keys in her pocket, but she's gone . . . "

Chris comes over and kneels in front of me. He takes both my hands. "Hey, don't worry about it. I have an extra set of keys." Looking down at our connected hands, he says, "You *are* cold." He lets go and grabs the blanket off the back of the couch and wraps me snuggly. Then he hands me a mug of cocoa. "This will warm you up. I'll be back in a minute."

He leaves the room, and soon I hear the back door open and close.

I sip on the delicious hot drink and clear my mind. I think about the concept of being virtually indestructible. How would I be able to know for sure? Tonight would have gone a lot better if I'd been tougher. Then again, maybe not. Crimson thought I'd be able to heal myself almost instantly if I was shot with a regular bullet. Of course, this one was made of obsidian, so that experiment went out the window. Am I going to have to be shot with a bullet to find out if I can heal myself quickly? I healed my burn once when I made tea. The rose thorn scratch didn't tear my skin, or if it did I healed instantly. But a teensy, tiny, bit of that black rock gets in me and I'm rendered helpless. I need to ask if I can have one of the Healer quartz from General Harding's compound on my body at all times. I already know a charged topaz isn't strong enough to heal major problems like when I had an enflamed appendix, and since the Healer quartz doesn't deplete like a topaz does, it would seem to be a good solution.

Tomorrow, New Year's Day, the other Bearers will learn of Marketa's death at the Diamond Bearer gathering. I'm still in shock over the whole incident. The more I think about it the more I remember. I'd rather not. I have to wonder if Marketa's reluctance to accept younger Bearers could have been worked through eventually. How am I going to get the older Bearers to accept us? To accept me and what I've been chosen to do?

I take another sip of my cocoa and consider that most of the Bearers are still in the dark about the upcoming Elemental blast that will hit Portland, Oregon in twenty months. Chris and I have only met with Jie Wen, Chuang, Kookju, Ruth, and Marketa. The rest of the Bearers still need to be told. I sure hope things go better than at the first meeting.

My mind shifts gears to the running list of dissident Bearers. Marketa wasn't a suspect in the first place on my list. Her mental communications were kept clean and positive, keeping her off my radar. Perhaps Jie Wen, Yeok Choo, Kookju, or Chuang doesn't belong on the list. Or maybe I'm wrong entirely. Perhaps I should suspect Fabian, Ruth, Aernoud, or any of the others, too.

The topic of capturing the Elemental blast in a diamond floats through my head. Apparently I'm supposed to be strong enough to withstand the radiation from the blast so a diamond can be charged with the power. The whole concept is confusing. No other cosmic ray has caused problems like this. Why this one?

I drink more of my cocoa.

Chris comes into the room carrying an armful of various sized logs and kindling. He's wearing an oversized winter coat and large boots that I assume were his father's. I have to wonder how he's coping with the loss of his father. Or rather, has he coped yet? I think I already know the answer to that.

He bends down, gently dumping the wood onto the rock hearth in front of the metal grate. "It's chilly out there. The thermometer said seventeen degrees."

"Fahrenheit?"

"Yeah. It's silly for us *not* to have a fire. The power bill will be astronomical otherwise." He piles the smallest pieces of kindling on the bottom and lights them with a long lighter. I'm surprised he's concerned about saving money for the Bearers. After he signed the house away for the use of the Bearers, he also parted with the responsibilities associated with maintenance. His frugality is kind of endearing, honestly.

The tinder crackles and pops as it ignites and burns. Chris carefully places bigger pieces on top and nurtures the growing fire. Then he stands, sheds the coat and boots, and puts them aside. He bends down again and tends to the fire.

Feeling the desire to be closer to him, near his warmth, I set my cocoa down and grab the nearby accent pillows off the couch. With the blanket still draped around my shoulders, I shimmy down by Chris. I say, "You've built a wonderful, warm fire."

"Thanks." He meets my gaze. His eyes hold heat of a different kind.

"What a good idea, Chris," Maetha says, entering the living room. "A romantic New Year's Eve fire."

I roll my eyes at the interruption and Chris smiles.

Crimson follows her and adds, "I find it interesting, Maetha, you refer to the fire as a mood setter and not a life-sustaining element. Fire is everything. A basic elemental ingredient to support life. Without it, humans couldn't live in extreme cold locations, cook food, or illuminate darkness to extend daily activities."

Maetha nods. "Yes, but in this day and age, with electricity and natural gas heating homes, the fireplace becomes a mood setter and alternative heat source."

Crimson nods. "Much has changed over the course of my existence, that's for certain. I remember when fires were positioned in the center of the floor, with the smoke filling the room. The invention of chimneys didn't come about till less than one-thousand years ago."

Chris clears his throat and says, "This is all really fascinating, but could Calli and I enjoy the warmth of this romantic fire without the history lesson?"

"My apologies," Crimson says. "We'll retire for the night to give you privacy." She walks over and places a hand on each of our heads and says, "No one will be able to hear you." The glittering blue mist of magical concealment encircles us. Then she leaves the room.

"Good night," Maetha says, giving us a quick nod. She turns off the remaining lights and exits.

Chris and I are left alone in the living room. For a brief second, the only sounds are the sizzling crackles of the burning logs. Chris pokes at the fire to reposition the flame for better efficiency. When he's finished, he sits beside me.

Breaking the silence, I say, "You know, I kind of like hearing what those two know about the past. They've lived it. They've experienced so many changes to normal life." I rotate on my pillow and face him. "Maybe someday in the distant future we'll tell our descendants about how we once used fire as a mood setter."

"Yeah. By that time they'll say, 'You actually got to light a fire?' "

I laugh and reach out and rest my hand on his thigh. His eyes drop to my hand, then travel slowly back up to my eyes. He lowers his voice and says, "I love to hear you laugh. It's something I didn't know if I'd ever hear again."

"What do you mean?"

He wraps his arm around my shoulders, pulling me

next to him. "When Crimson was trying to heal you and you passed out, I thought you might die. Well, actually, Maetha gave that impression because of how upset she became that you were injured in the first place. She said Crimson would not be able to heal you and she didn't know if we'd get there in time. I couldn't imagine what life would be like without you."

I sense his anxiousness and want to soothe his fears. "Everything worked out in the end."

"Sure, you can say that now. But it doesn't fix the way I still feel."

I wrap my arm around his back and turn into his hug. He lays his cheek on top of my head and rubs his hands up and down my back. I ask, "Have you thought about what you're going to set for your New Year's resolutions?"

He raises his head and cups the back of mine, gently massaging my hair. In all seriousness he says, "I want to catch that S.O.B Max Corvus. I can't believe he shot you."

"He wasn't trying to kill me, though."

"That doesn't matter. The obsidian made you powerless and Marketa was able to hurt you. If he hadn't shot you, you would have been able to defend yourself."

"You're forgetting that Crimson told me to let everything happen. Besides, if things hadn't played out the way they did, you and I wouldn't have the strong connection we now have."

"True. But it still makes me mad."

I go in for the hug again. I love being so close to his body and heartbeat.

He asks, "What's your New Year's resolution?"

"I want to find out if I'm really indestructible."

He pulls away this time. "What? What if you're not?"

"That's why I need to find out."

"But Calli," his words are slow and deliberate, "what if

you're not?"

"Well, I'm not going to purposefully put myself in a life or death situation, Chris. I just want to experiment a little to see if I'm injured or if I'm able to heal quickly."

"Okay, that sounds better." He relaxes and I settle my head against his shoulder. He says, "This year I definitely want to find more time to be with each other. Things are pretty hectic, but I think we can find the time to connect."

"I'd like that."

"I already know Crimson is sending me back to continue working at the Pentagon."

"Do you think you'll ever get to not be a spy?"

"This coming from the girl who will never have a normal life again," he jokes, then his body goes rigid and he pulls back. "I'm sorry, Calli. I didn't mean to upset you."

Why is he apologizing? I haven't even reacted to his statement yet. Chris *has* to be repeating, I just know it. But I don't know how he's doing it. Instead of voicing my suspicions, I say, "Normal life has flown out the window for both of us."

He smiles. "We'll just have to make a new normal." He drops his hold on me and tends to the fire, putting on another log.

"How do you think the Diamond Bearers will react when they hear about Marketa's death?"

"I suppose they'll be frightened. Think about it. In the last four months, Freedom, Neema, Rolf, Hasan, and now Marketa have died. These immortals who have survived centuries and millennias are now able to be killed. That's got to freak them out."

I nod. "Well, learning Crimson has had the ability to remove diamonds all along is disturbing to me. Maetha didn't even know. No one else knows this except us."

"Crimson is definitely a mystery."

"Chris, Max was about to post about Jonas and me. I saw the post. He would have stated both our names. Imagine the consequences. Jonas' mother thinks he's dead and buried. If she ever found out he's not—"

"She'd probably be very happy."

"I don't know about that. She wouldn't be able to have him come home. She'd have to keep the secret he's alive for the rest of her life or risk him being sent to jail for faking his death. It's for the best, I suppose. Jonas was going to die from cancer, that's for sure. I feel sorry for him."

"Do we really need to spend our evening talking about Jonas?" Chris moves into my space and nuzzles my neck. I tilt my head to the side and close my eyes, completely delighted by his touch.

"Are you jealous of him?"

He pulls away and stares me down with intensity. The blue mist reflects off his blue eyes making them seem to glow. "Should I be?"

I angle my head and lift one eyebrow. "No."

"All right then." He moves to kiss me but I move out of the way. His head drops. Then he takes a deep breath and lets it out slowly. "I'm sorry, Calli. I just feel like tonight should be focused on us. We don't get much time together and if Max hadn't come to Denver today, I wouldn't be here at all, near you."

"You have a point, but you don't need to be jealous of Jonas. Max was here to post about me and Jonas. I was only pointing out how disastrous it might have been."

"What about you? How would that have affected your life?"

"It wouldn't have been good, that's for sure."

He reaches with his hand and cups my cheek, his fingers extending back into my hair. With his thumb, he traces my lips. "I'm relieved the post didn't go up and that you're healed. I just want to be near you tonight and celebrate the countdown to the New Year by your side."

I'm surprised by his smooth response. I haven't seen this side of him before. I say, "Do you remember what you said to me on the plane ride back from Alaska?"

"Which part?"

"The part where you worried we wouldn't be able to have a life together because I'd be off saving the world all the time? Before you became a Bearer as well."

"Yes."

"Well, now you're a Bearer too and together we'll be saving the world."

"Interesting how things work out, isn't it?" He brings his lips to mine and kisses me fervently.

I return the passion and soon we're lying back on the floor. His hands move around on my shoulders and arms and under my back. Flutters, tingles, and lightning bolts race through my body all at once and I become abruptly aware of how exposed we are. Maetha and Crimson could come out of their rooms at any moment and see us.

I break the kiss and say, "It's weird to get close when either one of them could walk out at any second." I nod in the direction of the hallway. "I'm not comfortable with that."

"I don't think they would make a big deal about it. We're both adults, clearly in love."

"But I'm not okay."

His hands freeze and he sits up, pulling me up too. "We don't have to do anything that makes you uncomfortable." He stands and helps me up off the floor. "Let's sit on the couch and drink our cocoa before it cools down too much."

I nod and take my place on the couch.

"Too late, the cocoa is already cold. I'll go warm it up." He takes both cups into the kitchen, breaking our blue mist of privacy. Chris and I will have to make sure we don't discuss the happenings of tonight now that other Bearers could hear us if they wanted to.

Chris brings the warmed drinks in and together we sit and sip, watching the dancing fire flutter along the logs. Chris's earlier passion feels muted and I worry I've upset him. He's not acting put out, but I still worry.

"Calli, look at the clock. It's almost midnight."

Together we watch the second hand slowly climb to the twelve. I turn to him and say, "Happy New Year, Chris."

He takes my drink and sets it down next to his, then cups my cheeks with his hands and kisses me. "Happy New Year, Calli."

We linger in the living room for a little while longer, cuddled in each other's space and enjoying our time together. Then Chris walks me to my bedroom.

"Goodnight, Calli." He kisses me again and then walks away.

I'm left standing in my doorway thinking about our earlier passionate display and wondering when everything fizzled. I guess it was when I voiced concern over being exposed in the living room. I didn't mean we couldn't remain together and enjoy each other's company. Chris must have taken it that way. Oh well, it's probably for the best at this time. I close my door and get ready for bed.

I awake with a jolt, having just seen several disturbing images in a dream. Was it a dream or a vision? I can't tell. I was positioned on the roof of a tall building looking down at the streets and sidewalks. Many people of all ages were crying out in pain. Some were already dead. I ran down the stairs at Runner's speed and frantically tried to heal as many people as possible, but as soon as I healed one, more became ill. Others died before I could get to them. There were so many affected people. Too many.

Even though I'm awake, my heart still races and beads of sweat cover my forehead. The overwhelming situation in the dream/vision is a reminder of what I'm up against. I make a mental note to make sure we have plenty of Healers in Portland when the Elemental cosmic blast hits.

I check the clock on my nightstand: 2:30 a.m. I roll over and focus on my healing power to calm my body, so I can get back to sleep.

My eyes pop open and I turn my head to the window. Daylight illuminates the drapes. I get up and pull the drapes open. A thick layer of clouds blocks the sun. A man bundled in a winter coat, scarf, gloves, and a hat stands beside his car, scraping the heavy layer of frost off his windshield. Exhaust smoke drifts lazily through the air. I wonder fleetingly what kind of life he lives. What is his profession? What circumstances led him to live here a mile above sea level? I enter his mind and find he's a nurse and is presently worried about being late for work. He overslept after over-partying last night.

At least his evening was a party. I bet he didn't have any idea what was going on across the road.

I get dressed and put on my lucky necklace Uncle Don gave me.

Walking out into the living room, I find Maetha sitting on the couch with a laptop computer and headphones. She has a plate of cut-up vegetables and fruits on the side table. Chris is bent down in front of the fireplace, adding a log to the fire. He stands and greets me.

"Good morning. Sleep well?"

"More or less." I walk over and give him a hug. "Thanks for a wonderful evening last night."

"No problem."

"What's for breakfast?"

"Crimson food." He points to Maetha's plate. Then lowers his voice and says, "I could really go for a breakfast sandwich or a whole stack of hotcakes. This whole 'Unaltered' thing has increased my appetite. Come on." He takes me by the hand and we walk into the kitchen.

Crimson greets us and we dish up some fruit and nuts and take our plates out to the dining room table. Before we can sit down, Brand and Beth arrive.

Brand walks directly to me and gives me a big hug, saying, "I'm so glad Max didn't post about you yesterday. That would have been horrible."

I pull back, but still embraced. "For Jonas, too."

"Well, yeah. So, what ended up happening?"

Chris clears his throat, pulling my attention to the fact Brand and I are still in a half-hug. We let go of each other and take a step back. Brand puts his arm around Beth's shoulders.

I say, "Max shot me."

"What?" Brand and Beth exclaim together.

Crimson walks out of the kitchen holding her plate of food. "We will discuss what happened when the rest of the Bearers get here at noon. Understood?" Her statement is more of an order and not a question.

We nod our heads.

Crimson crosses the room to Maetha.

I say to Beth and Brand, "Have you two eaten

breakfast? There's some food in the kitchen."

Brand looks at our plates. "That's not breakfast. Maybe there's some real food in the fridge. Come on, Beth." Brand leads her into the kitchen.

Before Beth walks through the door she turns to Chris and me. "Happy New Year.".

"Yeah, you too." I smile. She looks confident and happy today. I don't know that I would be so upbeat following the holidays without my parents.

My thoughts go to my parents. I should call them.

Chris and I sit down. He hands me his phone and says, "Here Calli."

"Did you read my mind?"

"Yeah. Give them a call."

I sit back in my chair and dial their number. I realize I'll need to work more on my mind blocks.

My mother answers. "Hello?"

"Hi, Mom. It's Calli. Happy New Year."

"Allan, it's Calli." My mother's voice sounds frantic as she calls for my father.

I hear the other line pick up and my father says, "Calli?"

"Hi, Dad. Happy New Year."

My mother asks, "Are you all right?" I can tell she's incredibly worried.

"Yes." I wonder at the concern in her voice.

"Are you in Denver?"

"Yes."

She lets out a sigh of relief. "I just got off the phone with Mable. She said you're on the news and you were shot. I tried to call your phone, but I couldn't get through."

"I'm fine, Mom." *I was on the news?*

My father asks with deep concern in his voice, "What happened, Calli?"

"I can't really talk about it over the phone. You understand."

My mother's voice rises, "You're too young to be going through this. I want to talk to Maetha."

"Charlotte," my father says, "let Calli do her job. You don't need to talk to Maetha."

"I want to know why my daughter is being subjected to this kind of danger. She's too young."

"Mom, I'm fine. Honestly. My arm is all healed. I'll come visit you soon and tell you all about it. Maybe by then I'll have an update, too."

"Allan, I think we should hire that bodyguard we talked about."

"What?" I exclaim.

"Charlotte, we'll discuss it later with Calli."

"Mom, you are not hiring me a bodyguard."

Chris's head perks up and he looks at me with a "say what?" kind of expression.

"Besides," I add, "I'd end up protecting the bodyguard. I don't need the added responsibility." Not to mention we're not about to bring in someone who doesn't know anything about this world of powers, abilities, and diamonds. "Look, I've got to go now. I love you both, very much."

"We love you too," my father says.

"I'll talk to you later."

We end our call and I hand the phone back to Chris. My exasperated eyes meet his and all I can do is blink repeatedly and shake my head.

Crimson comes over and sits across from me with her plate of food. She reaches out her two hands, one toward me, one toward Chris. We clasp hands and the secrecy blue mist settles around us. Letting go, she picks up a raw almond and says, "I want you to lead the Bearer gathering,

Calli."

"Me?" *What?* "Why? I mean, wouldn't the news of Marketa's death be better delivered if it came from Maetha?"

"Maetha wasn't here. She only has hearsay to offer."

"I could project my memory to the others," I suggest.

"I don't want everyone knowing I can use telekinetic powers in the presence of obsidian."

"Are you hoping to expose the other dissenters by having me lead the gathering?"

"No. I want you to take charge and let the others know you are more than capable of handling this position."

"What if I don't feel that way myself?"

"But you do feel that way, Calli," she says. "Your conversation with your mother just now proves it. You know you're more than capable of holding your own and you wish she'd be able to see that."

"That was kind of a different topic."

"It's all the same. Remember what I said about not revealing you have the Blue Diamond's powers, and don't lose your cool with the other Bearers." She pauses, then looks beyond me with an unfocused gaze. "The news of Marketa's death will be disturbing to all."

We sit in silence for a few moments, picking at our food, but mostly just pushing it around. The blue mist fades away indicating we should be careful what we say out loud.

Brand and Beth return with their plates. Brand managed to find bread and, from the smell of it, strawberry jelly.

Chris glances at Brand's plate and lets out a whine as he turns his gaze to me. "No fair."

I appreciate his attempt to lighten the somber mood.

Beth's chosen selection of food is consistent with a

Runner's diet.

After Brand and Beth sit down, Crimson says, "Anika will arrive tomorrow."

Brand grunts.

"Do you have something to add?" she asks him.

"No, sorry," he states, slouching forward.

"I think you do. Let's get this settled, shall we. Anika does not grunt when she hears *your* name, Brand. Why do you?"

Brand's cheeks turn red. "I'm not religious. And if I was I wouldn't push it on anyone else."

"You allow yourself to be bothered by her opinions."

Brand waves his hand in front of him. "She firmly believes she's right and everyone else is wrong. And she's always going on about God's will."

Crimson pauses a moment. "I will say this to all four of you. Anika has an important role to fill, one that will save thousands of lives. It is in her ability to feel confident in expressing her religious opinion that will be key. Do not squash her gift."

Brand extends his neck forward. "That's a gift?"

"Yes. It is, Brand. I have yet to hear *you* speak so devotedly about anything important in your life." Crimson turns to Beth. "You chose Anika for your team. Why?

Beth replies matter-of-factly, "She is dependable and honest."

"Exactly. She doesn't try to trick you or play games to get her way. She does what she says she'll do and when she says she'll do it. And she holds firmly to her values. Religion or not, those traits are what make her special and of use in our cause."

Brand looks down at his plate with a blank face.

I ask, "What do you recommend we say to Anika when her ideals clash?"

Crimson looks around the table at each of us before speaking. "Every situation is different. There is no one answer to that question, Calli. But, consider the possibility that the five of you—should you all choose to become Bearers—might be around each other for hundreds or thousands of years and bickering with each other is not going to help you follow nature's will. When Bearers quarrel, humanity suffers. However, communication and calm discussions that allow both parties to fully express themselves help everyone appreciate and understand unique perspectives. Moreover, the choice to become a Bearer comes with it the understanding to put aside your pettiness. That goes for Anika, too."

Maetha comes over to the table. With a grimace, she says, "The bookstore shooting is all over the news. Calli will need to go to the police and clear her name."

I ask, "Are the news reports saying anything about Max or his blog?"

Maetha says, "No. The reports are based on cell phone footage caught at the scene. It's being described as an argument that escalated into a shooting. Basically, there isn't anything else for reporters to scoop right now, so, you've made the headlines."

Brand takes a big bite of his bread, a splotch of jelly sticks to the corner of his mouth. "You're famous, Calli. Can I have your autograph?"

I close my eyes and shake my head. "Splendid! I just got off the police radar."

Crimson adds, "They'll be looking for Marketa, too."

"What about Max?" Beth asks Crimson.

"Him also, of course."

Beth looks around the room and asks, "Where's Marketa?"

Not missing a beat, Maetha points to me and says,

"You'll need to appear wounded. They have footage of you bleeding on the floor. Your shoulder should be bandaged up. They also have witnesses who saw you take the flash drive."

Chris says, "We'd better make a clone of the flash drive in case they want it."

Crimson nods her head. "We'll do that before you go, Calli."

Chris reaches his hand out and covers mine. "I wish I could go with you, Calli, but I can't. We're not supposed to be on speaking terms, let alone friendly or intimate."

"I know, but like I told my mom, I can handle this, Chris."

Crimson wiggles a finger back and forth between Brand and me. "Actually, I want you to take Brand along. He can help you avoid bad situations."

"I could just give her my quartz and she could do it herself," he jests, but I know he's joking.

I roll a grape between my fingers. "I don't know how to use it, Brand. I suppose I'll just have to take you."

Jie Wen's bi-located form appears near Maetha. He addresses Crimson. "I need to speak with you in private."

Crimson nods, gets up from the table, and heads over to him. She walks around his form, leaving blue mist as she privatizes the conversation.

Brand leans in and with raised eyebrows and a big grin says, "So, you and Chris are on intimate terms?"

Beth smacks his shoulder. "That's rude."

I don't give him any attention. My eyes are focused on the fact Maetha has been left out of the blue circle. I hear Beth ask again about Marketa and hear Maetha respond with a terse, "She's not here." Maetha's expression remains unchanged, unaffected as she walks away into the kitchen. I can't help but wonder what she feels right now. I look back at Crimson and Jie Wen and spy on their conversation by reading Jie Wen's lips. His positioning behind Crimson makes it difficult for me to have a consistently clear view of his mouth, but I don't want to move or it might be obvious I'm watching them.

He says, "Doctor and his family . . . informant hasn't checked in . . . remote location. China."

He pauses while Crimson says something, then he continues. "The location . . . near my place." Jie Wen stops, listens to Crimson, then his eyes shift over Crimson's shoulder and connect with mine. His glare turns dark. I can feel his angry frustration as he asks, "Why does she need to be involved? She doesn't know anything about this. I want Brand." Crimson says something else. Jie Wen adds, with his nostrils flaring, "They could be dead in four days!" Jie Wen glares at me a moment, then disappears.

The blue mist dissipates, and Crimson comes back into the kitchen without looking in my direction. I let out my pent-up breath and try to refocus on the upcoming gathering.

Chris's hand covers mine as it lays motionless on the table. He gently squeezes my hand. I look over to him and find he's studying me intensely. "What's going on?" he whispers.

Using mindspeak, I say, *I think I'm going to China.* I intertwine my fingers with his, appreciating his atten-tiveness. His eyes reveal the deep level of concern he has for me.

With Jie Wen? Why?

Someone needs to be rescued. Crimson must have told him she wants me to go. He's not excited about it.

Go figure. When?

Pretty soon.

Well, I'll be leaving as soon as the gathering is over. I need to get back to D.C. by tomorrow.

My heart feels incredibly heavy. Are we ever going to get the chance to grow our relationship?

Chapter Two - The Gathering

The noon hour approaches, the beginning of the gathering is less than ten minutes away. To say I'm nervous would be an understatement. I sit alone at the dining table in deep thought, having sent Chris to get me some water. I'm not thirsty. I just needed a moment alone to listen to my thoughts. Being around Chris has a way of clouding my brain and muddling it with emotions and feelings. Not that that's a bad thing, but right now I need to focus on the task at hand.

I call in my mind to Crimson. *Could I use the obsidian fragments of the bullet Max shot me with to show the others?*

Yes, she answers. A few moments later, she enters the dining room from the hallway, holding the metal First Aid box. She sets the box on the table in front of me. *Do not remove the diamond, Calli.*

"I won't," I reply out loud and wait for her to leave the room before opening the lid. My powers rush out of my body upon exposing the obsidian within. Inside I find the pieces of obsidian bullet Max shot me with, the large non-powerful obsidian chunk that Crimson used to blast Marketa's heart out, Marketa's obsidian piece she had hidden on her belt, and her diamond.

The diamond is clean of the heart muscle and blood. I never felt the strumming sensation, so whoever cleaned it must have kept a large piece of obsidian exposed to nullify the diamond's power. The same way General Harding cleaned off Rolf's diamond.

I run my finger across the edge of the diamond that up

until last night resided within a woman who had been alive I don't know how long. Why did she have to try to kill me, I wonder? I reach inside and pick up one of the larger shards of the obsidian bullet with my thumb and forefinger. It has sharp edges because of the nature of obsidian and how it breaks apart. This small fragment, if it was the only piece in the whole house, would be enough to suck out all my powers. It's amazingly terrifying. I put the piece back and pick up Marketa's belt medallion. I saw her wear this belt day in and day out but never suspected it had a secret weapon.

I close the lid of the box slowly, waiting for the moment when the obsidian is blocked and my powers return. I pay close attention to what I'm feeling even though I've felt it many times before. I know the obsidian is an absorber of powers and once it's blocked or far enough away, my powers no longer get pulled out. The lid clicks closed and I feel the diamond infuse my body with an almost stinging sensation. I take a sharp breath and close my eyes. The Sanguine Diamond seems to continue to emanate powers in the presence of obsidian, it just can't make enough to overpower the obsidian, I conclude.

I look toward the kitchen and find Chris in the doorway, leaning against the frame, arms folded across his chest. One hand holds my glass of water. He has a soft smile and caring eyes, handsome as ever. He pushes off the frame and walks over. "I felt your diamond go dark with obsidian. I came to see what happened but figured you needed some time."

I reach out for the glass of water, feeling suddenly thirsty.

He motions to the box. "So, *it's* in there?"

I set my glass down. "Yes."

"Wow. It's a bit mind-blowing."

"I know." I get up from my seat and grab the cardboard box containing the prisms and charged quartz from the compound. Files and documents are slid in against the side of the containers. The outermost file reads: schematics. I put the box on the floor beside my chair and sit down.

Crimson and Maetha come in and stand behind me near the wall. Beth, and Brand come in from the kitchen and sit down, Brand on my right, and Beth next to Brand. Chris sits on my left.

The bi-located forms of Jonas, Mary, Amenemhet, Ruth, and Amalgada arrive before the others and sit their forms in the remaining chairs at the table. Jonas sits at the opposite end of the table from me. Yeok Choo, Kookju, Jie Wen, Alena, and Chuang materialize and stand along the opposite wall, almost symbolically. Avani, Merlin, Aernoud, Fabian, and Duncan arrive and stand behind the occupied chairs.

With eighteen Diamond Bearers in one room, plus Crimson, I can't help but feel intimidated.

I clear my throat. "Thank you for attending this gathering," I say, glancing around the room, making eye contact with everyone in the room except Maetha and Crimson. "Crimson has asked me to lead this gathering. As you know, we've—"

"Wait," Yeok Choo interrupts. "We can't start yet. Marketa's not here."

I don't know how to respond to her disrespect for my leadership, and I definitely don't want to begin the meeting by disclosing Marketa's betrayal. Some of the other Bearers look around the room, others seem perturbed. Clearly, Marketa didn't share everything she knew about the Blue Diamond's powers because I hear a couple Bearers speak telepathically to each other. However, again, I can't tell who is talking.

Maybe she knew ahead of time the gathering would be led by Calli. I can't blame her for not wanting to attend.

Why are you still here then?

Crimson is here.

I really wish I could tell who's saying these words, but everyone has a blank expression except for Yeok Choo.

Duncan says to Yeok Choo, "You can catch Marketa up when she gets here. Some of us have prior engagements we need to get back to. Let's begin."

I clear my throat again and continue. "We've been tracking Max Corvus as the prime blogger suspect. We recently learned the blogger planned on revealing me and Jonas as Diamond Bearers yesterday, on New Year's Eve. Coincidently, yesterday, Chris learned Max was headed to Denver. Chris and Maetha came as quickly as they could. Marketa and I waited for Max and followed him to a bookstore where he attempted to upload critical information to the blog, thus confirming he *is* the blogger. Marketa and I confronted him at which point he shot me in the shoulder."

Gasps and guffaws are heard around the room. I hear additional rude telepathic conversations between Bearers.

I say, "Max used an obsidian bullet that shattered during the firing process and pelted me with many tiny shards. My diamond powers were canceled, but my wound wasn't life-threatening. Max fled the bookstore after he shot me, leaving behind his laptop. He hadn't finished the post yet, and because he was still logged in, I was able to change his password to block him temporarily. I deleted the post. I also took the flash drive he was using. Marketa brought me back here and began to remove the obsidian pieces from my flesh. She told me she was unhappy with Crimson bringing in the younger generation into the

Bearers group."

She's not the only one.

Mmm hmm.

I speak a little slower and with careful deliberation. "When she removed one particular piece of obsidian, she intentionally cut open a vein and began letting out my blood."

Yeok Choo flails an arm pointed at me. "How dare you accuse her of harming you."

I decide not to address Yeok Choo yet. I continue. "Marketa also admitted to giving Max Corvus information about the clans and Bearers in an effort to frighten the 'kids.' The information was what Max posted to the blog."

Jie Wen stands a little taller and says, "I for one am not going to stay here and listen to these lies."

I'm feeling quite upset that Jie Wen would automatically assume I'm lying. And after the daggers he threw my way earlier when he spoke with Crimson, my confidence is strengthened. I fire back with, "Why would you think I'd lie when you have the power to view the memory in my mind?"

"Because you could be selective in what you allow me to see and paint any picture you want."

"Jie Wen, I'll let you *extract* my memories, so you can get the whole picture, but you have to let me extract yours to see if you were Marketa's partner."

Yeok Choo cries out, "Where is Marketa? She should be here to defend herself."

Crimson steps forward and says with cold finality, "Marketa is dead."

"Whaaat?" Yeok Choo's eyes widen and her skin pales further.

Everyone else, except for Chris, Maetha and Crimson, shift around in their seats, heads looking side to side, murmurs and whispers fill the air.

Crimson picks up the First Aid box and opens it. My powers rush out again and all of the bi-located Bearers disappear. Crimson pulls out Marketa's heart and closes the lid, separating the diamond and obsidian for the first time. My powers re-infuse my body and I experience the strumming sensation of a diamond without an owner.

Brand and Beth's mouths hang open in shock. One by one the other Bearers reappear once they can connect with my diamond.

Yeok Choo falls to her knees and wails. "Marketa!"

Aernoud asks, visibly shaken by the revelation, "How did this happen? How was her heart removed?"

Crimson answers him. "I will not be telling you how, but I will say why, Aernoud. Marketa dissented from her position as a Bearer even after Calli gave her the chance to renew her allegiance. A chance offered by Calli while Marketa was trying to kill her, mind you. If anyone in this room sympathized with Marketa and worked together to thwart my plans, then you need to rethink where your loyalties lie, or hand over your diamond. I will not tolerate any Bearer to be against me." The room is completely silent. No one even thinks aloud. "There is no room for dissention now, all Bearers must unite, or you'll be wiped out in the future. Failure to work together will result in Marketa's fate, and your diamond will be the next one in a box."

Merlin asks, "May I ask how exactly Marketa dissented?"

Crimson says, "As Calli already said, Marketa believed I'd gone mad by bringing in youngsters. She fed vital information about the Diamond Bearers to Max Corvus and orchestrated the meet up yesterday with the intention of having Calli mortally wounded with obsidian. She'd look like she did everything she could to save young, inexperienced Calli. Know this: the younger generation already knows more about this world than any of you could ever hope, and in this age, it is *their* word that holds power."

She steps closer to my side and places a hand on my shoulder. "Calli has more to report. Continue." She moves back beside Maetha.

I take a breath, trying to consider what I should say next. "Having been brought down by an obsidian bullet, I worry about all the Bearers being targeted. We will need to investigate these obsidian bullets further."

Kookju cuts in, "Why didn't you two run when you detected obsidian?"

"Marketa didn't worry about it and I trusted her judgment. She said we had our running topaz, so we'd be able to flee if we needed to. I believed her, not realizing she knew I'd be shot."

Jonas raises a hand. I nod at him to speak. "I tracked Max through the airlines. He boarded a flight bound for London. I called the authorities over there to alert them to his presence on an inbound flight, but because he doesn't have a criminal record, they said they couldn't detain him. Mary has some contacts in London, so we sent them there to meet him. Unfortunately, Max was able to slip past."

"He's there already?" I ask.

"Yeah. He caught a sixteen-hour flight out of Denver. He arrived a couple hours ago. We'll just have to wait till he resurfaces again. Hopefully it won't be through another blog."

"Thanks, Jonas. I'll have Max's flash drive delivered to you. Maybe you can find something identifying where he might be." I pause, then say to the group, "Something else we need to discuss is an upcoming threat. As some of you already know, coming in twenty months is a cosmic blast that will hit the city of Portland, Oregon. Crimson has foreseen the blast and the power it will bring."

Duncan says, "Which power?"

"A new one that gives the affected control over the elements of nature, to some extent. I've been assigned to lead the efforts to reduce casualties through prior preparation. I believe it's imperative the city is evacuated before the radiation hits. Special attention needs to be focused on pregnant women. They need to be relocated far away from the blast. To accomplish this, I need help from all of you. I will also need to call upon the clans to help teach those affected how to follow nature's will."

Jie Wen arrogantly states the obvious. "How do you expect to evacuate an entire city?"

"I don't know yet, but there must be a way."

Amenemhet says, "Diamond Bearers haven't ever successfully evacuated an entire city before. Most of us remember how disastrous our attempts were with Pompeii. No one would listen to us, and people back then were more accepting of cosmic powers and magical gifts."

Jie Wen nods his head. "Evacuating a city is a fool's idea."

She's so naïve

I don't think I want to be a Bearer anymore, not if she's going to lead us into ridiculous situations.

Let the blast hit and clean up later.

The three dissidents speak to each other's minds. I try not to stare or lead them to believe I can hear them, so I move my eyes methodically from one Bearer to another.

Avani says, "You say we have roughly a year and a half? That's plenty of time to figure out a way to evacuate."

Fabian joins in. "How do you expect to convince citizens to walk away from their jobs? And for how long?"

His tone is inquisitive not skeptical.

Alena jumps in, "I can't see any future containing this information."

"What about medical workers, patients, and law enforcement? Are they to evacuate as well?" Fabian adds.

"You don't have enough experience to lead an endeavor such as this," Chuang points out.

I focus on Chuang. "Are you wondering why Crimson would choose me over you?"

"Is this a test, Crimson?" Chuang directs his words to her. "Is there really going to be a blast?"

I pause for Crimson to answer. She doesn't, at least not to my knowledge.

A few other Bearers argue across the table, leaving me feeling like I've lost control over the meeting.

Beth slaps her palms on the table, startling everyone, getting their attention. "I can't believe any of you would doubt Calli's ability to do this. Have you forgotten everything she has accomplished in her short time as a Diamond Bearer? Crimson chose her for a reason. Are you seriously going to doubt Crimson?"

Alena says, "Why can't I view the future of this blast?"

Ruth asks, "Is it hidden from us?"

Crimson responds, "You can't see cosmic blasts; therefore you can't foresee the event happening. And, until you decide to support Calli and help with this project, your future sight on the matter will be limited."

"How so?" Chuang asks. "We were able to foresee Pompeii's destruction."

"That was literal destruction. Portland won't be buried under ash and pumice. If you're looking for the future of Portland, all you'll find is a city intact. The blast won't hurt the environment, which is the future sight you'd be able to detect."

"How are you able to foresee it?"

"The Primal Stone grants me the ability to see cosmic energy. Unless you know someone personally from Portland and look into their future, you'd have to travel there and read random people's future to see if they'll be affected."

The tension in the room calms down, but it does nothing to soothe the adrenaline flowing through my veins. I continue. "We need to unite the U.S. clans."

Duncan asks, "How?"

I reach down to the box and pull out two containers, one of quartz crystals and one of prisms. "With these quartz crystals and prisms."

Most of the Bearers move in for a closer inspection of the quartz. Yeok Choo, Jie Wen, and Chuang remain distanced.

Avani asks, "Is there a difference between the rock crystals and the prisms?"

"Yes," I say. "Both types of quartz were used in General Harding's government compound in conjunction with the power-removing machine. The rock crystals hold a single power. The prisms hold multiple powers." I stop and think about revealing the fact that each prism contains Repeating power. Then I check my own future for obvious consequences of divulging the sensitive information. I see a conversation with Crimson where she's furious because the prisms have been stolen. I return my attention to the gathering and say, "The multiple powers are weak, on the level of regular cosmic powers. However, to a clan member, these prisms would be similar to the diamond amulet without the deadly aspect."

Amalgada points to the quartz. "Why is there a difference between the two? And how were they infused with power?"

Kookju waves an arm wildly, cutting in before anyone can answer Amalgada. "Maetha, why was the fact that these stones have powers kept quiet? What else are you keeping from us?"

I look over my shoulder at Maetha to see if she's going to speak. She only nods her head in my direction. My stomach feels like a bag of rocks. My feet tangle at the ankles under the table.

Chris's voice enters my mind. *You can do this, Calli.*

I swallow hard and look at Kookju and then to Amalgada. "The stones were being studied to determine their power levels before sharing the results." My statement is kind of true. I sit a little taller and wrap my ankles around the legs of the chair to stop them from fidgeting. "The machine that harvested the powers and deposited them into these crystals has been dismantled. Here are the schematics we were able to get." I pull the paper schematics for Freedom's power-removing machine out of the box and lay them on the table. "Freedom's knowledge gave General Harding the ability to not only strip away power, but to also infuse it into a quartz crystal. These prisms were recovered from the machine. They seemed to be a power source, and due to the," *—I hope I pronounce this right—* "piezoelectric properties of quartz, that's probably true. The question is where did Freedom learn this type of technology?"

I pause and look directly at Kookju. "To answer your question about the secrecy of these stones, until it is determined Marketa worked alone, everyone can expect sensitive information being kept secret."

An awkward silence settles around the room. I say, "I think we've covered the topics of this gathering. If anyone has any thoughts to help with the upcoming evacuation or have any other questions, feel free to contact me. As we near the date of the cosmic blast, I'll give assignments to everyone. All right, I believe we're finished."

Jie Wen, Kookju, and Chuang disappear at once. Some of the other Bearers end their connections soon after. Yeok Choo remains, still distraught over Marketa's death. Maetha approaches Yeok Choo and talks quietly with her.

I glance at Chris who has a satisfied smile on his face. *You did great, Calli.* He stands and walks over to Crimson. Warmth radiates throughout my body from his approval. His reassurance during the gathering was much appreciated and gave me the courage to be strong.

Yeok Choo sobs. "She was my friend. I didn't know she was planning to betray Calli. I didn't get to say goodbye . . . and she didn't get to have a Surrendering."

A Surrendering?

I make myself look busy by scooping up the schematics from the table. I'm about to put them back in the box when I see something on the drawings I never noticed before. On the diagram, the location where the prisms were found shows two rows of seven slots. I count again, thinking I've made a mistake. Chris and I collected twelve prisms, yet according to the paper, there should have been fourteen. Two prisms might be missing. Who would have them? One of the guards? Max?

Brand and Beth are still sitting at the table and talk in low voices to each other. Without looking up from the paper, I listen to their conversation.

Beth says, "My brother is in good hands with Clara. She's a Spellcaster."

"You mean a witch, don't you?"

"No. Clara follows nature's will. Witches don't."

Brand laughs. "What's the difference?"

Beth's ire elevates. "There's a big difference, Brand."

"I'm sorry, Beth," Brand says with a completely different tone. "I want to learn more. Will you teach me?"

I look at Beth, thinking I'll see anger in her eyes. Instead, I find a soft expression. Brand's charm has won out again. He must have repeated to get . . . wait a second, he *repeated*!

My eyes instantly seek out Chris. He and Crimson are holding a telepathic conversation. I can't even read their lips to see what they're talking about. I can only assume they are talking about me. Why else would they communicate in this manner? I try to scan Chris's body for the prism but find nothing.

Chris walks from Crimson into the kitchen. Crimson makes eye contact with me and speaks to my mind. *We still have dissenters, Calli.*

I bring my focus away from Chris and back to the situation. *Do you know who they are and are they a threat like Marketa?*

I don't think anyone will try to harm you now. You must focus on uniting the Bearers in this common cause. They may not all like you or approve of you, but they can still perform their duties as Bearers.

Okay. Uh, Crimson, may I ask you a question?

Of course.

I noticed there's fourteen slots pictured in the schematics for prisms. Why are there only twelve prisms?

Crimson doesn't answer. Instead she walks over to me and puts a hand on my arm. "Call Chris so we can discuss this."

Yep, that's what I suspected. I mentally connect with Chris and ask him to come talk with us. He comes out of the kitchen popping a couple cashews into his mouth. "What's up?" he asks.

"Let's go sit on the couch and talk," Crimson says.

I get up from my chair and walk with Chris to the

living room area and take a seat on the couch. Chris sits beside me. My mind races with questions and memories of when he must have repeated. I knew he was. He never said he wasn't, but he deflected the questions. I want to know why.

Crimson pulls a small chair next to the coffee table and takes us both by the hand. The blue mist surrounds us. She drops the hold on our hands and says, "Calli noticed there are fourteen slots on the machine's schematics." Chris's head turns abruptly to me, eyes wide. He swallows hard, then drops his chin to his chest. Crimson adds, "She wants to know why only twelve prisms were pulled."

Chris swallows again and turns his body to me, pulling one of his legs under him. He reaches for my hand, takes it in his, and looks me in the eye. "I held back two of the prisms when we located them in the machine."

Struggling to keep a calm demeanor, I say, "We only removed twelve."

"I had already pulled out two before you started helping me."

I pull my hand away from his. "Why?"

He wiggles a little in his spot. "Well, actually, the first time around, I didn't keep two. When I almost tripped over my dad's boots, and I was still holding half of the prisms, I had a moment of regret, regret for not watching where I was going. That was enough to send me back ten seconds. I decided I'd keep two crystals that time. You were looking elsewhere, so after repeating, I put two in my other hand and gave you the remaining ones."

I am flustered. "Why two?"

"I figured I'd give one to you later on."

"But you never did. So why the secrecy?"

He leans a little toward me and continues. "I didn't tell you because I saw an opportunity to be able to communicate better and I took it."

"Huh?"

"Calli, I've been on edge around you since you rescued me from Justin's hideout. I seem to screw up everything I say to you. But with the prism, I found I could undo my idiotic words. Plus, I was about to meet with Agent Whitman and I wanted to feel confident. At that time, I wasn't going to keep the prisms a secret, but . . . " His head drops again.

"But what?" I press.

Crimson answers. "Once he told me about the prisms, I instructed him to keep one and give the other to me. I ordered him to keep everything secret until further notice."

I shake my head to keep the tears behind my eyes. "Have you both been repeating with me?" Neither answers. "I don't like that you made Chris keep a secret from me."

"You have the right to be upset, Calli. I've been keeping my eye on the long-range future of humanity and lost sight of the present. You should know, though, Chris asked several times if you could have a prism, too. I said no. Every time I look ahead with you holding one, the future is negative. I don't know why. I know you wouldn't abuse the ability to repeat, but somewhere along the line things will turn sour if you get a prism . . . at this point, anyway."

I don't know what to say. A sudden nausea wave hits me and I press a hand on my stomach. "Is that why you took the prisms from me after visiting Uncle Don?"

"Yes."

"But why have you let me be in close contact with the bundle of prisms since then?"

"You've never shown any desire to possess anything unless offered to you. I knew they'd be safe."

Chris asks, his voice quiet, "Are you mad at me, Calli?"

I turn to him, feeling frustrated, but understanding that he only did this under Crimson's request. "No. I'm not happy with the situation, though."

Chris lets out a breath of air. He cautiously responds, "I don't blame you. It's really hard to use the repeating power. With only ten seconds of a window, you'd be surprised how quickly that time passes and then you can't undo something. I have a new admiration and respect for Brand. He is a true superhero; just don't ever tell him I said so."

Crimson nods. "I share your respect for Brand. I wished I had a better understanding of how to use the power when Marketa was working on you, taking out the shards. One second the future showed everything was going to be fine, eleven seconds later you were probably going to die. I couldn't undo the moment to where you'd be all right."

"Is that why you let me get shot at the bookstore?"

"Yes. I could still view a future where you would be fine. The same scenario happened when Marketa was removing the obsidian. But then in the blink of an eye you were going to die. I stepped in, almost too late." She pauses, clears her throat, then continues. "When I flew you to Tennessee, I used the power to determine how fast I could fly without causing you too much discomfort. I pushed the boundary over and over again, knowing we had limited time to get your name cleared before Max showed up." Crimson pauses, her focus pulled away. She stands and says, "Would you excuse me?" She leaves the blue mist circle.

I'm left with Chris, wondering how to best say what's on my mind.

Chris is still facing me. He says, "You probably already know most of the times I used the repeating power on you."

I say, "I don't think you realize exactly how much time I've spent with Brand. I spotted a few identifying Repeater moves, times when your behavior or tone of voice changed from one word to another."

"I wanted everything to be perfect with you."

I turn my body to him. "Why? We've been over this before, Chris. No relationship is perfect."

"I guess I didn't want you to run you off like what happened with my other girlfriends."

"Didn't they leave you because you wouldn't open up?"

"Yes, among things."

"You had to keep the secret you were a double agent and that didn't leave room for relationships."

"Exactly."

"But Chris, I know all about your past and your father. Why do you still worry I'll run off like the others?"

"I don't know. I guess I worry I won't be good enough for you. You know, Calli, after I survived having my power removed and I became Unaltered I put two and two together and realized I could possibly be your equal. Frankly, it scared me to death."

"You were feeling that at your father's compound? I couldn't tell."

"Yeah, well, that's part of my well-disciplined outer demeanor. I'm trained to hide my true feelings. Another reason relationships don't work out for me. And, another excuse to hang on to the prisms."

"Chris, I need you to be honest with me. I understand Crimson made you keep the secret after a while, but in the beginning, you chose not to tell me *you* kept two prisms. Why?"

"There wasn't time to run that by you, Calli. The

authorities were on their way."

I rub my temples. "All the more reason to tell me. Instead you had me standing by in case you needed me to control minds. Come to think of it, that was probably just in case you couldn't handle the repeating power."

"Calli—"

I put my hand up. "What bothers me is you and I were alone. You had enough time to realize the prism had repeating power and didn't tell me. Instead, you made a snap decision, one that can't be blamed on Crimson."

He moves back a little. His face tightens. "What can I say other than my brainwashing runs deep."

Memories start flooding into my mind. "Then, in Denver you and Crimson put on an act when Beth discovered the prisms had repeating power. "I feel like a fool."

"Come on, Calli," Chris says. I can tell he's worried. His tone of voice is calming, making me wonder if he's trying a line on me. Is he repeating now?

I stop rubbing my head and look directly at him. "Do you have a prism on you?"

"No. That's probably why we're fighting."

"This isn't fighting. We're communicating. I want you to feel you can talk to me about anything, that you can share your innermost worries and concerns. If you already felt that way, you wouldn't have wanted to keep the two prisms a secret."

He takes a deep breath, lets it out, and pulls his brows together. "So, let me get this straight. You'd rather see the real me, my real fears and frustrations?"

"Yes."

"Okay." He scoots to the edge of the cushion and leans toward me. A look of boldness flashes across his face. "This is me not repeating. I've seen the way you act around

Brand. I totally understand how much time you've spent with him. You have inside jokes. He knows what you're going to say, and that upsets me. I've tried to hide my frustration, my worry, but deep down I know I can't compare to the relationship you have with him."

"You're right, Chris. I am comfortable around Brand, but not in a way you should be worried about."

"The same way you didn't worry when you saw me with Kikee?"

"I was jealous. Then you reassured me I didn't need to be jealous and I trusted you. So, I dismissed it."

He pauses, and I look across the room at Brand. He's talking to Maetha. As I watch, Jonas bi-locates to Maetha. Jonas looks my direction and makes eye contact. He smiles and nods.

Chris must have noticed his arrival as well. He says, "Okay, what about Jonas?"

"Huh?"

"How about the way he looks at you?"

"That's not my fault."

"I was there when you thought Jonas was dying."

"He *was* dying."

"Yeah. And you were more concerned with his wellbeing than with the knowledge you got by seeing my vision of us. Do you know how that made me feel?"

"No. I'm sorry. He was dying."

"Well, there he is. He miraculously made it."

"Not by my hand. Maetha saved him. I don't have a relationship with him, Chris."

"You've been inside his mind and he in yours. You definitely have a relationship with him."

"Because of the shared diamond, not because I wanted to be in his mind. Big difference, Chris. I think you're being overly paranoid."

"Paranoid? Do you want to know the real reason Maetha saved Jonas?"

"She was trying to figure out how to heal DNA and it finally worked with Jonas."

"No. He's the backup guy, Calli."

I cough. My voice shakes as I answer. "What?"

"He's here in case you and I don't work. You have to have someone to save for all this to work out. If you and I don't work, someone else needs to be in place."

"I don't . . . what makes you think . . . "

"Crimson told me. When Maetha foresaw the events with the Death Clan, there were two possible love interests: me and Jonas."

Why would Crimson tell Chris something like that? Unless she could see the possibility of us not working out.

Chris continues. "You were so drawn to Jonas, attempting to heal his cancer, feeling like he shouldn't die at that time."

My mind replays how I wanted to heal Jonas once I learned I actually could with Maetha's help, yet Jonas turned down the opportunity. I meet Chris's worried eyes. I feel sick. "I'm not attracted to Jonas. I don't want to kiss him. I don't want to be with him. He's like a brother to me. Same with Brand."

"Yeah, but he's a Diamond Bearer now. He's been placed, strategically positioned, and protected in case I'm not the guy for you."

"You're worrying about things that don't exist."

"Am I? Or am I seeing things you don't or that you refuse to admit?"

"Chris, why are you being so jealous and insecure?"

He makes a scoffing sound.

I realize the communicating has evolved into quarreling. "Have you asked Brand how many times he tried to pick up on me and I shot him down? He has told me repeatedly that I'm the strongest willed girl he's met. Brand can get any willing girl. I'm not willing. Don't you get it?"

"What's to get?"

"I want *you*, Chris! *You*. Not Brand. Not Jonas. I love you."

He moves forward, taking me by the hand. He cups my cheek and swiftly brings his mouth to mine and kisses me like his life depends on it. I kiss him back feeling as though I've finally met the real Chris. And I can't get enough of him. My whole body warms with passion, the likes of which have me wishing we weren't presently on display in the living room. He slowly pulls away from my mouth, then he hugs me and rests his cheek on my head. "Thanks for hearing me out. I've needed to get those fears off my chest for a long time and I've been so afraid of how you'd react."

"Thanks for being honest." The old adage goes through my mind: be careful what you wish for.

"I'm sorry I didn't discuss the prisms when I first kept two, but I hope you can understand a little bit better about what goes on in my mind."

"I do."

He kisses my forehead and stands. He extends his hand to me which I take and stand next to him. "I'm going to miss my flight if I don't move along. I really wish I didn't need to leave. I love you, Calli."

We hug again, then he leaves the blue mist circle. The mist dissolves and vanishes. I watch him stride across the room and disappear down the hall. My warmth turns to chill. I wrap my arms around myself to try to hold onto the warmth a little longer. I notice the fire needs a log added. I walk over and crouch down, grabbing the last piece of firewood and moving the screen far enough to set it inside on the coals. Closing the screen, I consider that last night Crimson told me there was more information she wasn't telling me. I guess now I know what she meant.

I glance over at Brand, Beth, Jonas and Maetha, who are having a conversation about inserting the repeating quartz under Brand's skin. Ever since I learned about his power, I've respected his ability to use it effectively. I agree he should insert it somewhere so it won't get stolen.

While watching the four interact, Jonas looks at me and quickly diverts his eyes. Was he not expecting to find me looking at him? I don't understand his reaction. What about his feelings toward Anika? I don't know where the two of them stand relationship-wise. I analyze my feelings for Jonas. He is a good-looking guy, with dark hair and thick brows. He's a Runner by nature so he has the ideal body for that power even though he is now Unaltered. I didn't want him to die young, I remember. But that didn't mean I wanted to be with him. Am I attracted to Jonas? Yes. Am I giving him signals of possibilities between us? Not that I'm aware of. Do I feel anything could come about between him and me?

Chris enters the living room, pulling my attention away. The feelings that ignite to life when I see him are unmistakable. They always have been. I am completely, wholeheartedly attracted to Chris. Without a doubt.

I decide not to mention any of my inner dilemma and discovery of Jonas being the backup guy to Crimson or Maetha. I already sort of know what they'd say: "The will of nature required a sacrifice for love in order to bring down the Death Clan. Who that love was didn't matter. In your case there were two options"

Chris comes back toward me and pulls me into an embrace and holds me for a few extra moments. He continues. *Calli, while I was in getting my bag, Crimson told me to take a prism with me back to D.C. I have one on me right now, but I promise you I won't use it unless lives depend on it. That includes your life. I won't use the prism to manipulate anymore conversations with you. Okay?*

Thank you, Chris. I hug tighter.

Then we kiss and say goodbye. He closes the front door behind him and I feel a wave of uncertainty creep into my mind and take hold. I'm not worried about my feelings for Chris. I'm concerned as to why Crimson and Maetha think they need a backup guy. And why exactly does Crimson want Chris to be able to repeat?

To get my mind off the matter, I walk to my bedroom. I remember I'd promised Anika I'd charge her a Seer topaz so she could better understand the power. She'll arrive tomorrow and I'd like to have it ready.

I strap on a topaz with a piece of medical tape and sit on my bed to meditate. In a little while, Brand and I are going to go to the police station to discuss yesterday's shooting. I need to be focused.

Chapter Three - Repeating With Police

A knock on my door pulls me out of meditation.

"Come in." I unfold my legs and move to the edge of the bed.

Crimson enters the room. "How are you doing, Calli?"

"As well as can be expected. Don't you already know?" I point to my head to indicate I know she can hear my thoughts at will.

She walks over and sits next to me. The blue mist of privacy surrounds us. "Calli, I don't always hear what goes on inside your mind. I have to pay attention or purposely look. It's time I pull back and give you and Chris privacy. I've intervened many times and protected you from misery, but it's time you experience life as everyone else knows it."

"What exactly do you mean?"

"I think you know."

"Is my life going to fall apart or something?"

"No, but you may notice more things go wrong or unfavorable simply because I'm not intervening as much. I won't be reading your mind or inserting thoughts as often, either. You shouldn't worry, though, you're level-headed, compassionate, smart, and have a strong grasp on life."

I look over at her. This woman of many millennia, possessing knowledge and foresight the likes of which I can't begin to imagine, giving me compliments. I say, "Thank you. Does the future still look optimistic?"

"Yes. I wish you could understand how I see the

future and what causes me to intervene in lives, but that's not possible. I'm constantly watching for alterations to the overall existence of humanity. It's not often that one person's choice affects the future of all, but it has happened through the course of history a couple times. Actually, recently."

"Really?" I'm thinking like in the last month or last couple of weeks.

"Of course. The concept of the A-bomb alone changed the future for humans. Then the tense situation between Cuba and the United States was another example of the weight of the world resting in the hands of one person. Another example came down to one person—Maetha—halting the ability for terrorist groups to get hold of enriched uranium, thus preventing a catastrophic global disaster in the late 1990s."

I say, "About the A-bomb, why didn't Bearers step in and stop the bombs being dropped on Japan?"

"Many tried, believe me. We couldn't stop the number of balls rolling once they got going. Too many brilliant scientists were involved. Our job is to preserve humanity not eliminate those who use their intelligence for progression. The situation was a first for me and I regret my inaction and the amount of devastation that followed. That's why when the Cuban Missile Crisis escalated, I put Maetha on the task to prevent the foreseen destruction. She performed exceptionally. She alone saved millions of lives."

"Wow. I'd love to hear that whole story."

"Later. You have the potential to save hundreds of thousands of lives, if not millions, as well. In fact, it's safe to say if we cannot capture the Elemental blast—that one act—humanity is doomed. Billions of lives will be lost over the next century and a half. Now, it is not my intention to frighten you, but you are the only person who is physically strong enough, and with access to the greater healing power, to help me capture the energy in two diamonds."

My mind spins after hearing her words concerning me. What if I cannot pull it off? *Wait,* "Two diamonds?" My voice shakes.

"Yes. The one you'll be holding, and the one in your heart. I'm unsure at this point how you'll survive, I only know you will. But, as I said before, you need to figure out how to succeed at this task. Unfortunately, I feel that my continual contact is influencing you to make decisions you think I would want you to make. You need to make your own choices, Calli."

"What if I choose wrong?"

"Here's something to consider when it comes to choices: most choices don't affect the overall outcome of the future of humanity. That said, consider everyone has choices and can change their own futures. For example, if a person chooses to take harmful drugs, they alter their future until they choose to stop and become clean. If they do not stop, they continue on with their altered future. They may go on to influence others to take drugs. They may kill someone while under the influence, but the overall future of humanity won't be affected unless that 'someone' killed is you." She pauses a moment, then continues. "When Chris asked if you could have a prism also, I looked to the future and suddenly everything had changed. The answer was no. I don't know what choices you'd make or if you'd think you were acting in nature's best interest, but something would go horribly wrong."

Huh, go figure.

She continues. "That's why I took the prisms when we were at Don's house. Each time you held one in your hands, the future darkened. I don't want to alarm you," she pats my arm, "just know that's the reason you can't have a prism." Clearing her throat, she continues. "I also want to talk to you about the process of choosing Bearers. Everyone has tendencies and inclinations, these are important to monitor when choosing new Bearers. Those with the tendency to be quick to anger are not suitable candidates. Those inclined or drawn to gambling are not suitable candidates. They take unnecessary risks. Bearers shouldn't be risky. They should consider all options then take the smartest course. Not the quickest. Not the one with the least effort. Also, those with unnecessary, mind-controlling addictions are not good candidates to become Bearers.

"When I choose Bearers or approve of Maetha's choices, I don't see their entire futures. I didn't know Henry—or Freedom—would turn against nature so quickly. I only knew he had the tendency to be too emotionally attached to possessions and relationships. He was not a good candidate." She looks me in the eye. "Chris and Jonas were not preselected to become Bearers. They are not good candidates."

"What?" The air rushes out of my lungs.

"But with the help of the prism, Chris, at least, can undo any rash decisions if he catches them within ten seconds. That's the main reason why I told Chris to keep the prism. Jonas, on the other hand, is a different matter."

"How so?"

"He has repressed anger. He won't open up about it either."

I know she's talking about how Jonas's father murdered his brother. I ask, "Can he be healed of his anger?"

"He has to do it himself. This is not an illness where hormones or chemicals are out of balance. This is a choice to avoid, a choice to resist. He and I have had many conversations. He and Mary have had many more. Throughout all of them, he becomes frustrated and insists he's not angry deep down."

"Why did you allow him to have the remaining shard then?"

"The diamond was already living within him. Not to worry, the long-range future is still optimistic with him being a Bearer. And, he may yet have a different purpose to fill."

"But what is his future?" I want to ask if he really is the backup guy, but I don't.

"Like I said, I don't see individualized futures. He has many choices he can make and if he's smart, he'll make good ones."

"What about Chris?"

"Chris is dealing with his anger. He has a long road ahead of him, however, he doesn't have the diamond fully yet. I've given him private instruction that he needs to wait to have you insert the diamond until he's mastered his anger, preferably after the Elemental blast. If he never reaches this level of mastery, he can at least be your companion for the rest of his life."

She stands from the bed. "You and Brand need to get ready to go to the police."

I shake my head a little, trying to fathom what she's just told me about Chris and Jonas. Why does she keep flipping new cards on me? I calm my racing heart and take a deep breath. She's right about needing to go to the police. I remember I wanted to ask her about the Healer quartz. "Crimson, should I have a Healer quartz on my body at all times? You know, in case something similar to last night happens?"

"The Healer quartz only contains modern era power.

The Sanguine Diamond's healing power is so much more effective. You are better off charging top quality Imperial topaz with the diamond's power instead of using one of the Healer quartz."

"Okay. But I already know the topaz doesn't hold a charge long enough to heal major health issues."

"Yes, that's right. However, if you were wearing either of the two stones last night Marketa would have just taken them from you like she did the others. It would have done you no good."

"All right. I'll make sure I charge up an Imperial topaz after I get back from the police station."

Beth helps me attach bandages and tape to my shoulder, making it look like I'm injured from the shooting. While she does that, Brand works with Maetha to copy the files on the flash drive to her laptop. She'll transfer the files to Jonas.

After my shoulder looks adequate, I rehearse with Maetha some answers to possible questions the police might ask. I know I can repeat with Brand, but I don't want too many pauses in our conversation, in case some-one is recording my interrogation.

The decision is made to use my phone to contact the police station. We don't want a link tying Chris's father's house to me, and as I'm using my real name and identity, calling from my personal phone makes sense.

After a couple minutes on hold, following an ex-planation of who I am and my involvement in the shooting last night, I'm connected to the detective in charge, Det. Albert Gardner. He tells me to come to the station promptly.

Brand and I arrive shortly thereafter. As we approach the building, Brand says out of the blue, "You're going to have to use some persuasive words with this guy."

I glance over at Brand as he holds the door open for me and walk in the main door. "Which guy?"

"You'll know."

The chairs in the waiting room are sparsely populated indicating a mild start for the New Year, well, except for the shooting last night.

A tall, lean, bald man wearing a white shirt and a tie with blue jeans stands by the far wall, perusing through papers. He appears to be in his forties. The man looks up and asks, "Calli Courtnae?"

"Yes."

He straightens the papers and jams them into a file folder he's holding. I use my Hunter's eyesight to see my name on the tab of the file. The man approaches us and extends his hand, which I politely shake. "I'm Det. Gardner. Come with me, please. He can wait here," Det. Gardner says, nodding toward Brand.

I say, "I want him with me. There is a crazy person trying to kill me."

The detective seems put out. "Ms. Courtnae, you are in a police station. You're completely safe."

As per Brand's recommendation, I use a bit of Mind-Control to convince the detective. "You want me to be as open as possible for a successful, short investigation. You know he will help me relax and you'll be able to get back home with your family to enjoy the holiday."

"All right. Both of you come with me."

Det. Gardner leads us down the hall to an office. We enter the room and sit in the two chairs across the desk from him.

"How's the arm?" he asks. His thoughts reveal he knows I was shot in the shoulder. I'm not sure what he's fishing for in my response. My gut reaction is to be on guard.

"It hurts," I say, reaching up and placing my hand gingerly on my bandages. "But I'm going to be okay."

Det. Gardner scratches the top of his head. His thoughts tell me he wonders if the itch is from a piece of insulation that fell on his head as he climbed into his car this morning. He turns his attention to Brand. "I'm sorry, I didn't catch the name of your friend."

"This is Derek, my boyfriend. He patched me up after I got home."

"Yeah, and I'm not gonna let her leave my side until this is over," Brand declares.

Det. Gardner says, "I'm glad to see you're doing okay. We were worried when we couldn't find you at any hospitals or clinics." *Thought you might be dead, especially with such a strange type of bullet,* his thoughts add. He scratches his head again.

So they found some of the obsidian at the crime scene. "Yeah, I didn't want to risk him finding me at any public place. I didn't want to call the cops, either. Besides, it was just a flesh wound . . . well, several."

"What do you mean?"

"The bullet must have been made of something breakable. When Derek pulled out the different pieces, they looked like some kind of glass. None of them went very deep."

Brand adds, "Yeah, like shrapnel."

Det. Gardner says, "Yes, I know. We are waiting for the lab results of the stray-bullet pieces retrieved from the scene, but we think it was made of obsidian." His mind reveals he has reviewed Max's blog.

Too bad I didn't have time to deactivate the whole blog.

I play along. "Obsidian? Wow! That nut was going off on obsidian a while back on his blog."

"How do you know the shooter?" Det. Gardner asks.

His mind shows images of the truck-stop robbery from the blog, and that he's resisting the urge to scratch his head again.

"The question is how did he know me? A friend made me aware that a video of me was on a blog. A recent post said he was going to reveal my 'secret identity.' My friend hunted him down with some of her friends so I could confront him. And, well, you know how well that turned out."

"I assume you're talking about the woman with you in the footage. Where is your friend now?"

"I don't know, she told me to run home while she went after him. I told her not to go, but she took off without me. I haven't seen her since. I'm really worried about her."

"What is her name?"

"Marketa Jones." Jones is the first name that pops into my head. I lay on a little more Mind-Control to move the conversation along and away from Marketa.

He says, "We'll keep our eyes open for her. This guy had a blog, huh? What was he blogging about?"

You already know, sir, I want to say. "It was all about people with magic powers who are 'walking among us'," — I use air quotes— "and he thinks I'm one of them."

"Magic powers?" Det. Gardner scrambles for a pen and writes something down on the notepad near his computer. "Why does he think that?"

I resist shaking my head after reading his thoughts. He's already searched the law enforcement databases and is well aware of the video footage of me fleeing the robbery. I won't give him more than he already knows.

"Well, I got caught in the middle of a truck-stop robbery in Tennessee a few months ago and the footage was hosted on his blog. That was the video my friend showed me. I got scared and ran away as fast as I could, and the way the cameras caught it made it look like I have some kind of superpower. He thought it was real and posted it to his blog."

"You're a fast runner, then?"

"Well, I *did* set a record at my high school track meet."

"What do you think the significance of obsidian in the bullet is all about, Ms. Courtnae?"

"He seems to believe it cancels superpowers. He sells it on his blog."

"The video footage shows you getting on the shooter's laptop. What were you doing?"

"Deleting his post about me. This stupid blog has already made my life miserable at college. I didn't want him putting a target on my head, too."

"Why didn't you take this to the authorities for their help?"

"I have some law school friends. They said the blogger hadn't hurt me or my reputation so there wasn't anything the law could do. My tech friends said the blog was anonymously hosted offshore, so we wouldn't be able to do anything about it other than maybe issue a cease and desist. However, who knows how long that would have taken."

"You have a lot of friends."

"Yes. I do. I'm just glad Marketa was able to find him before he posted my picture and name to millions of people." I read his mind again and see he wants to ask about the flash drive. I address it first. "Oh, hey, I have the flash drive I took from his computer."

"I was just going to bring that up." Det. Gardner scratches his head and a crazy realization spreads across his face. *Can she read minds?*

"You look like you're wondering if I just read your

mind, detective. That's funny. You see, on the blog, it says you know when someone reads your mind because your head itches."

Brand pipes up. "Either that or you have lice." He tilts his head to the side and points and waggles his finger at Det. Gardner. "Not you, though, because of the no-hair thing."

I say, "Isn't it interesting how some paranoid person can take a simple body action and put a ridiculous reason behind it?" I pause, then add, "Just so you know, I've had several people tell me I'm quite intuitive. Does that make me a mind reader, sir?"

Det. Gardner's eyes narrow as he looks me over.

Brand elbows my arm and says, "This time don't bring up the flash drive. Let him ask for it." Then the room starts to spin around as Brand repeats to the moment just before I volunteered up the flash drive.

Det. Gardner says, "Yes, I think you're right about stopping him. However, you did take a piece of evidence from the scene: a flash drive."

I act surprised. "Oh, right. I brought it with me." I retrieve the small device and give it to the detective. "I just hope it helps you find this guy."

"Why did you take it?"

"I knew it held his next post and I didn't want to leave it behind in case he came back."

"Why did you leave the scene, Miss Courtnae?"

I let out a sigh. "I was afraid the guy was still in the store, and I wasn't hurt that bad so Marketa helped me leave."

Det. Gardner sits perfectly still, staring at me. I wait for him to speak. He takes a deep breath and opens the file in front of him. "Okay. We have all the evidence we need to put out an arrest warrant for this guy. We know his name, employer, home address, and Social Security number."

"You know his name?" I try to act shocked.

"Yes. The cashier who traded laptops with him gave us the information."

"Well, what is his name?"

"I'm not going to tell you. I don't want you getting shot again. No more vigilante justice, do you hear me?"

"He's gone now, so how could I continue?" I sit back in my chair and cross my arms over my chest in a huff, trying to act put out.

"Exactly. However, there's something else I want to talk about with you."

"Yes?" I uncross my arms and sit up straight.

"When you didn't show up at any hospital, I entered your picture into the system. I found your name associated with the Tennessee truck-stop robbery. This morning, I contacted Det. Webb and asked for a photo of you. I wanted to see if your two pictures matched. Det. Webb was more than accommodating to email me a screenshot of you being interviewed. But, as she watched the video, she was, how shall I say—spooked. Apparently, she hadn't viewed your video yet."

"What are you talking about?"

"Well, you just have to see for yourself." He pulls a printed photo from the file and passes it to me.

I glance down at the paper, showing the upper-corner surveillance shot of me sitting at the table and *Crimson standing behind me!*

I take a slow breath and say as innocently as possible, "Who's that?"

"That's what Det. Webb wondered as well."

"There wasn't anyone else besides the two detectives in the room." I fidget in my chair and pick up on Det.

Gardner's thoughts that my body language says I know who the woman is. I turn to Brand and say, "Take me back to when he hands me the photo, please."

"Yes, ma'am."

The room spins and comes to a halt as Det. Gardner passes the photo to me.

"Who's that behind me?"

"That's what Det. Webb wondered as well."

I let my mouth fall open as I look between Brand and Det. Gardner. "I don't understand. Is this a . . . a joke?"

"Do you recognize this woman?"

"No. There wasn't anyone else in the room."

"Well, there's more. When your companion, Chris Harding, came in the next day for his interview," Det. Garner slides another paper to me, "the mystery woman is seen standing behind him, too."

I open my eyes wide. "Okay, now I'm spooked."

"Det. Webb searched the surveillance archives for when you arrived at the station. The woman entered the building with you. She seamlessly slips inside the open doors without anyone noticing otherwise. The same happened with Mr. Harding. She arrived with him."

I shake my head and rub my temples. "This is, ah, freaky."

Brand startles me by whipping around in his chair to look at the space behind my seat. "Is she here right now? Are you recording?"

"No, I'm not recording. I guess I should be."

Brand puts an arm around my shoulders. "And you said the police station was safe," he says to the detective.

I reach forward, making sure to have visibly shaking hands. "There must be a logical explanation for this. Would be able to have a copy of this picture? That way if she ws up somewhere, we can report her."

"Sure. Take that one. I can print another."

"Thanks." I carefully fold the paper.

Detective Gardner says, "Has any of your contact information changed since you gave it to Det. Webb?"

"No."

"Okay. I'll use that information if I need to get in contact with you."

We enter the house and I walk straight up to Crimson. I hold the printed photo up for her to see.

She takes it from me and stares at it. "Oh dear."

Maetha takes the paper. "Didn't you know, Crimson?"

"I've never had to accompany one of my Bearers to law enforcement before."

Brand walks casually between us. "Crimson, you could totally cover this up, you know. Just go back there and haunt the security cameras. Toss some stuff around, leave some eerie messages, let out some blood-curdling screams here and there. Can you imagine how freaked out they would be? They'd easily dismiss you as a poltergeist and not related to Calli and Chris."

The thought of Crimson pretending to be a ghost makes me chuckle.

"More proof of the supernatural would not be a wise use of my time and may create more problems. They'll come to the ghost conclusion on their own. However, this is good information for you, Calli. Now you know you're not invisible on camera either."

"What about bi-locating?"

"I would assume that is not safe either," Crimson says. "I recommend you stop short at producing a form and hold at hearing when you bi-locate."

"I'm not sure I follow."

Maetha says, "Remember when we flew from Florida to Washington D.C.? Freedom connected to my diamond and listened. He didn't materialize, but I knew he'd connected."

"Is this different than when I speak to Chris through the diamonds?"

"Do you feel like you're in the room with him? Or do you only hear his responses?"

"I'm not sure. I don't remember anything about his location, just his responses."

Maetha says, "Try bi-locating to Jonas right now but don't materialize."

Interesting she wants me to connect with Jonas when there's so many other Bearers I could practice with. I mentally connect with Jonas's diamond and go to him in my mind. My vision goes black and a slight whirling sensation tickles my senses. I hear waves crashing in the distance. Jonas comes into view. He's sitting on the sand, shirtless, staring out to the distant horizon. He turns his head, jumps up, and faces me.

"Calli," he wipes his sandy hands down the front of his cargo pants. "What is it?"

"Uh," my eyes dart around, catching glimpses of his muscular form, but not wanting him to know I notice. "I'm practicing bi-locating but not materializing. I guess I failed."

"Why?"

"Security cameras can see us. I'm going to try again. You should feel my presence but not see me. I should feel that I'm here but not materialized."

"Why don't you use Invisibility?"

"Crimson was captured on film invisibly, so that won't work. I'm going to try again." I let go of my connection to his diamond and open my eyes in Denver.

"Well?" Maetha asks.

"I need to practice. I materialized."

"Yes, it does take some practice. I stop pursuing a connection once I can hear surrounding sounds associated with the Bearer I'm connecting to."

"Oh, I'll try that." I'm wishing I didn't need to master this right away. I don't want to see Jonas's half-naked body again. Wait, maybe that would help me stop pursuing. I close my eyes and try again.

After a moment, I hear Jonas say, "I sense you are connecting, Calli."

I can't hear the waves yet. Jonas comes into view. "Ugh." I disconnect. Images of his body flow through my mind. I send him a mental message. *Jonas, would you please put a shirt on?*

He chuckles. *Of course.*

I try again and connect carefully, methodically, until I hear waves. Jonas speaks, "I don't see you but I sense your connection. It's stronger this time."

Did you put on a shirt?

"Yes."

He comes into view, shirtless. "Jonas!"

A broad smile lights up his face. "If you'd stopped at auditory, you wouldn't have known I lied."

I drop connection and open my eyes. "I'll practice more later," I say, frustrated with my inability and even more upset with myself for being bothered by Jonas. I blame Chris for this. If I didn't know Jonas is the backup guy, I wouldn't have been bothered by his overexposure. At least I think so.

The next day Anika arrives. I notice how Brand is on his best behavior around her. After Crimson's talk, I feel much needed light has been shed on the reality of our situation. As I struggle to figure out how to save the most amounts of lives in Portland, I'm relieved to hear Anika will play a big role in the endeavor.

I approach Anika privately after lunch. "I charged you a Seer topaz." I extend my hand, holding the golden piece of crystal.

"Oh, thank you." She takes it and twists it between her fingers. "What should I look for?"

"That's up to you."

She puts the topaz in her pocket. "I think I'll wait till I figure out something important."

"I'd love to hear what you end up using it for," I say, hoping the Seer topaz will help her to better understand the power of being able to foresee things ahead of time.

She and Beth will remain behind here in Denver while Brand and I go to China. At first I thought Brand was going to be my protector, but then Crimson revealed Jie Wen wants Brand on this mission.

The plans are set for China. Brand and I will leave Denver tonight on Maetha's private plane and stop off in Washington D.C. to pick up Duncan. It feels wrong that we'll pass through Chris's area without seeing him, but we just saw each other and honestly, I'm all right with a bit of a break to let my head clear. From D.C., we'll fly to Bermuda to pick up Jonas and Maetha, then we'll continue on to China with fuel stops along the way. Barring any unforeseen maintenance, we'll be in the airplane for close to thirty-five hours.

I start packing my things in my bag. The good thing about a Runner suit is it has microbial prevention properties. They don't stink even after a few uses. Plus, the material is thin and folds into a small size, leaving room in my bag for more things. I put a pouch of Imperial topaz crystals in the side pocket of the bag. I'll be charging these with Mind-Control while on the flight.

This is the only reason Maetha is coming with us. She needs to appear as if she's the one charging the topaz to keep up the ruse she still has the Blue shard. Instead, she'll charge topaz with the Healer power. I don't know how long we'll have to keep up this pretense, but I think this is for Jie Wen's sake alone as I know not many Bearers know she even has the shard in the first place.

Jie Wen sure isn't happy to hear I'm coming along. At least that's what I gathered when he spoke with Crimson. I wonder if Jie Wen or anyone else for that matter will ever see me as an equal in terms of our abilities. I understand I need to go because Crimson will be able to view events through our Blue Diamond connection. Not while I'm around obsidian, of course, but later she'll be able to connect to my mind. However, as she told me earlier, she won't be intruding much in my decisions or thoughts anymore. So, I'm not quite sure how this will all work out.

One thing bothering me is we won't be wearing Runners topaz. I've made an effort to always have one of these topaz with me at all times in case I need to escape the effects of obsidian. The reasons given are that we'll already be wearing Mind-Control and Healing topazes. Adding a third would confuse the powers or at least confuse the wearer. I don't know if that's true. All I know is I'm a little uncomfortable without mine, especially after searching the future and finding we'll encounter obsidian in China.

The voice of Rodger Rutherfield fills the plane after

our obvious descent. "Buckle up, folks. We're landing in Bermuda."

I find myself wanting to go see Maetha's island, but she and Jonas are already waiting at the airport. Capt. Rutherfield helps Maetha and Jonas with their luggage and greets Maetha as Ms. Lightner.

Maetha's appearance has been altered. Her skin coloring is the same, but her bone structure is different. All these changes made with the purpose of throwing off facial recognition software looking for Janice Johnson.

Duncan says to Maetha, "Staying with your Egyptian heritage, I see. Good choice." She smiles and joins the captain up front.

Now that both Jonas and Brand are on the same flight with me, I'm able to look at them and compare my feelings to that of what I hold for Chris. I'm sure of what I want. And besides, all Brand and Jonas can talk about are Beth and Anika. Neither one is hitting on me or trying to capture my attention.

I take a deep cleansing breath and relax. We have many hours of flight ahead of us. We are, after all, flying to the other side of the world.

Somewhere over Western Europe, I have the opportunity to chat with Duncan. I'm hoping to learn more about Duncan's history as a Diamond Bearer.

"What was your life like before you became a Bearer, Duncan?"

"Well, I was a mercenary in my mortal years, back in the age of muskets and cannons. I became a "vampire slayer" when the clan grew large enough to terrorize small towns. Vampires were much smarter than the Death Clan and weren't as easy to trick. I had no idea I was an Unaltered until I was approached by Maetha, whom I believed was a witch."

"Were witches viewed with the same hesitation back then?"

"Absolutely. But they were far and few between. I realize now they were all Spellcasters. That's what Maetha is."

Brand and Jonas lean closer to join in the conversation.

Duncan continues. "Me and my group of slayers hit a dead end concerning how to kill Vampires. They outsmarted every technique we had, almost as if they were being counseled by a Spellcaster. Maetha presented a new option—luring the leaders of their clan to accept a valuable peace offering: The Sanguine Diamond."

I add to his story. "They were under Freedom's control. I saw it in his mind before he died." My eyes meet Brand's and his clenched jaw. I'm filled with immediate regret for bringing up his biological father's death.

Duncan doesn't seem to be aware of Brand's inner conflict and continues. "Maetha gave me a diamond with the instructions to arrange a peacekeeping meeting where the legendary diamond would be given in exchange for harmony and safety of my village. I followed her instructions against my wife's wishes. My wife felt the Vampire clan wouldn't honor the peace treaty, but I knew without it she and our children would be slaughtered. I had to try.

"In a scene similar to what you experienced with the Death Clan, the Vampire clan arrived and among them was my wife."

Jonas gasps. "Was she their hostage?"

"No. She was a member. She'd been one of them all along.

My mind envisions Maetha. She would have known his wife was part of the evil group, yet she set him up to inadvertently kill her. A deep, roiling anger within me heats up another notch and I feel immense pity for Duncan.

Jonas says, "That's horrible!"

"Yes. It was. Following the destruction of the Vampire clan, I became the recipient of a shard from the exploded diamond. Maetha offered me the opportunity to become immortal and join her clan that serves the will of nature or return to life as a mortal. Obviously, I accepted the diamond. After a while, I was taken under Jie Wen's arm and taught everything he knows about battle and tactical ingenuity. He learned from the best. He personally knew Genghis Khan."

"Holy crap," Brand exclaims.

Duncan continues. "I have high respect for Jie Wen and see him as a strategic genius. In my opinion, he's every bit as formidable as Amenemhet."

My ears perk up. "What about Amenemhet?"

"He's been a part of almost every major war since Ancient Egyptian times. He found Jie Wen and recommended him to be a Bearer."

"Amazing!" Jonas shakes his head and blinks his eyes. "I mean, I've tried to imagine some of what the Bearers have seen or been involved with over the thousands of years, but this is *awesome.*"

Jonas, Brand, and Duncan continue to talk about different aspects of the Bearers. My mind replays the information Duncan told me about his wife when we were at my parents' cabin and how he became obsessed with bringing her back from the dead. I noticed how he rushed past that part a second ago. I can't say that I blame him.

Crimson's words echo in my mind that Chris may not become a full Bearer in the end. Even if he lives a full life with me, he'll still die. I'll have to let him die. But only if he doesn't choose to have his diamond inserted. I don't want to think about this right now. I'm still trying to pick through the revelation that he's been carrying a prism, using it on me.

I rub my temples and close my eyes to clear my mind. What I need to focus on is the upcoming Elemental blast. I need to think beyond myself and find a way to save as many lives as possible. I know what needs to be done, I just don't know how to do it.

Are you all right, Calli? Jonas speaks to my mind.

Without opening my eyes, I reply, *Yes. I have a lot on my mind, that's all.*

You have so much responsibility on your shoulders. I wish I could help lessen the load.

You already do, Jonas. I open my eyes, realizing Brand and Duncan are still talking. I'd blocked them out entirely. I meet Jonas's worried gaze.

With a subtle, barely noticeable smile he says, *I'll always be here for you, helping you accomplish your tasks.*

Thanks. I switch to verbal language and address Duncan. "I'm going to go in the back and lay down."

I walk to the bench seat, remembering I need to charge some topaz. I stop and open my bag and pull out the six topazes and bandages. Charging these with Mind-Control for Invisibility seems counterintuitive since we now know cameras and video recordings can see us. Hopefully we'll be long gone from the facility we're going to by the time it's realized we're there.

I strap on the stones and lay down to rest.

I wake up from my nap and am met with a startling, awful sensation. I'm nervous, paranoid, and hypersensitive for some reason. I feel like everyone is looking at me, noticing everything I do, almost as if I'm on stage in front of an enormous crowd. I walk to the front of the plane where Maetha sits with Capt. Rutherfield. I sit in a nearby chair.

I speak to Maetha's mind. *I feel strange.*

Are you sick?

I don't know. I've never felt like this before. I explain my symptoms.

She responds, *I know the answer. You're experiencing the exact opposite of Invisibility. Remember that you're charging multiple stones with the same power. It's not only draining on your body, it's giving you a sense of reverse invisibility, one where it feels like everyone 'sees' you.*

I peer over my shoulder at the three guys, none of which are looking at me. As soon as I turn forward, the overwhelming feeling of exposed, vulnerable, paranoia invades my body. I squirm in my seat wanting nothing more than to rip the topaz off my body.

Maetha says, *I'd offer you some healing right now, but because I'm charging six stones with that power, my stores are drained, like yours. In fact, I'm experiencing flu-like symptoms. I haven't felt like this since before I obtained the Sanguine Diamond.*

I hadn't thought of that.

She continues. *Remember, you and I will need to exchange the charged stones prior to handing them out so everyone believes I charged the Invisibility topaz.*

I understand.

Maetha turns to the captain. "Rodger, what is our estimated arrival time?"

"We'll land in Bangkok in three hours. From there we'll have to wait till Jie Wen secures clearance for us to pass into Chinese airspace."

"He hasn't done that yet?"

"He's only had two days. Normally it takes a week to

get clearance. But he has connections."

"Excuse me, Rodger." Maetha leaves her seat and walks to the back of the plane and sits down. I notice how wobbly she is on her feet—so unlike Maetha.

I get up and go back to her. "What's wrong, Maetha?"

"I need to communicate with Jie Wen. Give me a moment."

I sit nearby and wait while she connects with Jie Wen.

"We have to land in Guangzhou in Guangdong, China to have the plane searched before we can continue to Jie Wen's personal landing strip."

"Searched?"

"Yes. A bit of Mind-Control will be needed to rush the search." She nods at me. "Come on, let's go relay the message to Rodger."

After speaking with Rodger, with Duncan, Brand, and Jonas overhearing, Jonas asks, "Is it cold there, where Jie Wen lives? I mean, it *is* January."

Maetha answers. "Not really. It's a subtropical climate. Your Runner's jackets will keep you warm enough. If all goes to plan, we'll be there less than twenty-four hours. We still have a few hours of flying. I recommend all of you practice your meditation and clear your minds. Rescuing the scientist and his family is risky. I want you to be mentally ready.

Chapter Four - China

I'm guessing this isn't Capt. Rutherfield's first time in China. The Cantonese chatter on the radio is impossible for me to decipher, but Rodger handles it well. Who knew he was fluent in Cantonese?

Another surprise: Duncan speaks Cantonese, too. He effortlessly translates some of the conversation for the rest of us one-languagers. I guess I should have already known. He told me Jie Wen trained him long ago. Jie Wen probably taught it to him.

Jonas says to Brand and me, "We're probably going to have to learn other languages at some point."

"Yep," Brand says.

Guangzhou International Airport is busy, busy, busy. Constant streams of planes are lined up in the sky to land and several are in line for takeoff. The flight traffic controllers are obviously skilled with the high volume of flights rolling in and out.

Capt. Rutherfield receives instructions of where to drive the plane once we're on the ground. The location appears to be a checkpoint where several people in official-type suits stand waiting.

Duncan says to me, Brand, and Jonas, "You three need to remain quiet during the inspection." His order has a let-the-adults-handle-this feeling.

Maetha speaks to my mind. *I'll tell you what you need to do to speed this up.*

Okay.

Capt. Rutherfield unlocks and opens the door then

lowers the steps. He steps outside and begins conversing with the officials.

Duncan translates for us. "They're asking about the cargo . . . he needs to open the hold . . . they want us off the plane while they conduct their search for illegal items."

"Do we take our bags with us?" I ask.

"No."

Capt. Rutherfield enters the plane. "Everyone off."

Brand mutters as we exit, "Good thing I left my exotic animals and fly-infested fruit back home."

Duncan places a hand on Brand's shoulder. "Keep your sarcastic attitude to yourself. It will only make things harder for Maetha to control if they suspect we're smuggling."

"Sorry." Brand hangs his head.

We step off the plane and find several armed guards with the officials. The hatch is open and the captain and an official are inside the cargo hold. Three officials move forward and enter the plane. We stand still. A woman approaches us and points to Maetha's neckline where some medical tape holding her topazes is exposed. The woman says something to which Maetha responds in Cantonese.

No surprise, she's fluent as well.

Maetha's voice in my head says, *Calli, she wants me to take off the bandages so she can see my injury. Tell her mind she doesn't need to see.*

I don't speak Cantonese.

You don't need to. Just think about the action and stop her from doing it.

I try to control the woman, but I don't know what I'm doing.

The woman raises her voice slightly and sounds bothered by Maetha not following orders.

Maetha slowly raises her hand to her neckline. *Now*

Calli! Tell her she doesn't need to see.

I'm trying! I focus intensely on the woman, willing her to stop wanting to see what's under the bandage.

Maetha grasps onto the tape and pulls it off slowly, no doubt hoping I'll be successful before she removes it.

I'm not.

As the tape comes off, the topaz are exposed, stuck to the backside of the tape. The woman points and says something, to which Duncan responds. The woman holds her hand out, most likely wanting to confiscate the topaz.

My heart sinks even though it's racing like crazy. I've failed. What's worse is the woman will probably want my topaz as well. I send my thoughts to Brand. *Repeat with me back as far as you can.*

The ground spins and I soon find myself at the moment just before Capt. Rutherfield opens the door to let the stairs down. Maetha is about to tell me she'll instruct me on what to do, but I cut her off. *Maetha, I can't control the woman's mind. She's going to seize your topaz and probably mine.*

You repeated?

Yes. I can't control her actions.

In the background, Duncan translates what's going on outside the plane. I know the captain is about to tell us to deplane. Time is running out.

Maetha reaches up and strips off her bandage. The topazes are stuck to it. She crumples the mass into a small ball and tosses it in the trash located by the galley. She nods in my direction, indicating I do the same thing with the Mind-Control topaz on my body.

Won't they find these? I ask as I rip the sticky tape off my chest and wad it up like Maetha did.

I don't know, but at least they won't be on our bodies.

"Everyone off," Capt. Rutherfield orders.

We stand to exit the plane and I toss my "garbage"

into the trash. The normal garbage bin is now equivalent to a treasure chest with healing and mind-controlling stones for the taking. I sure hope no one thinks to go through the trash.

Outside the plane, I watch as the scene plays out, only this time I don't need to control the woman. A couple of men enter the plane and rummage through bags and cupboards. I focus on their bodies and press my thoughts their direction, thinking, *You don't need to search. You don't need to be concerned,* over and over again.

Our bodies are scanned with a handheld metal detector and we're told to empty our pockets, which we do. No alarms are raised, no concerns are expressed, and other than Brand giggling and wiggling when he's being patted down, claiming he's ticklish, we are given the all-clear to proceed to our destination.

We board and my eyes are immediately drawn to the upside down garbage can, the contents scattered. I throw a glance at Maetha and find her concerned eyes directed to the pile of trash too. I bend down and right the can and begin searching for the two wads of stones. Maetha stops me and speaks to my mind, *Wait till the door is closed. They're watching.*

But, did they find the topazes?

No. They're safe. I can see both bandages.

After the door closes and Capt. Rutherfield locks it down, we all breathe a sigh of relief. Maetha helps me retrieve the two bundles from the garbage pile, and together we clean up the mess.

Our plane lands on Jie Wen's private air strip with a slight bump. I stare out the small window trying to take in the natural beauty.

After stepping off the plane at Jie Wen's private estate and being driven to the main buildings, I'm blown away at the majesty of his estate. Beautifully manicured gardens with koi ponds and waterfalls are bordered with pathways of precision-laid rock. Carved wooden statues of dragons accent several outbuildings and covered sitting areas which are painted in gold and deep red tones. Everything matches the breathtaking architecture of the main house that could be suitable for royalty. I guess I figured he'd live somewhere stark and extremely clean, lacking in anything natural. Instead, his estate reflects an unknown personality I wouldn't have guessed. Maybe I've misjudged him.

Chuang meets us as we step out of the car. He wears an ornate robe deep blue in color with a perfectly tied band around his middle. He walks with controlled fluid motion.

"Maetha, Duncan," he says, with a slight bow. His eyes move in Brand's, Jonas's, and my direction then back to the others. "Jie Wen is meditating. Come, I'll take you to him."

Brand looks at me and rolls his eyes. Then he rubs his upper arms with his hands as if he's cold. I know he's communicating his dislike of Chuang's cold greeting and I try not to chuckle.

Jonas speaks to my mind. *It's like we're back in high school and we're not in the cool crowd.*

Let's just try to stay focused on the mission. I'm not impressed with Chuang's behavior either.

We follow Chuang along the immaculate stone pathway away from the landing strip. He turns to Maetha and asks, "What does the future show as far as our success with this mission?"

"I can't tell. Whenever Brand is involved, I can't determine the outcome because there are so many. Plus, there will be obsidian."

"Good thing we have the Mind-Control topaz then. It is ready, I assume."

"Yes," she says. "The group needs to experiment with the invisibility ability before attempting the extraction, and without using too much of the power stored."

Duncan asks, "How long will a topaz last?"

"I don't know the exact length of time. If the power is used for invisibility, then you should get several uses out of it. However, if it's used to control someone's actions, perhaps one or two uses. Altering perception is easier than controlling actions. We also need to distribute the Healing topaz Calli charged on the way here. Calli," she turns to me as we walk, "may I?" She extends her hand for the topaz I've charged.

I hand her the bundle of topaz, knowing the whole "show" is for the sake of maintaining the secrecy of the Blue Diamond. I have the sudden realization I'm in the same situation as when I carried the real Sanguine Diamond and Chris had the decoy. I almost feel like I'm protecting the Blue from would-be takers, but not quite. This time around, I'm helping expose dissenters.

We arrive at the main building and find Jie Wen waiting. He also wears an ornate robe with the knot of perfection around his middle. His robe is deep red and gold, like the color of his estate I have to wonder, since I haven't seen him in anything else, how he fights in that kind of attire.

Customary bows are made and the younger members are ignored once again. *Oh well.*

Jie Wen leads us inside his home. Rude or not, this man has impeccable taste. His decorations are probably antiques like Maetha's and most likely have an interesting story behind each one. Too bad we have neither the time nor the camaraderie to delve deeper.

Maetha sits on a floor pillow and separates each of the two bundles of topaz. She then performs a switch-up to confuse anyone watching, namely Duncan. By intermixing the stones on the floor and then separating them into groups of two, one for healing, one for mind-controlling, then giving each person in the extraction group a set, she's able to keep him in the dark.

But why? Should I be concerned with Duncan being a dissenter?

Brand clears his throat and says rather unceremoniously, "So, Jie Wen, tell us about the people we're going to rescue."

The look on Jie Wen's face is priceless. He seems shocked by Brand's lack of manners, yet I know he requested to have Brand on this mission, so it would seem he needs to adjust his normal uptightness. Jie Wen motions to other floor cushions, indicating for us to sit. "Two scientists and their daughter," he says.

Brand moves his hand in a circular motion to encourage Jie Wen to continue. "And . . . what makes them so special?"

"Dr. Toddkhuslan—he goes by the name Tod—and his wife, Mishell, are developing healing blankets using quartz. Their daughter, Sarangerel, is a computer genius and has been hacking the bunker's system little by little."

Jonas clears his throat and scoots forward in his spot. "You don't say. How is she doing that if they're captives? I mean, if we're going to rescue them, I'd assume they're captives."

Jie Wen seems bothered. "Dr. Tod joined the group so Sarangerel could get in behind the facility's network firewall, and, as a family team, spy on the workings of the facility."

"Doesn't sound like she's as good as me, if she

couldn't get behind the firewall." Jonas sits back, grinning.

"She's the best in all of China, believe me."

"I'm excited to meet her and compare notes."

Brand says, "Sounds like you'll be *taking* notes, dude, not comparing."

My mind is still processing Jie Wen's words. I ask, "Are you saying the parents aren't as important as the girl?"

"Not at all. The parents are deeply involved in the science behind charging powers into quartz. Their research, coupled with the information Sarangerel is able to get from the computers, will help the Bearers immensely."

I press further. "How long have you known about this group empowering quartz?"

"Long enough."

I glance over to Maetha, wondering if she knew about this. She doesn't look at me. I ask Jie Wen, "Longer than, say, five months?"

Chuang jumps into the conversation. "Our research is not your concern."

I sit up a little straighter and respond to Chuang. "You know, a whole lot of stuff happened not too long ago that your knowledge might have helped with."

His chin rises with his lips clamped together.

I continue. "People died over experiments with quartz. Good people."

"Good people die every day, Calli," Jie Wen says, as if I didn't know. "Our place as Diamond Bearers is to prevent groups like the one at the facility from becoming too powerful. You accomplished that with your team six months ago when you prevented General Harding from rising in power. Imagine how many more would have died if you didn't act when you did."

I find myself frustrated with his redirect, but I calm my mind and ask, "How did you discover this group?"

"Local clan members were being abducted, held for medical testing, then released with threats against their families if they retaliated in any way. They all reported seeing various quartz crystals while in captivity."

My attention is piqued. "What kind of medical testing?"

"A scan of some kind and blood work. The clan members all report their cosmic powers disappeared after being inside the bunker and having the tests performed."

I scoot a little closer as my stomach drops, loaded with dread. "They have one of General Harding's power-removing machines."

"Perhaps. Or maybe Harding had one of theirs."

"Whoa! I hadn't thought of that. Who designed or invented the machine? Freedom or someone else?"

Maetha finally enters the conversation. "If you go far enough back, everything we're fighting against today originated with Freedom. He either enlisted others or joined in others' cause. We don't know for sure. We're hoping the remaining files Sarangerel needs to get will reveal more information."

Jie Wen says, "My informant says the bunker has a security system that will wipe the computers if the alarm is sounded and not deactivated in a short amount of time. Because of this, we need to enter the bunker in two waves. The first will be Brand and me. We will take out the front guards, enter through the main door, find the security room, and unlock the front doors. At that time, the rest of you will enter the compound, using invisibility. We don't want anyone sounding the alarm. Dr. Tod works in Lab 1, and the two females are either with him or in their living quarters in room 8. We will be swift, concise, and armed, leaving as little evidence of our presence as possible."

I choose to ignore his obvious blow-off of the

females, and say, "Wait, armed?"

"Yes."

"No." I shake my head. "We're Diamond Bearers, plus we have Brand who can repeat us out of anything, Right Brand?"

He shrugs his shoulders.

I continue. "We'll be invisible, quick, and they'll never know we were there. Gunfire would raise alarms."

Chuang jumps in. "Weapons give us protection and speeds up the process. I vote we take them."

Jie Wen asks me directly, "How do you propose we enter the bunker if not with force?"

Brand suggests, "Knock on the door?"

Chuang scoffs and shakes his head.

Brand continues, "I say we try it Calli's way first. If it's not going to work, I'll repeat and we'll try something else."

Maetha says, "Yes. I agree with Brand. I also agree taking weapons can offer protection. Perhaps weapons should be used as a last resort."

I look at Brand, then Chuang. I turn my head to Maetha. "I agree with Maetha. Only use weapons as a last resort."

Everyone nods in agreement and I feel we've made it across our first hurdle as a team.

Maetha says, "Now, we need to practice harnessing the perception-altering power of Mind-Control." She stands and issues everyone a set of topazes. "Keep these in your pocket, not against your skin, until you're ready to use them. That way you won't accidentally drain the power." She tosses a box of four-by-four, self-adhesive bandages to Duncan. "Use these when it's time to attach the stones."

She goes on to give instructions concerning how to use the power. I already know, so I don't pay much attention and push the topazes into my pocket.

My mind is preoccupied with what-ifs. What if we'd had more knowledge going into General Harding's compound concerning quartz? What if we'd known about Healers quartz before I carried Freedom's pocket watch? Things would have been different. But how different? Would Brand still have his power in his body, not in a loose stone?

I notice him and Jonas practicing Invisibility with each other. Because I have the Blue shard, I can see everyone whether they're invisible or not. Brand is especially fun to watch as he masters the art of manipulating perceptions. I imagine he'd love to have this ability full-time.

He looks directly at me and our eyes lock. The excited expression falls from his face. "I guess I'm not doing it right," Brand says. "Calli can still see me."

Jonas laughs. "You're doing it, Brand. I can't see you. I can feel your presence, though."

Jie Wen leans forward and looks my direction. I see his movement with my peripheral vision and resist making eye contact with him.

After everyone masters the art of appearing invisible, and recognizing the locations of others when not visible, we change into provided camouflage fatigues and get ready to leave.

I walk out to the courtyard and find Jie Wen and Maetha in a hushed discussion. Maetha glances in my direction and says to Jie Wen, "This is not my decision. Take it up with Crimson."

I can't tell if Maetha is upset with the decision, whatever it is, or if she's at a loss for words and wants their discussion to end.

Jie Wen looks over his shoulder and sees me. He motions for me to join them, to which Maetha closes her eyes and inhales deeply. I walk over to them.

Jie Wen says, "Calli, there's no tactical advantage of having you participate in this extraction. You should stay here and Maetha should come."

"I'm supposed to come with you."

"You'll be a liability."

I stand my ground. "I'm a Diamond Bearer, Jie Wen, and not as experienced as you or the others. I need to learn from you, from your expertise."

"Don't patronize me. This is not the time to be learning."

"I'm coming. End of story." I half-expect him to fight the topic further, but he doesn't. He narrows his eyes and purses his lips, studying me. I try to read his mind but am blocked. I wish he'd try to communicate with Chuang so I could get an idea of what's going on in his mind.

He turns his head to the others. "Let's go. We have an hour-long drive ahead of us and no time to waste."

We arrive at a location deep in the forest/jungle. After we loaded into the six-seat Jeep back at Jie Wen's home, I wondered to myself where he planned on putting the three people we were headed to rescue. However, I kept my thoughts to myself. I didn't want his scrutinizing glare again.

One thing I found amusing before we left was Chuang and Jie Wen shed their robes, revealing tactical gear underneath. I guess that answers my question about fighting in robes.

Piling out of the Jeep, Duncan hands each of us one of the self-adhesive bandages for our topazes. "Put it in your pocket for now."

"Let's go." Chuang slings a long pack over his

shoulder and begins walking into the thick undergrowth.

Brand hops around, panting. He looks like he's about to enter a boxing ring. He says to me, "Are you ready for this?"

"Not really sure what 'this' actually is, but yes, I'm ready."

Jonas moves close to my ear. "I've got your back, Calli. I won't let anything happen to you."

"I don't think that's a promise you can make. How about we keep an eye open for each other and help wherever we can?"

He smiles. I realize I haven't seen him smile much lately. He always seems to have a worried look on his face.

"Keep quiet back there," Chuang orders over his shoulder.

Duncan looks over his shoulder and affirms Chuang's words.

Jie Wen nods.

A shiver climbs my spine, leaving me feeling on edge.

We walk in silence on a trampled path through the dense undergrowth. Ragged, machete-cut branches stick out precariously, threatening to snag or scratch passersby. I watch my step and keep my distance from anything dangerous.

Chuang stops the group and motions for us to crouch down. Then he creeps forward to a moss-covered boulder, easing his head up just high enough to see over the top. He moves away and motions for us to look over the boulder like he did. One at a time each of the team peeks over the boulder.

When it's my turn, I see a small valley about one-hundred yards across drop down below us. On the other side, a large metal doorway is built into the side of the hill with a narrow road consisting of two muddy ruts leading through the valley. Two armed guards stand on either side of the door. I lower my body and slide out of the way so Jonas can take a look.

I sit down by Brand who pulls out his topazes and bandage and attaches the stones to the side of his neck. The other Bearers follow his lead and attach their topaz as well, including me.

Brand gets up on one knee and addresses everyone. "Okay, so there's obsidian at the doorway, but not inside the bunker. Jie Wen and I will be let in peacefully if he acts like he's bringing in a new candidate for experimentation."

"What?" Chuang wrinkles his nose and shakes his head back and forth. "You don't know—"

Jie Wen hushes Chuang, then asks Brand, "You've already repeated?"

Brand throws a frustrated glance my direction. I think he wants to say, "Duh!" but instead he says, "Yes."

Jie Wen moves to a squatted position. "They'll let us in? Do they question my affiliation with the group?"

Brand tilts his head to the side. "Uh, no, I don't think so. Are you part of their group?"

The question hangs in the air for a brief second, then Jie Wen says, "What happens after we get inside?"

"The guy with the clipboard leads us down the hallway. That's how far I got. Look, all I know at this point is we'll be allowed to enter, and once the doors close behind us, the obsidian effects are canceled. Are we doing this or what?"

"Let's go," Jie Wen rises to a crouched stance and moves toward the bushes.

Brand grabs his arm. "Let me lead. I know the fastest route." Brand turns to Chuang. "Don't go beyond the bush with the red flowers or they'll see you."

Jie Wen and Brand leave the group, but not before

Chuang speaks with his thoughts to Jie Wen. *You trust his judgment?* Chuang asks.

Yes. We can't get what we need without him.

I don't let on that I hear their exchange. I have to wonder what Jie Wen meant with his words, "can't get what we need." He must be referring to the hostages, but it bothers me that he didn't answer about his affiliation with the group. I hope "we" doesn't mean someone else.

Duncan sidles over to the boulder and glimpses over the top. He speaks to our minds with his diamond. *Watch through my eyes.*

I access Duncan's diamond and look through his eyes the same way I looked through Chris's at Cave Falls. *Chris.* I wonder for a moment what he's doing. I send out my thoughts to him. He responds.

Calli, you have obsidian in your near future.

I know.

Please be careful.

I will. I instantly feel better just knowing he's watching out for me.

Duncan's view of the bunker reveals the two guards at the door are taking defensive positions, aiming their guns in front of them. Jie Wen and Brand come into view having exited the forest. I can see the guards' mouths moving but can't read their lips because I don't know their language. One guard speaks into his radio. Then the huge doors open slowly and a man in a lab coat holding a clipboard walks out to them. Jie Wen pushes Brand forward rather rudely and they enter the bunker. The doors close at the same slow pace and the guards take their position.

Chuang says, "Let's go." He moves forward and the rest of us follow.

We tread carefully through the undergrowth, keeping our heads down. The path is steep and winding to get to the bottom, but we make it within a minute. We pick our way through the bottom of the valley, jumping across a small stream. As we near the clearing where the road ends at the bunker's doors, Chuang puts his hand up, signaling for us to stop. To his left is a bush with red flowers. We squat down and hold perfectly still.

Duncan speaks to my mind. *Now we wait.*

Time ticks by at a tortoise's pace. I try to imagine what might be happening inside the bunker. Brand is probably delivering his trademarked groin kicks, knocking out any who stands in his way. I don't know if we'd be able to hear any gunfire. The doors are so immense and thick. This bunker is probably designed to withstand a nuclear blast.

What's taking them so long, Jonas says to my mind.

Don't worry. Brand is the best at these things.

I know. I lived with him for a couple months.

I clear my mind and try to imagine what Drs. Tod and Mishell and their daughter Sarangerel will be like. Do they speak English?

A loud clunk is heard and the doors begin to creak, causing the guards to stand at attention. Little by little the doors open

Now, Chuang announces non-verbally. *Invisibility. We're running inside.*

I activate my invisibility. The others do as well. Then we all run at super speed until we enter the obsidian field, slowing us down to normal human speed because we don't have Runners topaz. As we run past the two confused guards and into the building the doors slowly pull together behind us. The obsidian field is canceled.

Brand comes running down the hall, visible to anyone watching cameras. "Come quick," he says in a hushed voice. "You don't need your invisibility now."

Dropping my connection to the topaz, I hear

Chuang's telepathic voice, *This kid is crazy.*

I reply, *No, he just knows we're safe for the next two minutes.*

We follow Brand to the control room where we find two unconscious guards on the floor. Jie Wen searches the multiple surveillance screens. Jonas dumps himself in the main chair and goes right to work trying to hack the system. A voice comes across the radio. Jie Wen picks up the receiver and responds.

Duncan translates. "The guards are wondering about the main door malfunction. That's all."

Jie Wen hangs up the receiver and points to the diagram on the wall of the bunker floor plan. "The females are here in room 8. We need a four-digit code to gain entry. Dr. Tod is here in Lab 1. We need a keycard for the lock."

Brand points to the guards on the floor, "I already tried their cards on the lab door. They don't work." I look up at the monitors and see four guards standing outside Lab 1, talking to each other. Brand adds, "My Mind-Control topaz loses strength each time I repeat. It's half-way gone now."

I rip mine off my neck, holding onto the Healer topaz. "Trade with me. You need it more than I do."

We exchange topazes and re-attach our bandages. I focus on re-infusing his topaz with more power. As long as I'm not around obsidian I can use the Blue shard instead of the topaz.

Brand pauses, points to the monitor displaying the four guards outside the lab, and says, "Okay. That guard's card, the one standing by the lock, opens the door."

Chuang asks. "How do you know that?"

Brand ignores him. "Jonas, how's it going? In yet?"

"No." Jonas furiously types on the keyboard trying to find a way into the system.

Brand says, "Jie Wen, Chuang, and Duncan, go disable

those guards, get the scientist and bring him back here. Calli and I will go get the wife and kid. Use invisibility."

Brand doesn't wait for anyone to agree or disagree. He takes my hand, activates his invisibility, waits until I do the same, then we run down the hall to room 8. Brand halts abruptly, putting his hand up to signal a stop. A door further down the hall opens. Voices filter out into the hallway, then the door closes. Footsteps are heard, fading as they move away from us.

I'll never stop being grateful for Brand's ability.

We reach the door and Brand becomes visible again. "Keep your invisibility up, Calli. I don't want to drain mine any more than I have to." Brand stands still, staring at the number pad by the door to room 8. He enters a code and the light turns green.

"That was fast," I say. "How many repeats did it take to figure that out?"

"None. I saw a four-digit code written on the board by the monitors. Figured I'd try that one first. Ta-da. Oh, and you better stop being invisible. It freaks them out to see you reappear."

"So, you *did* repeat." I discontinue my use of the Blue's power.

"Just now, yeah." He pulls the door open. Inside the room, a woman gets up from her chair where she was reading a book. A girl around my age peeks over the top of her computer. Both look confused. Brand puts his finger to his mouth, signaling silence. I really hope they don't scream or sound an alarm.

I say, hoping they speak English, "We're here to help. Come and I'll take you to Jie Wen." *Boy, I really hope he used that name with them.* What if he's like Maetha, using a different name at each town?

"Jie Wen is here?" the girl asks, her voice rising.

"Yes. We have to go *now*."

They both run over. I look to Brand, wondering if we need to be invisible. He answers before I ask the question.

"No. We'll be fine, but we have to be silent." He turns on his heel and leads us back in the direction of the control room.

On the way there, I notice Sarangerel's height is close to mine, her frame is petite, and her skin is perfect like porcelain. Her mother Mishell is a bit taller, also petite, yet clearly more mature. Both are beautiful.

We enter the control room, closing the door behind us. I ask Jonas, "How's it going?"

"Not good. It's not working." He doesn't look our way, he just keeps typing.

Sarangerel hurries over to him and says, "Move." Jonas reluctantly glances up at her. She repeats, "Move!"

He jumps out of the chair and she sits. She clicks on the login screen and begins entering keys.

Brand moves to the wall of monitors and focuses on Lab 1's. "Hurry," he mutters to himself. I look at the monitor and see Duncan, Chuang, and Jie Wen slowly moving in for the attack, invisibly I presume. The guards talk animatedly, not knowing what's coming their way.

Bam! They attack. Jie Wen takes two down faster than the others. Chuang flattens his guard and grabs the keycard, swipes it, and opens the door. On another monitor I see Tod in the lab as he looks up to see who's coming. He rushes over to Jie Wen, who must be visible at this point.

Brand turns to me with a frighteningly panicked expression on his face. "This is going south. They have obsidian bullets! We need more time."

The room whirls around and around.

We arrive at the point where Brand and I stand

outside room 8, invisibly.

Brand says, "5591 is the code." He turns and starts running away. He calls over his shoulder, "I have to go help the others. Get those two to the control room."

Crap! I disconnect with my invisibility, open the door, and raise my finger to my lips. The two females look at me and I say, "I'm here to help."

Sarangerel looks over the top of her computer. "Who are you?"

"Friends with Jie Wen," sort of.

"He's here?"

"Yes. We must go *now*."

They jump up and join me in an instant.

We arrive at the control room. Jonas is still trying to crack the code.

"Jonas," I say, "move so Sarangerel can work."

Sarangerel looks at me and I read her mind. *She knows my name?*

Jonas states, "I've almost got it."

"Move!" Sarangerel and I both say at once.

He jumps up, possibly on the verge of firing off at Sarangerel. Then he notices the monitor for Lab 1. He points. I follow his finger and watch as Brand single-handedly takes down three of the guards as Jie Wen takes down one. Chuang opens the door and rushes into Lab 1.

I try to figure out how much time Brand has saved with this change. It can't be much, mere seconds, but to Brand, that's huge.

"Are they saving my husband?" Mishell asks.

"Yes," I say, not knowing if I can promise anything.

Sarangerel says, "I know the password for the system is seven characters long and consists of only lettered keys on the bottom row."

Jonas crosses his arms and scoffs. "A password

consisting of seven characters will be impossible to crack before we're discovered. Are all letters used once? Are any letters repeated?"

Sarangerel doesn't answer and begins entering letters.

Jonas moves back and forth in his spot. "Do you realize how big of a number seven to the seventh power is? I say we keep on my path of working around the pass-word."

Sarangerel's attempt fails. She types a second in the blink of an eye. Failure again.

"This method will take too long." Jonas points to the unconscious guards. "They're going to wake up, and the system is going to lock down."

She says, "I know for sure the first key is Z and the last key is B."

Brand and the other Bearers enter the control room with Tod. Brand responds as if he's heard the whole password conversation. "Hang on, that narrows it down a lot. Let me try." He grabs a pad of paper and a pen, then pulls the keyboard closer to him.

Now Sarangerel acts a bit slighted. She gets up and moves over to her father, who has an arm around Mishell and the other wrapped around a bundle the size of a basketball.

Brand stares at the paper, pen in hand. Ten seconds tick by.

Chuang paces behind us.

Ten more seconds pass.

Sarangerel comes back to the computer with a confused expression as she looks Brand over. "I don't know what you think you're doing—"

Brand jots down letters on the pad, then types them in. The computer accepts the code. "Got it!" Brand ex-claims, moving from his spot so Sarangerel can take over.

"Okay, do *your* magic."

She throws him a wary glance. "How did you know the code?" She doesn't wait for his answer. A new screen opens. She maneuvers through the files and moves them to the flash drive file. As the progress bar slowly moves across the bottom of the screen, she looks at the security monitors and the unconscious guards on the floor.

Brand announces, "Bearers, we need to give her time while the files load."

Jie Wen, Duncan and Chuang pull the guns they've brought with them. Before I protest, I remember Brand mentioning obsidian bullets. And it's only a matter of time before someone finds the unconscious guards on the floor by the lab. I figure it's better to be firing the bullets verses getting fired at, so I hold my tongue.

Brand says, "You four," pointing to Jonas, Sarangerel and her parents, "when the files are done uploading, run to the front entrance. We'll meet you there." Brand looks at me and I read his mind. *Hopefully.* His eyes change slightly, almost as if he's deciding the best way to save everyone. *Maybe you'd better go with them, Calli . . . no, wait . . . come with us. Maybe you can use your Mind-Control on them.* Brand swirls his finger above his head and says, "Let's go, Bearers. Invisibility!"

We run out of the room and follow him further back into the bunker. I figure we're leading the guards away from the others. We round a corner and see three guards waiting with guns pointing our direction. One of the guards has a bloody nose and broken bottom lip.

Chuang says, *They can't see us. Should we attack?*

Hold. Brand puts his thoughts to the front of his brain as he cannot send them telepathically.

One of the guards asks the bloodied guard while looking our direction, "Are you sure someone's there?"

"Do you think I did this to my own face? Yes. They are invisible. Why haven't you sounded the alarm?"

"They'll ask for descriptions of the intruders. I'm not going to say they're invisible. We need something more than that."

"Four guards taken down, three still unconscious, isn't enough to sound the alarm?" The bloodied guard cocks his gun and says, "I'll sound my own alarm." He begins shooting.

Chuang fires back.

Gunfire erupts in a deafening roar. Stings and burns rip through my flesh as I realize I'm being pelted with . . . stuff. *What is this?* It's not obsidian. Yet my powers are unusable. Around me I see Chuang and Jie Wen on the ground in growing puddles of blood.

"Calli," Brand grunts, "something needs to happen differently or we're all going to die." Brand has been shot too, but the substance can't stop or remove his power, obviously. He's already repeated back from this situation. At least I think he has.

I say, "Next time I'll control the guards actions."

The floor and walls spin around and around. Everything stops. We're in the control room at the moment after Brand's group arrived with Dr. Tod from Lab 1. Sarangerel is trying to crack the code on the computer.

Brand rushes over and pulls the keyboard closer to him, away from Sarangerel.

"Excuse me?" Sarangerel protests. "Who are you?"

I remember this moment. Brand is about to blow about twenty seconds figuring out the code. But not this time. Instead, he types it right in and access is given immediately. Sarangerel stares at him with strange admiration, as if she's seeing him for the first time. In reality, she is.

She says, "How did you do that?"

I say to Brand, "You just saved twenty seconds. Is it enough?"

"I don't know."

Three simple words from Brand I'm not sure how to process. *I don't know.* I don't know? Of course you know! His words leave me feeling similar to hearing Maetha say the same words. I feel the incredible need to get out. I'm cornered. I'm vulnerable. I'm in danger. *Get me out!* My heart races uncontrollably. Five Bearers are in danger of losing their lives, their diamonds captured. Where's Crimson? Seriously? She's nowhere? Come on!

The ground spins around my confused mind as Brand performs another repeat. Am I ever going to see Chris again? My parents? Are any of us going to get out?

We arrive at nearly the same point as before, only this time Brand doesn't grab the keyboard. He takes the nearby pad of paper and quickly jots down the computer code. He pushes it toward Sarangerel with a nod. He says, "Hurry."

"What?" she asks. "Who are you?"

"It's the code. Go!" Then he turns to me and says, "We need to create a clear pathway to the front entry. Once the files are transferred, we all need to run with superpower running. Otherwise, none of us will get out."

I hear Jonas telling a reluctant Sarangerel to enter the code before the system locks up. As she types the numbers, Duncan and Chuang shift back and forth on their feet.

"Does this plan look good?" I ask Brand.

"I can only see two minutes. So far, so good."

Chuang asks, rather demandingly, "What are you talking about?"

Brand raises his voice and puts his hands up in front of him, "No more questions and maybe you'll live this time." Jie Wen's mouth hangs open as Brand points to

Chuang and Duncan. "You two stand guard while Sarangerel downloads the files. Then run with her to the main doors. When you see people wearing white coats, lay flat on the ground. Understand?" Brand turns and points to me, Jonas, Jie Wen, Tod and Mishell. "Come, now." He runs out of the room and we follow.

Jonas sends his thoughts. *Calli, does Brand have this under control? He seems like he's losing it.*

I don't know.

We run a little way then Brand halts us. "Jie Wen," Brand points to the wall, "stand right here and shoot the guard that's coming around the corner. Keep the hall clear for the others." Brand motions for the rest of us to follow him as he continues down the hall.

The main doors come into view. I breathe a sigh of relief.

Brand grabs my arm. "There's a fire extinguisher in the room by the doors. Use it to smash the keypad on the wall by the doors. Hurry, before the grenade goes off."

Grenade?

A gunshot echoes from Jie Wen's direction. He must have fired his weapon. I don't hesitate. I run into the side room, locate the extinguisher, and yank it off the wall. Hustling out into the hall, I see Brand and Jonas in a defensive stance, holding two large guns, pointed down the hallway. I run over to the keypad and ram the bottom of the extinguisher into it as hard as I can. Little plastic pieces and buttons fly and slide across the floor as crackling sparks shoot out of the keypad.

Brand shouts, "Push the doors open before they re-lock."

I run over with Tod and Mishell and push against the massive doors. The doors move a little, hopefully enough to prevent them from locking. We keep pushing.

"What do you hope to accomplish?" a male voice with a German accent sounds from down the hall.

I turn and look beyond Brand and Jonas. Several people wearing white lab coats stand in the hallway. Coming up behind them is Jie Wen, Chuang, Duncan, and Sarangerel. The lab coated individuals seem harmless, as if they are caught in the crossfire, but the tone of voice the German-accented man used says otherwise.

"Get down, guys," Brand mutters under his breath.

Jonas asks, "Us?"

"No. Them, Jie Wen and the others. I told them to get down. We can't shoot the bad guys without hitting them."

In unison, "the bad guys" grab onto their breast pockets and pull out black stones in one movement. Obsidian.

My diamond and Blue diamond powers rush away from my body. I quickly access the topaz attached to my neck. It's mostly drained. Can I use it for Mind-Control? No. Can I still use it for invisibility? Yes.

The same man as before says to us, "Is this little black stone troublesome to you? That's a shame. We don't have a problem with it." The man looks at the others who chuckle with him. He then turns to a couple accompanying guards and says, "Capture them. Alive."

Brand says, "Not gonna happen. Get down!" he shouts to the others who fall to the ground instantly. Brand and Jonas open fire on the lab coats and guards. More guards come behind Duncan, Chuang, Sarangerel and Jie Wen, trapping them. Jie Wen rolls over on his back and fires his gun at the approaching guards. The ear-splitting shots from the guns echo through the hallway.

The lab coats duck for cover into open doorways. Tod and Mishell push against the large doors, and I can hear the guards outside yelling indiscernibly.

Brand yells, "Now, Chuang!"

Chuang and the others jump up and run toward us as Brand raises his hand holding a small metal ball. With his thumb, he flicks the small metal pin out of the device and drops it to the floor. The firing stops momentarily, long enough that I hear the pin hit the ground. Brand throws the grenade as Jonas grabs my hand and pulls me toward the side wall, pinning me with his body.

The grenade detonates. The force knocks me and Jonas off our feet. Everything sounds like I'm underwater, then my ears start to ring intensely. Ceiling tiles and lighting fixtures fall all around me as dust and smoke clouds fill the hallway. Yellow emergency lights begin flashing overhead, illuminating the scene. The large doors have blown open. The two guards outside lay unconscious on the ground. Across the way, all of the team members, including Brand lay in a heap. No one moves.

My powers are still gone, and now that the doors are open, I have to assume the exposed exterior obsidian is the reason.

Jonas sits up. "Calli, are you all right?"

"I think so." Nothing hurts, so I get up and rush over to the others. Jonas is only one step behind.

Coughing on the dust and smoke, I help separate the group. Everyone is alive, but some are slower to gain their wits than others.

Brand rubs his head. "I don't think we can get that any better, guys. We're all in one piece for now. We've got to run, though."

I hear yelling down the hall. Then small square panels open on the walls spaced about ten feet apart. I look inside the nearest one and see what looks like the bell of a trumpet.

Sarangerel shouts, "Get down!"

Before I can follow her orders, things start shooting out of the opening in random directions. I can hear them hitting the walls across the hall. Each of the square panels are shooting out whatever the stuff is. A sharp pain rips through my thigh, but I don't have time to think about it.

The main doors begin closing. Brand yells, "Out! Everyone out."

It's painfully clear everyone has been injured by the stuff that came out of the walls. After getting outside, I look down at my leg and find something sharp and shiny sticking out. I grab it with my hand and pull out the small object. Blood oozes down my pants. I can't use my diamond's power, so I access my healing topaz to stop my bleeding. I don't try to heal completely as to not drain the topaz. Behind me, Jie Wen, Duncan, Mishell, and Tod push on the big doors to close them faster. As soon as they shut, a loud clunk is heard.

Tod says, panting for breath, "They're in lockdown now. No one in or out for at least fifteen minutes."

Jie Wen marches to Brand, "You were supposed to protect us!"

"You have *no* idea what I just did! You'd all be dead right now if it weren't for me." Brand shoves past Jie Wen and heads over towards me, blood running down the side of his face. "Next time let's follow Jie Wen's plan. Give me a gun and I'll go all Deus Ex on em'. Let's get out of here!"

Chapter Five - Confusion

We hustle as quickly as we can back to the Jeep with Brand in the lead. Duncan is the least injured so he brings up the rear. I help Sarangerel by wrapping my arm around her waist and letting her lean against me. Her knee is injured and she's struggling to walk.

Chuang appears to be in the worst shape. Jie Wen and Jonas have to nearly carry him, he's so bad off. Jie Wen's and Jonas' injuries aren't minor, either. However, they've used some of their Healer topaz to stop the bleeding like I did. Mishell and Tod have obvious injuries to their upper bodies but are mobile. Tod supports Mishell's weight with one arm and carries the bundle under the other.

We reach the vehicle and the same question hits me: how are we going to fit everyone inside?

Chuang says to Jie Wen, "I told you we needed two jeeps."

"We'll fit. We'll just have to get creative now that no one can use their running power."

Tod says, "We can use the blankets now." He opens the bundle and separates the golden, silky, shimmery material into four pieces. "Put your friend in the front seat." He points to Chuang.

Jie Wen and Jonas help Chuang into the front passenger seat. Then Tod lays one of the blankets on top of Chuang and closes his door.

Duncan announces, "I'll drive."

Jonas, Brand, and I climb awkwardly into the back two seats. I try to find a comfortable position but keep bumping Brand's injured arm. Jonas pulls me onto his lap so my shoulders are away from Brand and my back is up against the side of the Jeep. Not that it's any more comfortable for me. My shoulders are now crammed between the back of the seat in front and Jonas's chest. He places one arm behind me and the other across my legs, holding onto my knee.

Tod and Mishell take the middle seat directly in front of us, and Jie Wen sits in the other with Sarangerel. Tod hands one of the blankets back to Brand, which he spreads over himself and extends the edge to Jonas and me. Jonas pulls the blanket onto my legs. The remaining two blankets are used by Tod and Mishell, and Jie Wen.

Duncan begins the bumpy drive back. "Sorry, everyone. I'll try to miss the big holes."

My leg hurts every time I tense up from a bump, then again, I'm tense simply from the situation. I feel Jonas's hand moving on my leg and look down.

He's pulled the shimmery blanket back and is examining my leg. He says, "Your leg is hurt real bad, Calli. Do you have any more topaz power left?"

"I stopped the bleeding. It only looks bad." I pull the bandage off my neck and feel the two topazes. I reach my hand forward between the seats. "Jie Wen, give my topaz to Chuang. There's still some power in it."

He takes the bandage and separates the topaz and hands the healing stone to Chuang. Jie Wen throws a suspicious glance over his shoulder at me with the Mind-Control topaz between his fingers, then he puts it in his pocket.

Chuang grunts and lets out a hiss. He holds up a bloody chunk he's just pulled from his body. "What is this? It's not obsidian."

"No, it's not," Tod says, but this substance also blocks

the ability to use powers."

Brand asks, "Well, what is it?"

"Fused silica. Finely ground quartz mixed with sand, melted, molded, charged with the anti-power, then broken into pieces and put in everything from dirty bombs and grenades to bullets and the emergency weapons system installed inside the walls."

"What is the anti-power?" Duncan asks, not taking his hands off the wheel.

"I don't know."

I've already drawn the conclusion Tod and his family know a lot about the cosmic powers, especially if there was a power-removing machine at the bunker.

I hear Chris's voice in my mind. *Calli, what's going on? Can you hear me?*

I hear you, I answer.

Calli, can you hear me? Are you there?'

Yes, I hear you.

I can't seem to be able to bi-locate to you. Can you hear me, Calli?

I want to tell him I've been hit with Confusion Glass, but he wouldn't know what that is.

Speaking to the group, I say, "I was only hit with one piece, which I've removed, yet my powers are still confused. I can hear Chris trying to connect with me, but he can't hear me."

Jie Wen says, wincing as he yanks out a shard from his upper arm, "Well, you're fortunate. The rest of us have been pelted."

Jonas pulls the blanket over my legs and tightens his protective hold around my waist.

This is going to be a long ride back.

We arrive at Jie Wen's home and see Maetha waiting for us. Chris is bi-located by her side.

Maetha opens Chuang's door. "What happened?"

Duncan comes around to help her carry Chuang inside. "Let's get him inside first."

Chris's eyes are zoomed in on me, sitting on Jonas's lap. His voice sounds in my head again. *Why didn't you respond to me?*

I speak, "I did, but obviously it didn't work. We were hit with a confusion substance. I could hear you, but I couldn't use my powers."

The rest of us exit the Jeep one by one. Chris remains by Maetha's side to stay connected to her diamond. I wonder how it must look to Tod and his family to see an able-bodied man not helping injured people. I can't read their minds, but I don't have to. Their gazes keep flicking towards him, frowns and furrowed brows indicating their disapproval.

Jonas helps me out of the Jeep and we follow the others to a room inside. Jie Wen directs Maetha to the storage area to retrieve several floor mats and first-aid supplies. After she spreads out the mats, the others sit or lay with the quartz blankets covering them. Jonas helps me over to a mat next to Brand. Then Maetha kneels beside me and assesses my injury.

I angle my head and ask under my breath, "Shouldn't you work on the worst injured first?"

"No. Healing you first will give us two Healers to work on the rest." She grabs my torn pants and rips them more.

Chris sits by me and reaches out for my hand only to have his bi-located form pass through mine. Obviously frustrated he can't be here with me, his eyebrows lower. "I don't understand why you were all injured. Why didn't

Brand protect you?"

Brand glares at Chris. "I did the best I could! All right? Sheez, no one appreciates my efforts."

"I do," I say to Brand. "How many times did you repeat to make sure everyone lived?"

His pissed-off expression softens. "Too many to count. Each time I risked not being able to repeat."

Chris says, "What do you mean? Your quartz isn't affected by anything now."

"If I'm dead, I can't use my repeating quartz, *Chris*."

I say, "I thought the power always repeats you out of death."

"If the quartz is not in my possession, I can't use it to save my life. It's all quite precarious, really. This whole situation has made me absolutely sure I want the quartz inserted into my head—and I want it done before I leave China."

Wow! Brand's change of attitude is a big indicator of just how hard he worked to make sure we lived. I wonder if he'll change his stance on receiving a diamond.

Maetha says, "Calli, I can see a piece of shrapnel in your leg.

"I pulled it out."

"You still have a piece just below the entry wound of the other. Brace yourself. I'm going to remove it."

I look away and flinch when I feel her fingers dig into my flesh, reminding me of the pain I endured only a few days ago when Marketa did the same thing. I squeeze the edges of the mat, breathe in sharply, and hold back the yelp that wants to escape my lips.

"There," she says. I look over and see her holding a jagged piece about one-inch long. She examines it closely, then puts it down. "Are you able to use your powers now?"

I focus on the healing ability and feel myself access the

diamond. The strength is muted a bit but seems to be coming back into my control. I nod my head.

"Great," she says. "Help me with the others."

"Okay." I remove the quartz blanket and focus my power. Soon I'm able to stand up with no pain. In the far corner, I see Crimson. I didn't see her before Maetha removed the second piece. She's obviously invisible to everyone else. I ask her with my mind, *How long have you been there?*

The whole time.

So, the confusion substance doesn't affect your ability to use powers on people? I mean, that's why they can't see you, right?

That's correct. This substance is not as disabling as obsidian. Now that your power is restored, you'll be able to heal others like Maetha did with you. It seems this substance would be effective to disable an opponent long enough to kill them either with a power or with traditional means. Now, go help the others.

I hurry over to Chuang, figuring his injuries seem to be the worst. Plus, he's a Bearer. If he's healed, he can help with the others.

Chuang waves his hand in the air as if he's shooing me away. "Get away from me. I'll wait for Maetha."

Jie Wen also declines my help, although not as rudely.

I move on to Duncan.

Duncan says, "Don't waste your time on me, Calli. Help them." He motions to the scientists.

I don't argue with him and move to Tod and Mishell. Tod points to Sarangerel and says, "Help her first."

Is everybody going to decline my help? I glance over to Maetha. In the time I've tried to help someone, Maetha has removed the glass from Brand's leg. However, I do understand why Sarangerel's parents would want their child helped first. My parents would do the same thing.

Positioning myself in front of Sarangerel, I remove the

Healer blanket and scan her body. She has three wounds, none of which are deep. I give instructions for her to lift her sleeve to her shoulder. As she does so, I overhear Bearers' voices in what they think is a private conversation.

This is her fault. She shouldn't have tried to run the show.

She can't help herself. She knows she's Crimson's pet.

I don't like that we have to listen to her or else we risk Marketa's fate.

Sarangerel cries out as I pull out the first piece. I issue pain relief and stop the bleeding with my diamond, then move onto the other two injuries. Some of her clothing has to be moved aside or ripped to gain access.

Look at her. She thinks she's a doctor.

I resist the intense urge to fire back a retort and stay focused on what I'm doing. Maetha has moved onto Jonas's injuries. I become aware of what's going on. Maetha, probably under Crimson's direction, is healing in the order of importance, not urgency. The younger Bearers are apparently more important. Even though Brand isn't a Bearer, his power is *definitely* important. After what he declared about having his quartz inserted, I think he's getting closer to accepting a diamond.

Maetha moves to Jie Wen after finishing up with Jonas. Interesting she chooses him over Chuang, or Duncan for that matter.

I help Tod and Mishell. While doing so, I read their minds. Collectively, they wonder how Maetha and I are doing what we're doing, but they know better than to question at this time. Clearly, they don't know about the diamonds.

I overhear Maetha and Jie Wen talking. Maetha says, "You should have your power back. Try again."

"It's still muddled."

"Keep the blanket on until you gain control of your

powers." Maetha then moves to Chuang. She says, "You have shrapnel and a bullet wound. I'm going to remove the bullet from your side first."

I finish with Tod and Mishell and move back over to Duncan to begin working on him. His injuries are flesh wounds, minor, with no remaining shards of confusion glass. Yet, his powers are still jumbled for some reason. I delve deeper with my mind into his wounds, searching on the cellular level. The small specks of glass are easily identifiable to me. No bigger than grains of salt, and some being the size of a grain of powder, I try to determine the best way to clear out his body. Should I use my greater Healing power? Or should I tell Maetha's mind, alerting her to the presence of the tiny fragments and let her remove them. I have to imagine this is also the reason Jie Wen doesn't have his powers back yet.

I decide to ask Crimson. I describe what I see to her then ask, *What should I do in this situation?*

She replies, *The health of those three Bearers does not change the outcome of the overall future. Revealing the fact that you have the greater Healing power, however, does. The choice is yours. If you feel the time is right to let them know the extent of your powers, then go ahead.*

Is there anything I can do for him without exposing my greater Healing power?

No. With enough time, Duncan's body will push the substance out like a splinter.

I overhear Maetha's words to Chuang. "The bullet was full of powder, which is now inside your belly. I can't get it out."

I move over to Maetha and say, "If he was operated on, the powder could be removed with the same tool they use to suction excess blood."

"Get her away from me. I don't want to hear any of

her nonsense."

I walk over to Chris by the other two guys and sit down.

Brand says, loud enough for Chuang to hear, "Well, that's a fine insult. She's just trying to help your sorry butt."

"She's the reason I'm hurt like this."

"No, she's not. I am," Brand defends.

"What do you mean?" Chuang turns his head and looks at Brand.

Brand says, "I positioned you to be a shield to protect Sarangerel from being killed. It was the last repeat I performed—the one where everyone lived. You're just a whiner because you probably haven't felt real pain for a long time and you want to blame Calli for it."

Chuang, offended good and well, says, "If we'd followed Jie Wen's plan and used weapons first—"

"Ha! Jie Wen's plan," Brand scoffs. He speaks to Jie Wen, "Do you want to tell him how well *that* worked out for us?"

Jie Wen doesn't respond. He only narrows his eyes and crosses his arms.

Brand looks back at me with an irritated expression and shakes his head a moment. Then he speaks in a more serious tone. "So, you're going to be like that? Well, Jie Wen, you asked specifically for me to be on this mission. I took you on several repeats to show you what was going to go wrong. And now you're going to sit there and support Chuang in his bull-headed stupidity? You know what? Don't bother asking for my help again."

The air crackles with tension. I want to look behind me to see if Crimson is still there hearing this but decide not to.

Brand adds, "I completed what you asked for: safe entrance into the bunker, safe retrieval of the family, computer files extracted, quartz blankets acquired, keep everyone alive upon exiting. What I want to know is what was so damned important?"

Tod speaks up. "Young man, the importance lies in the computer files. They detail all the studies and tests that have taken place over decades, manipulating DNA, creating strange powers, removing powers, etc."

I pick up on the Bearers speaking with their thoughts. *Why don't you have your powers back, Jie Wen?*

Why don't you?

The question you two need to be asking yourself is why does she?

The hair prickles on the back of my neck. The last comment made had a new energy to it, one I haven't detected before when the dissenters talk to each other. Could it be Maetha's thoughts?

You're right. Jonas's powers aren't restored yet, like ours. Why her?

Brand and Tod's discussion goes on in the background as the Bearers conspire. When Tod talks about the quartz Healing blankets, I think to myself how one of these blankets would have been useful on New Year's Eve.

I turn my thoughts to Chris and speak to his mind. *Guess I'm not invincible yet. Or indestructible.*

His expression softens and his lips pinch at one corner. *I wish you weren't determined to find out if you are or not.*

I didn't get injured on purpose, Chris.

I know. Calli, I have to go now. I need to get ready for work.

What time is it there?

Twelve hours behind you. I'll come see you as soon as I can. He winks at me and vanishes. I use the opportunity to look around the room only to find Crimson is gone, too.

I reflect on the events and decide I should never knowingly put myself in a situation where I can be killed again. I have a responsibility to keep humanity alive, and I must survive. I'm only virtually indestructible. I can't bank on that keeping me alive.

In the background, I listen as the Bearers and scientists and Brand discuss the goings on at the bunker. With the exception of the quartz blankets and confusion glass, it sounds like an identical setup as General Harding's facility.

I absentmindedly say, "We need to find the source, the manufacturer, of the machine."

All heads turn my way.

Chuang protests, "How? We don't even know if there is one."

"There was a company listed in the files from the Denver compound. Vor-hair, Vor-something. Anyway, I'll bet they're in the files from the bunker, too."

Maetha says, "We'll have to examine the files. For now, we need to get back to Bermuda."

Jie Wen sits taller and says, "I'm staying here."

"That's your choice. Capt. Rutherfield has alerted me the flight plans are in place. Chuang, I suggest you come with me so I can help you through your healing process." She turns to Tod and Mishell. "Your family will be safest on my private island. We have a fully functional lab where you can continue your work, plus we are in the process of building our own power-removing machine."

"What?" I interject. "Why are you building one?"

Jonas turns to me. "Calli, we're in an arms race. If they've already figured out how to disable us, we need to know how to counter it."

Brand jumps in. "Hey, I want my quartz inserted before I go anywhere."

Maetha looks Brand up and down. "I don't think that's a good idea at this time. You'll need time to heal and an appropriate place to do so. The island would be perfect, not 30,000 feet in the sky."

Brand grumbles loudly but concedes.

I can't believe how quickly we're up in the air again and on our way back to Bermuda. One thing's for sure: everything goes smoother when you're leaving Chinese airspace than entering.

For the first many hours, I listen to Chuang and Duncan speak Mandarin to Tod, Mishell, and Sarangerel. Even though I can't understand them, I know they are being educated about cosmic powers, clans, governments, and the little that we know to date, based on their hand gestures. The exhaustively long stretch of hours that lay ahead of us is not fun to think about. However, with the newly acquired files and information, at least it won't be boring.

Brand and Jonas sit by me, Jonas on his laptop computer, Brand on his phone texting Beth. I send a few texts back and forth with my parents, then I settle back and take a nap.

I am awaked to Brand complaining. "I don't want to wait any longer."

Maetha shrugs her shoulders. "I won't have time to help you for a few weeks. There's no point in you living on the island for that long without a purpose."

"Huh?" Brand sounds dejected.

"Every soul on the island has to be cared for. From food and extra electricity usage down to toilet paper. If you don't have a purpose for being on the island, I'd rather you not be there. I'll let you know when I have the time to devote to inserting the quartz. Until then, don't lose your head."

We arrive in Bermuda and drop off Maetha, Chuang, Jonas, Sarangerel, and her parents. Duncan, Brand and I begin our flight to the U.S., with a quick stop in Washington D.C. to drop off Duncan.

Brand and I don't talk much for the rest of the way to Denver. He sits by Captain Rutherfield, asking unending questions about flying. My mind swims with topics, including the upcoming cosmic blast to hit Portland. I'm feeling a bit overwhelmed with the knowledge the enemy has confusion quartz glass and can't decide which is worse: the confusion glass or obsidian. Both stop the use of powers, but confusion glass is easily created with an unending supply where obsidian has a finite amount. Of course, without the power-removing machine, the quartz cannot be charged with any power.

All of this information needs to be shared with the clans and they need to join together to help one another defend against our common foe. I don't know what I can say to convince them how serious this is. I don't know if they'll even listen to me. More pressing is I need them to unite to help with the Portland blast.

I let out a deep exhale and lay my head back on the seat, closing my eyes. To say I feel overwhelmed is quite the understatement.

Our taxi comes to a stop outside Chris's father's house in Denver. I pay the driver and Brand pulls our luggage out of the trunk. The freezing temperature and layer of snow and ice is a stark contrast to what we left in China.

Chris's voice enters my head as soon as we get inside.

Calli, you're not going to believe this. Max called me.

He did?

Are you in a secure location that I can bi-locate to you?

Yes.

Chris's form materializes next to me in the living room. He looks around. "You should bring everyone in here so they can all hear."

"I think it's just me and Brand."

"Where's Maetha?"

"She stayed in Bermuda to help Chuang."

Brand comes out from his room with a note in his hand. "Oh, hi Chris." He waves the note. "Beth and Anika are on a task and should be back tomorrow."

Chris looks at me. "I wish I could be there with you."

"You are," I say with a smile, trying to calm his worry. I know he's uncomfortable with Brand and I being alone after what he divulged before we left for China. "What did Max say when he called?"

Brand's attention comes to full stop and his eyes widen.

Chris says, "He called to ask for money. He said he had to flee the country because the Diamond people knew who he was. I was surprised he admitted he ran the blog. I asked him why he lied to me about it and he said he didn't know for sure which side I was on. He warned me about 'their' plan to take over the world. He said people with powers want to rise up and take over governments, countries, and everything and we must fight back. I asked him what he thought I should do. He told me to get some obsidian from my father's compound and stick close to the government. Only they could save us now."

I ask, "Did you ask where he was?"

"Yes. He said overseas, then apologized, saying he

couldn't risk giving that information over phone lines."

Brand says, "Didn't he say anything about shooting Calli?"

"He didn't, but I did. I was careful not to let on that I personally knew what happened. I said the news showed cell phone footage of him holding a gun aimed at Calli. He had already shot her in the arm. His reply was, 'Yeah, I did that.' "

Brand grunts insults.

Chris continues. "I pressed him further, saying he's a better shot than that. With that close of range he should have been able to hit her right between the eyes." Chris pauses, looks at me, "Sorry, Calli." He continues. "Max said he wasn't trying to kill you, just as you suspected, Calli. He wanted to test out the bullets he stole."

I ask, "If he stole the bullets, he would have a limited supply. What about his connection with Marketa? Did he mention that?"

"Only that he wondered if the news reported what happened to you and the other woman. I said only that you reported to the police station to give your side of the story. The other woman wasn't with you. He didn't like that answer."

"Do you think he's waiting to hear from Marketa? I mean, they were in this together. Maybe they had a place chosen to run and he's frustrated she hasn't joined him."

Chris says, "Anything is possible. He still seemed to treat me with suspicion."

Brand adds, "It sounds to me like he's suspicious of everyone. He can't tell who has a superpower and who doesn't. He's threatened by anyone and everyone."

I say, "He did this to himself."

"I have to go now, Calli," Chris says apologetically. "Would you relay my news to the other Bearers?"

"Yes."

We say our goodbyes and Chris's form disappears from view.

Brand stands and paces back and forth. "I wouldn't be able to keep my cool like Chris if I was in the same situation with Max."

"Yes, he's extremely level-headed in tense situations."

"I wasn't when we were in China. You didn't see it, but I lost it several times. Most of them because you had just died and it was my fault."

I don't know what to say. My memories of the bunker are vivid enough without knowing the might-have-beens. I look into Brand's eyes. "Hey, you were successful. No one died. You did great!"

"Thanks." He sways his shoulders back and forth and looks to the floor. "I wish Beth was here. I need a hug."

I know what he's trying to do. I think for a second that a hug would be appropriate right now, as a thank you for saving my life. But is that how Brand would interpret it? Or Chris, for that matter. What about Beth? Instead I say, "I wish Beth was here too. Be sure to give her an extra big hug when you see her next. I'm going to make some tea. Would you like some?"

He smiles, says, "Yes," then follows me into the kitchen. "Calli, I didn't mean to make you feel uncomfortable just now."

"Don't worry about it." I fill the tea kettle with water and put it on to boil. Brand sits at the counter. I turn to him and ask, "Are you going to become a Bearer?"

"Eventually, probably, most likely . . . I think."

"Is there something in particular that's bothering you?"

"I don't know. I guess I realize just how long forever is. It's exhausting doing all those repeats, Calli. And I know you understand how repeating makes my day seem more like a week, and a week more like a year. I feel like I've already lived a lifetime."

"Every time you pull me with you, my mind takes a little while to adjust to reality. It is exhausting, but I use the Diamond's healing power to calm my body and restore my energy."

"Why do I need a whole diamond just to use the healing ability? Why don't I just carry a Healer's quartz?"

"That's a good idea. But what about the running ability? You're Unaltered now. You can't have the power passed on to you."

"Runner's quartz."

"Hunter abilities?"

"I don't want to smell people."

"Mind-Reading?"

"Not interested." He gets up and walks to the cupboard, removes two cups, and sets them on the counter.

"Seer?"

"Now that one I'm most afraid of getting. I don't know what would happen if I could see the way I should resolve an issue."

"Maybe it would prevent you from having to repeat so much."

"Huh. I didn't think of that."

"Don't forget the Diamond connection we all share. We can communicate with each other's minds from around the world, view memories, bi-locate, and extract memories."

"Well, I seem to always be around a Bearer, mainly you, so why would I need those extra powers? Just get me a Healer's quartz, and maybe a Runner's, and I think that will be good."

"Okay. One more thing, Brand: until you have the

Repeating quartz inserted in your body, you could die."

"Yes."

"The diamond's Seer power could help you keep an eye on your own safety."

Brand grabs the tin of tea bags and pulls the lid off. "Calli, I have my whole life to decide if I want to be a Bearer. Once the quartz is in my head, I'll be just fine."

"True, but once the unowned diamonds have owners, which they will, you'll have to wait till someone surrenders one or gets killed. You might die of old age before that happens. I don't think you can repeat out of a heart attack, can you?"

"Hmm, good question. But if I had a Healer quartz, I could repeat and heal the problem."

"True, I suppose. But here's one last thing to consider: Sanguine Diamonds hold powers originating from the cosmos 5,000 years ago. The powers were stronger then. The Bearers are able to keep their appearances because of this. You never got to see the Death Clan. They were Healers from only a couple hundred years ago who used the modern power to heal their heart attacks and other deadly diseases. They looked like aliens. The Healer quartz you want was made recently, extracting modern power and putting it in the quartz, the same power the Death Clan used. The power is dramatically weaker than what's in a diamond. Just something to think about." I pat him on the shoulder as the tea kettle whistles.

We pour our tea and sit in silence at the counter. I'm not sure why I feel I need to convince Brand to become a Bearer, but maybe it's because I understand how powerful he is and I believe he would enjoy it. Plus, he's kind of grown on me. I've watched him mature and come into his own over the last few years. He's a good guy, a good guy with an amazing power.

Crimson's voice enters my mind. *I'm arriving at your location. Tell Brand so he doesn't attack me when I enter the door.*

Okay. Why would he do that?

To protect you.

Oh. I turn to Brand. "Crimson is almost here."

The words barely escape my mouth when the front door opens and Crimson enters the house. She comes into the kitchen and after greeting us says, "I'm taking Chris's uncle, Don, to Bermuda so he can help Jonas and Dr. Tod decipher the schematics and narrow down manufacturers of the different machine parts."

"You're not 'flying' him are you?" I ask.

"Goodness no. He'll fly on a plane. Would you tell Chris his uncle is going to the island?"

"Yes."

Brand jumps in with a sarcastic chuckle in his voice. "Maetha will be pleased. Now she'll have to buy more toilet paper."

Crimson pours herself some water for tea. "Maetha only discouraged you from going to the island to keep you with Calli."

Brand and I look at each other, both of us with admittedly surprised expressions.

"So Maetha *could have* inserted my quartz now?"

"No. That part was true. She didn't want Calli to be alone."

"She could have just told me that. I would have stayed with Calli, no problem."

"Not everyone is as comfortable at sharing their exact thoughts and emotions as you, Brand," Crimson says with a smile. She turns and addresses me. "You will travel to meet with Clara Winter next week to discuss a clan gathering. I'll let you know travel details later."

Chapter Six - Clara's Apprentice

When Beth found out I was going to meet with Clara, she begged to come with me. I looked to the future to see if this was a good idea and saw her hugging her brother Nate with Clara standing nearby. To see how happy Beth will be to be with her brother again tugged at my heart and helped me make my decision. With the many different doomed outlooks potentially coming our way, Beth should be able to see Nate as often as possible.

After Crimson gave me the final travel details, Beth and I boarded Maetha's private plane, headed for Bozeman, Montana. When we arrive, we head to the car Clara sent for us. The sliding doors of the airport open, creating a wind tunnel, whipping snow and bitterly cold air in our faces.

Exiting the building, I see a man in a Runner's suit jump out of an SUV and run around to the sidewalk.

"I guess that one's for us."

Beth grabs my arm and squeezes. "Do you know who that is?"

I peer at the man. "No."

"That's Will. Justin's friend . . . uh, I mean, he was Justin's friend."

I hear the slight panic in her voice and instinctually look to my future to see if I'm in danger. I see myself giving my parents hugs, which if everything goes according to plan, I'll be visiting them after Clara. I say to Beth, "You don't need to be worried."

"I didn't say I was. I just haven't seen him since he left the compound after Justin was kicked out."

Will waves and grins, motioning us to him. He opens the back door for us.

Beth says, "Hi Will. You're our driver?"

"For today. Good to see you, Beth." He looks at me and smiles warmly. "Calli."

I nod my head. "Will."

We get in the car and are soon traveling down the familiar roads toward the compound. Will asks many questions, most directed to Beth. I listen to them catch up about all things "Runners' World" but notice Will dances around the subject of Justin, the deceased clan leaders, and the missing amulets. At one point I slip into Will's mind and find he's always had a crush on Beth and views her as available. I direct my attention out the window to avoid prying into any more of his thoughts.

After rounding the last corner on the road, the huge building complex comes into view. Nothing seems to have changed at all other than everything is covered in a couple feet of snow. A carved out trail leads to the leaders' cabins near the wood line, the basketball courts are covered with snow, the once manicured lawn is now a pristine white field, and the ever present floodlights are already turned on even though dusk is several hours away and the Shadow Demons haven't been a threat for several months. I guess old habits are hard to break.

Will parks the car and escorts us inside the front door. Several Runners walk the halls and stand on the stairway talking. Will says, "Clara is expecting you. I'll talk to you later, Beth."

We turn and head to Clara's office but before we reach her door, I hear female voices behind us.

"It is too her. I know it."

"Calli?"

I turn to see Shanika and Ashley from the delivery

team.

Ashley waves. "Hi."

Shanika asks, "Calli, what are you doing here?"

"I need to talk to Clara."

Ashley rubs her hands together. "My friends are going to be so jealous I saw you and they didn't."

I don't know what to say. My mouth falls open a bit.

"Mmm hmm." Shanika nods. "Did you really steal the amulets?"

There it is. "No." I want to excuse myself and move on to more important business with Clara, but I remember why I'm here in the first place: to have Clara set up a clan gathering so I can clear my name over the stolen amulets and the Readers, Seers, and Hunters leaders' death. Yet, here are two Runners who still believe I stole the amulets. I think I can use this opportunity to feel out the misunderstood sentiments I might encounter at the gathering. I respond to Shanika's question, saying, "Justin orchestrated the whole thing."

"Mcintyre?"

"Yep."

"No way." Shanika's voice trails off in disbelief.

"You hadn't heard that before?"

"His name came up but more like he was helping you."

Oh great. "No. You can ask Chris. He was there."

Ashley puts her hands on her hips. "Wasn't he helping you too?"

Shanika adds, "Yeah, he just walked out of the compound with the amulet to go meet you."

"This is why I'm here. I'm going to have Clara schedule a Clan Gathering so I can explain what really happened. If you'll excuse me, I need to—"

Shanika presses, "Where are the amulets?"

"They're safe."

"So, you *do* have them?"

Beth jumps in. "Ladies, we have to go now. Leave Calli alone." She doesn't wait for them to respond. She wraps her protective arm around my shoulders and directs me down the hall.

I think this small verbal exchange indicates I'm in for a long haul in trying to get the clans to understand what happened. I'll have to give up more details than I thought, if these two girls are any indication of the common sentiments.

Clara sits at her desk talking on the phone. She sees us through the windowed door and waves us inside. We enter the office. Beth sits in a chair across the desk from Clara. I choose the soft couch I sat on once upon a time. Sinking into its buttery leather, I close my eyes and inhale the scent and remember the day Chris walked into my life.

The scene plays out behind my eyelids. I've witnessed and experienced his confusion through his own memories. I know what he thought and felt the moment Clara told him I was a Runner, not a Healer. He's been through so much. I'm glad I came here and remembered this.

"Calli," Clara hangs up the phone and greets me. She stands and comes around the desk to me. I get up from the couch. She opens her arms for a hug and I accept. "It's good to see you here again."

"Thanks."

She lets go, turns to Beth and hugs her. "Come with me. I'd rather we wait to discuss anything until we're in my private quarters."

I ask, "Do you have a cabin like the others?"

"No. Follow me."

We walk out into the hall and turn left. Good thing, too. To the right is a large gathering of Runners, with

Shanika in the front, all wanting to see if she was telling the truth.

"Never mind them, Calli," Clara motions over her shoulder. "You're kind of a legend around here."

I squirm inside.

We walk to the end of the hall and climb a smaller staircase that leads to two doors at the top. She pulls a key from her pocket and opens one of the doors. She holds it open, motioning for us to enter.

I walk into her room and look around. I feel like I've just walked into Maetha's Lake Patoka residence. The walls are covered with shelves holding similar collectibles and oddities. Bookcases are lined with old, well-read books and new titles, side by side. Antiques and old photographs hang on the walls. I say, "I didn't peg you as a collector, Clara."

"How did you 'peg' me?"

"I don't know. I guess my first impression of you was that you walked off a soap opera film set, of course that was a shallow assessment based on your appearance. If I'd known what your interests were, I'd have thought differently, I suppose." I walk further into the room and examine some of the book titles. "Did you inherit these?"

"No, they're mine." She closes the door and locks it.

"Is this where you keep your Spellcaster journals?"

"No." She waves her hand for us to follow and walks toward the hallway. "Come with me."

I feel for her thoughts and find she's not comfortable discussing the journals at this time.

She knocks on a closed door. The door opens and Beth's little brother, Nate, appears.

"They're here," Clara says.

Nate has dark brown hair and Beth's light eyes. He's young, too young to have gone through the misery he's already endured.

"Hi Calli," he says, beaming ear to ear.

"Hi Nate."

Beth steps forward.

"Beth!" he exclaims, running over to her. The two of them embrace in a tender moment.

Clara turns away and says to me, "Let's go into the lab and give them a moment to talk."

She opens the next door over and we enter a room that looks completely different from the living quarters. The lab is all white, with a large square machine the size of a clothes dryer humming softly along the wall. A computer screen displays what looks like a recipe.

I wander around the room, observing and taking it all in. This is where Clara makes her magic juice.

Nate and Beth come in and Nate walks over to the humming machine and pushes a button on the front. "Twenty more minutes on this batch, Clara."

"Are the bottles ready?" Clara asks.

"Yes. They're still in the sterilizer."

Clara turns to me. "We have a little time to talk then. Have a seat."

I look to where she's pointing and see a couple chairs pushed under a table. I pull one out and sit. Beth sits beside me.

She says, "Nate, would you bring us cold juice?" He nods, opens a refrigerator on the wall, and pulls out four bottles and hands me one. I open mine and take a sip.

"Mmm. Good and refreshing as always."

Nate beams with pride and I read his mind. This batch was made completely by him, without Clara's help. He sits down and opens his juice.

Clara opens hers as well. "You need me to line up a Clan Gathering. Am I correct?"

"Yes."

"Well, first of all, the clans don't like to group together, so you'll be lucky to get a few from each clan to show up."

"How come?"

"In the past, there was a falling away. Clans in other regions of the world get along, or so I've heard. But here there seems to always be a struggle for power. The Death Clan was a good example of that. For the mythical Sanguine Diamond to surface, successfully bring about their end, and then get divided between the clans, the clans were reminded that larger forces are at work. Unfortunately, everyone became defensive with their amulets. The clans turned inward, relying on their amulets for direction."

I interrupt. "And then I go and run off with the Healers' amulet."

"Exactly. Getting any of the clans to listen to you isn't going to be easy. However, I do think that if I set up the gathering and let them know I'll be bringing you—basically, I'll be in charge of you—then maybe they'll agree to show up."

"In charge?"

"Like your parole officer, so to speak."

"Oh."

Clara takes a sip of her juice, then continues. "Secondly, with the first being they don't like to gather, they wouldn't want to do it just anywhere. I think the gathering should take place at the Hunters' village."

"Where's that?" In my mind I picture the Pacific Northwest as the perfect location for the Hunters to have a compound. Perhaps I feel this way because the Runners are based in Montana, and the Healers are in California.

"In South Carolina."

"The East Coast?

"Yes, they have a protected, hidden location."

Beth asks, "But aren't the Hunters dangerous?"

Clara looks at Beth. "Not these ones. Every group has their rogue members or dissidents. Hunters seem to have more than the rest. The ones living in the Hunters' village are peaceful. When we need to hire a Hunter for a task, we always recruit one of these members. I'll contact their leader and ask if they'd be willing to host a gathering."

I ask, "When do you think the gathering will take place? I need to plan for it."

"Not for a few months. That's assuming the Hunters are okay with hosting the event. The other clans will have to be softened to the idea."

Nate says, "Is there anything we can do to help the clans agree?"

I ask, "What do you mean?"

Clara smiles. "Nate is referring to Spellcasting."

I shake my head. "I don't know, Nate, I'm not entirely familiar with what Spellcasters can do."

Nate says, "Well, when Clara and I were held captive at General Harding's compound, we helped everything work out for the good."

"You did, did you?" I'm not sure what to think and I don't know how to react to his words.

Clara says, "What Nate is saying, Calli, is we tapped into the energy of individuals in the compound and found one who was on the edge."

"I don't understand."

Clara continues. "Well, imagine using your Reader power and sensing the minds of a small group of people. You might be able to determine one person who has ill thoughts or who has bad intentions. What we do is evaluate the energy given off by individuals."

I ask, "Nate, do you have a cosmic power?"

"No. I'm just naturally aware."

Clara says, "When Nate and I were captured, I realized he possesses an innate talent for Spellcasting. I taught Nate to meditate, clear his mind, and sense possible futures and the factors leading to them. I found he was able to do this better than most kids his age, and with me nearby, the two of us could sense the leader of the military forces was a 'solid' player in the compound, like a big brick wall preventing anyone from escaping. The leader's mind was too strong to be swayed by impulse, and he certainly would not make a mistake. As long as he was in charge, nobody would leave the compound alive."

I wipe my mouth with my hand. "That leader was Chris's father."

"Yes, I know." Clara's expression softens. "I understand Chris's personality all the better now, after seeing with my own eyes the man Chris had to deal with on a regular basis. However, one of General Harding's associates, a woman with a very strange essence connected to the flow of time, was unstable. She was quite explosive, determined, and dangerous. We could sense a lust for power in this woman, and a struggle to keep herself from murdering the leader and all witnesses."

"That's amazing to hear you talk about Deus Ex that way. She was everything you describe."

Nate points to me. "I sensed you too, even though I couldn't see you."

"Me? Really?"

"Well, I didn't know who I was sensing, but now being around you, I recognize your presence. I've felt it before. Someone else was with you at the compound, but they didn't want to be sensed."

What? My confused expression is answered by Clara. She says, "You were with a 'force of nature' who wished to remain hidden."

Beth's hand flies to her mouth and she looks at me. "You were with—" Her head twists to her brother. "You could *feel* her. Nate, you could feel her." I can tell she's proud of her little brother and rightly so.

The only explanation I can come up with for Crimson being able to be sensed is she allowed them to feel her. Crimson did, after all, adjust Beth's vision to be able to see Unaltereds. Maybe she knew Nate would become instrumental as well.

Clara continues. "We sensed that if the unstable one's mind was 'nudged' in just the right way, it would lead to a chain of events that would not only destroy the military leader, but herself as well; the outcome of that future would be freedom for everyone in captivity. I taught Nate to focus his mind on the future we wanted to happen, the future of every friend getting out of there alive, and together, we determined the quickest path to that goal was to inspire greed in the woman."

I don't know what to think about their possible influence with the events at the military compound. Part of me wants to believe Clara is a psychic of some kind, but she's a Runner and can't be both. I don't know enough about Spellcasters to determine one way or another.

I tread carefully, saying, "I'm curious how you felt you had any effect on Deus Ex. It seems just as likely she would have shot Harding and tried to steal the diamond anyway, with or without your 'psychic powers' interfering. Are you sure it wasn't just coincidence?" I take another sip of juice. I am reminded of how my father grilled me about my ability to see the future. I'm doing the same thing, ironically.

Clara tilts her head slightly and smiles. "I cannot prove what we did had any effect on the female's behavior. It is just as likely she was going to lose self-control in that moment anyway, and maybe Nate and I were just engaging in wishful thinking. It is a sign of good mental health for Spellcasters to doubt the efficiency of their own abilities, as many things do come about by chance alone whether we influence them or not. However, Deus had already come close to a diamond before, I could feel the need for it strongly on her mind, but some part of her held back until a more opportune moment to strike presented itself. All we did was give her a little 'nudge' in the right direction, one that made her think that moment was then and there, and you know the rest."

I say, "Whether or not you two influenced her, Deus Ex's sudden betrayal to General Harding was fortunate and in line with nature's will. However, I'm saddened that she died. She didn't have to."

Clara nods. "When we sensed her death, we were saddened also. We were aiming for her to incapacitate General Harding, which she did. Her end came by her own choice."

I look down at my hands. "I tried to convince her to let go of the diamond, but she wouldn't. She was too greedy."

Beth reaches over and places a comforting hand on my knee.

Clara says, "Once people cross over to greed and selfishness it's extremely difficult to change back." She pauses.

The air feels heavy with loss. So many people have died in such a short amount of time, it's hard to fully grasp the magnitude. I simply haven't allowed myself to stop and think, to remember. I place my hand on Beth's to let her know I appreciate her thoughtfulness.

Clara clears her throat. Beth removes her hand and we

both wipe our eyes. Clara says, "On a different note, Nate and I have been experimenting with topaz crystals ever since they were discovered to store cosmic powers. Topazes are actually very useful for storing just about any kind of power, cosmic or not, and in the right conditions we can enchant the crystals with some of our own Spellcaster abilities. Some of these enchantments haven't been very noticeable, others have been dangerous, but there are a few useful ones we have stumbled across. The most useful topazes we created can send signals between each other. When one is rubbed the other will vibrate or hum like a pager device." She hands me a small clear plastic container with two yellowish topazes.

"Thanks, Clara." Just by looking at their pale color, I can tell they aren't Imperial Topaz.

She continues. "We have also been using the same spell to detect passing animals in the woods, so in the future we might be able to tell if intruders are approaching the compound before they reach us."

Nate grins proudly. "Motion detectors. Those were my idea."

Clara nods and says, "Nate and I are curious to know how well the pager-topazes work in the field and how many times they can be used before they must be charged again. I'm sure you could help us gather that information, Calli."

We talk for a while longer then prepare to head back to the airport. Before we leave, Clara gives us two boxes of freshly bottled juice. "Be sure to give a box to Captain Rutherfield," she says.

I raise one eyebrow.

"He's one of my loyal customers." She smiles. "I will let you know when the Clan Gathering will take place."

◇ ◇ ◇

Once Will drops us off at the airport and delivers us to our waiting plane, I ask Beth, "Do you want to come with me to Ohio? I need to visit my parents and reassure them I'm all right. You wouldn't see Brand for a couple days, if that's okay."

"I'm just fine with that. If I'm not around him he can't repeat with me."

"Are you getting tired of him doing that?"

"Yes."

I double-check with Rodger Rutherfield to make sure it's all right for Beth to continue to Ohio with me.

Rodger says, "That shouldn't be a problem at all. We will still need to make the planned stop in Denver to refuel. I'll call ahead and have food service waiting for us."

"That would be great," Beth says, having overheard.

"I have a contact inside the airport who helps me out quite often."

I ask, "Rodger, how did you meet Maetha?"

"I met Ms. Lightner twenty-years ago when I applied for the position of private pilot."

"I've noticed you are always alert, no matter what kind of schedule you're asked to undertake. What's your secret?"

"No secret, really, just healthy living. That and Clara Winter's juice."

"That makes sense." I smile. "Speaking of, one of these boxes is for you."

"Great! Ms. Winter thinks of everything."

A few hours later we arrive in Ohio where my parents are waiting by the small municipal airport hangar—the same location my mother watched me jet off with Chris not long ago.

"Calli." My mother smiles brightly. Her Unaltered aura

energizes with her excitement. My eyes water and my throat constricts with the knowledge of why she and I have the same aura—we've been genetically altered. She hugs me tightly. "Good to see you."

We release and I wipe my eyes. I turn to my father and give him a hug.

"Mom, Dad, this is Beth Hammond. Beth, these are my parents, Allan and Charlotte Courtnae."

They shake hands and exchange greetings. Then we climb in their car and drive to the house.

My mother says as we drive, "We want to hire a bodyguard for you."

I let out a slight groan. I knew they'd bring this up.

My dad's eyes connect with mine in the rear-view mirror. "We're worried, Calli."

My mom obviously doesn't like my resistance and protests further. "You were shot! You need to be better protected."

I lean forward. "I was being protected. You two don't know the whole situation or what we were trying to do."

My mom says, "Why don't you tell us?"

I note the drained countenance of my father and realize he's lost sleep over me and my situation. I consider the possible consequences of saying too much and wonder how much I can tell them. A little guidance from Crimson would be great about now. But no.

"Well," I say, "you know I have the diamond in my heart. The man named Max Corvus was about to post on the Internet about me and my diamond. He's afraid of me and the people with powers in general and thinks we're trying to take over the world. We stopped him before he uploaded his information about me, but he also escaped."

"He's out there right now?" my mother asks, her hand flying to her mouth.

"We know he fled the country. He's most likely in Europe. But he might put his information back up on the Internet. Because of that, I've been staying out of sight, which includes not going back to college at this time. I need to stay out of public places to minimize the possibility of innocent bystanders being injured should I be attacked."

My dad nods his head. "Which is exactly why I think you need extra protection!"

"The only bodyguard I can have needs to be someone from within my group."

"What about Brand Safferson?" my mom asks. "You and he make such a cute couple."

"Charlotte," my dad objects, "an effective bodyguard needs to be unattached to their client. Brand and Calli are too close."

Beth coughs, or chokes, I can't be sure. "You and Brand?"

"No!" I speak slowly yet firmly to my parents. "I was never dating Brand. I was assigned to him by Maetha to teach him about his power and this new world. That's why we hung out together. Brand is actually going out with Beth."

My mother blushes and averts her gaze from Beth. "Oh. I guess I completely misread his behavior around you, then. What about Chris?"

"Chris has to keep his position with the government. He can't be with me all the time. But that's not even the point. I can take care of myself. I can see my own future, heal my injuries," for the most part, but I leave that bit of info out of my tirade, "I can flee a situation in a flash. I don't need a bodyguard, Mom and Dad."

An awkward silence settles over the car.

My dad clears his throat and asks, "Are we going to have to go to the cabin again if Max resurfaces?"

"I wouldn't rule it out."

My mom asks, "So no college?"

"Not till this clears."

◇ ◇ ◇

After a night at my parents' house, Beth and I are back on the plane.

Beth says, "It's interesting your parents identified Brand's crush on you, Calli."

"That doesn't mean I have a thing for him. I like Brand as a friend, I didn't always however. He kind of grew on me."

"Well, to be honest, it's always bothered me the way he looks at you."

I want to say, *get in line.* I don't. "Beth, did Justin ever tell or more like accuse you of Will having a thing for you?"

"What?"

"Will liked and still likes you."

"Yeah, but I don't . . . "

"Do you see what I'm getting at?"

Beth stares at me, then starts to laugh. A giggle at first, then an all out belly laugh.

I start laughing too. The whole thing is really silly. I try to speak through my laughing. "Beth, Chris doesn't like how Brand looks at me either."

"Really? Brand gets jealous when other guys look at me, too."

We laugh some more.

"I was pretty jealous of Kikee and Chris."

"You should be. Chris actually did stuff with her."

My laughing comes to a halt. "He didn't know what he was doing."

"Is that what he told you?" Beth is still chuckling and

wiping her eyes.

I become completely serious. "Yes. I believe him. I even watched him break things off with her in D.C."

"She came here from Alaska? For Chris?"

"You know what? I don't want to talk about this anymore. I think it's safe to say we all have normal jealousy levels, but deep down none of us would hurt the others."

"I sure hope you're right," Beth says in a quiet voice.

"Me too. If we all become Bearers, it would be 'unbearable' to be fighting all the time."

"I agree, and I like your pun."

Chapter Seven - The Surrendering

The remaining days of January seem to fly by. After visiting Clara and my parents, Beth and I returned to Denver. Brand, Anika, Beth and I scour the Internet ever day. We look for signs of Max's blog, any newly posted paranoia topic, paranormal sightings, and UFO articles. Nothing yet raises suspicion of Max resurfacing or other people taking his ball and running with it. Most of the other articles, photos, and video we've watched are easily debunked or determined to be photoshopped.

Crimson has kept to her word and not interfered with my day-to-day life. I know Beth is a little let down to not be in her presence. She really admires Crimson. I'm still a little uncertain when it comes to decision making, feeling like I should decide what Crimson would decide. It's hard for me to make my own big decisions and not second-guess myself.

Anika and Brand are finally getting along. She's lightened up on expressing her beliefs and Brand has lightened up on expressing his.

Jonas has bi-located several times to talk to Anika. He has to do this through me because I'm the only one in Denver with a diamond which also means I have to be nearby so he's able to keep his connection. Even though I feel like their relationship isn't working out, I don't interfere.

Today, we're having a Bearer Gathering. I received word from Jonas to bi-locate to Maetha's diamond at noon. I go into my room and close the door so I'll be able to meditate without distraction. Sensing diamonds and their owners is second nature to me now. I don't struggle one bit determining who belongs to which.

I connect with Maetha's diamond and focus on her surroundings. She sits in a plush chair in a living room of sorts. Seated in person on other chairs are Yeok Choo, Chuang, and Jonas. Other Bearers bi-locate and arrive all around me, including Chris. He moves his form by mine. He looks good and I can't help but smile.

Speaking to my mind, he says, *I wish I could hold your hand.*

I know. This is kind of strange for both of us to be in our bi-located form.

Maetha begins. "I've called this Gathering for an announcement to be made." She turns her head to Yeok Choo and nods.

Yeok Choo stands from her seat, appearing tired and defeated. She clasps her hands in front of her, cinching her pale blue robe around her waist. "I'm choosing to surrender my diamond."

As if choreographed, many Bearers react with sounds, words, and actions, all expressing sadness and loss. Chris and I exchange confused glances.

Yeok Choo continues. "The pressures of being a Diamond Bearer in this new era are too much for me to handle, and Marketa's death . . . I can't go on." She sits down and wipes her eyes.

Maetha says, "A Surrendering will be held the last weekend of February. I'll be communicating with each of you to give traveling instructions. Due to the increased risk of detection, we're going to need to be careful. That is all."

I'm stunned by the lack of emotion displayed by Maetha. In fact, she seems a little mad. But I may be misreading her.

A few Bearers approach Yeok Choo and talk quietly.

Maetha stands and walks over to me and Chris. She motions to Jonas for him to join us. I look into Maetha's eyes wishing I could read her mind.

"Calli," she says, "I want all of the Bearer candidates in attendance for the Surrendering. You will travel with Brand, Beth, and Anika." She turns to Chris. "You'll be traveling with Mary. She'll be in your area at that time and will be in contact with you. Now, return to your places and continue with your duties."

"Wait." Chris leans closer to Maetha and whispers, "What is a Surrendering?"

Maetha looks at each one of us for a moment, then says, "Yeok Choo is choosing to give up her diamond. She will die. A Surrendering is a funeral prior to death, although in the past this only happens when a diamond needs to be used to wipe out a clan. Like with Gustave when he surrendered his diamond for you, Calli. Yeok Choo is the first to simply give up."

I want to ask her how Yeok Choo will die, if we'll have to witness her death, or if this is considered suicide, but I feel that might be insensitive and a little morbid, so I don't. Instead, I ask, "Is this frustrating to you?"

"Extremely."

Chris says, "What do we do at a Surrendering? What's appropriate?"

"Well, imaging attending a funeral or wake and the kinds of things you'd say to the surviving family members about the deceased, maybe memories, things you'll miss. Those are what you'd say to Yeok Choo at the Surrendering."

Jonas says, "Oh, like what you might say to a dying grandparent?"

"Yes." Maetha says. Her attention is pulled away and she leaves us.

We linger a little longer then Chris and I say goodbye. Chris's form vanishes, then Jonas says to me, "Calli, wait. I wanted to thank you for letting me communicate with Anika through you. I know it puts you in a bad position."

"No problem, Jonas."

"Well, thank you." He dips his chin.

I let go of Maetha's diamond and open my eyes in Denver. I go out to the others and inform them of Yeok Choo's Surrendering.

I can't believe how quickly the last couple weeks have flown by. Nothing of any kind of concern to Bearers has happened on the world-wide-web, none that we found anyway. Chris has bi-located to me only a couple times. He's been busy with his job. I've seen Jonas more often, however. He and Anika are unraveling relationship-wise and I'm sad for them. Beth and Brand seem to be struggling as well. I imagine being confined to the house 24/7 isn't easy for any relationship. Throw into the mix the fact that I'm in the same house and it makes for a bad combination. I've tried to keep my distance from Brand for Beth's sake. I've thought about having a repeating session with Brand where I tell him what's bothering Beth but decided against it. If Beth ever found out, I think it would destroy our friendship.

We've arrived in Bermuda and are being driven to the docks in a large van Maetha arranged for us. I stare out the window and am mesmerized by the many different flowers, all bright pinks and oranges and trees with huge fronds and peeling bark. This is paradise.

The waiting boat is more like a large yacht. Sleek lines, polished wood trim, with three levels of windows, seating in the bow and open area in the stern. Workers haul wooden crates of supplies up the gangplank and hand them off to others who take them down below.

Beth and I look at each other with excited expressions.

Brand whistles through his teeth. "Money, money, money"

Beth, Brand, Anika, and I board the boat. Beth and Brand roam the boat, exploring. Anika and I take a seat in the front. I notice every employee on the boat is a person with powers of some form or another. It makes sense to only hire people who are going to be loyal and keep sensitive information quiet, like the island's location.

Once we leave the docks and head out onto the open ocean, I turn to Anika. "Have you used the Seer topaz?"

"A little. There's still a lot of power remaining in it."

"What do you think of it so far?"

"Honestly, I think it's wrong to dwell on the future."

"How so?"

"The future is already set, so why look for it."

"Well, that's why I charged the stone for you so you could see the benefit in knowing certain things ahead of time and make necessary changes to fix potential problems."

"But I don't believe we can change what's going to happen. So, a Seer stone is only useful to view what's going to happen."

"That's not true. Otherwise, Chris would have died several times already. I saw his future and made changes to keep him alive."

"My belief system says you didn't change the grand plan. You only think you did."

My frustration levels are mounting. "Well, you don't have to keep it, you know."

"I know." She glances down at the ocean waters below

us. "I have one more future I want to look for, out of curiosity of course, then I'll give it back."

I assume she wants to know if she and Jonas have a future together. I'm certainly not going to look, even though I could. Anika and I make small talk for a little while longer, then she lays back in a reclining chair and closes her eyes.

My mind is on Chris. I'll be seeing him in person for the first time since New Year's Day, since finding out he'd been using the prism, and discovering how he feels toward Jonas and Brand. I'm tempted for a moment to seek him out in my mind, but I hold back. He's probably already on the island, waiting for my arrival.

After an hour, the boat slows. I look off the bow to see why, but all I see is ocean in every direction. The boat continues forward. Then before my eyes a shimmering hole begins to open in the air before us. Through the hole I see an island in the distance. The hole grows larger as we approach and our boat glides through. I look behind and watch as the hole shrinks to nothing. The island in front of us is large with mountains, cliffs, and beach area. As we near, I admire the palm trees lining the pristine beach and make out the dock where we're headed. Using my Hunter's vision, I identify Jonas on the dock waiting for us.

The boat comes to a stop and a shipmate throws a rope to Jonas who ties us off. The gangplank is extended to the dock.

"Hey guys," Jonas greets us. "I don't get many visitors here. I feel like I'm welcoming you to my personal island, which is kind of true. I've certainly explored every inch of it since I've been here."

Brand steps onto the ramp first and jumps off at the end as a wave moves the plank a little. He turns around to help Beth.

She pushes his hand aside. "I don't need your help, Brand. I can do it myself."

"Okay, have it your way." He steps back a half step and drops his hand a little. I notice his positioning. I think Brand knows Beth is about to fall.

Beth starts down the plank and is about to step onto the dock when an excessively large wave rocks the boat, causing her to slip. Jonas dives forward and catches her before Brand.

"See," Brand says.

Beth stands with Jonas's help and glares at Brand. I choose not to read her mind to see what she's thinking. Their relationship would be difficult to navigate under the best of circumstances.

Jonas moves aside so Beth can pass, then he holds his hand out for Anika. She gladly accepts after seeing what happened with Beth. She doesn't let go and gives him a hug. He hugs her back and I decide to get myself off the boat instead of waiting for help.

"Jonas," I call out, after I step onto the dock. "Has Chris arrived yet?"

"No. Not yet. Come with me, guys, I'll give you the tour."

Anika turns. "What about our luggage?"

"They'll bring it. Don't worry." Jonas points to the dock workers.

We follow Jonas up the path toward the buildings. One large building is surrounded by many smaller structures. Each has a Southern plantation look to them, something straight out of *Gone With The Wind.*

Jonas points to the biggest building and says, "Maetha and the Bearers have used this island for centuries, living in huts and a large cave on the other side of the island. The main house was built in the late 1700s and is just that, the main house. That's where the food is prepared and laundry washed. Maetha employees a team of twenty people of various powers to run the details and specifics on the island. The smaller units or bungalows were built as they became needed. They are basically individual dwellings for each Bearer. Mine is over there," he says, pointing to the right.

Brand says, "Yeah! Let's go see your bachelor pad."

Jonas's eyes shoot to me first, then to Anika. "Actually, I . . . um . . . it's a mess. I'll show you later. Let's go see other parts of the island. Follow me." He turns in the opposite direction of his bungalow.

I speak to Jonas's mind, *What's the matter?*

I have pictures of you pulled up on the computer screen because of the research I was doing. I don't want Anika to see that and leave the island thinking all I do all day is look at images of you.

Oh, gotcha. I think to myself how I wouldn't want Chris to see the images either. I add, *Would you make sure you remove them before Chris arrives?*

Uh, yeah.

Jonas says out loud, "Most of the other Bearers are here already. They're at the main house and the surrounding grounds. Sarangerel and her parents are located on the far side of the complex. They won't be joining us for the Surrendering. I overheard Maetha instructing them to stay in their bungalow till morning. Don Harding is also here, but he was given the same instructions as the others. I guess the Surrendering will be a little intense." Jonas stops abruptly at a fork in the path. "Come with me. I want to show you the best beach on the island." He leads us along the pathway through the trees and bushes for a few minutes until we emerge on a beautiful white sand beach with a gentle slope. The water level, which is at high tide right now, laps against the sand about thirty yards out.

Beth and Anika let out gasps and fluttery sounds at the beauty of the setting.

Jonas motions toward the horizon where the ocean meets the sky. "That's west. This is the best beach for sunsets, if you ask me. And over here is the beach house bungalow."

Brand asks, "Who lives there?"

"Probably Crimson," Beth answers.

Jonas states rather bluntly, "No one lives in that one right now."

Brand shouts, "Dibs! I want dibs."

"You have to be a Bearer to get a bungalow," Jonas says. Then lowers his voice and becomes serious. "There's a couple empty bungalows right now."

His words bring grimness to our conversation. I have to assume they're empty because of the recent deaths of Diamond Bearers. This beach bungalow probably belonged to one of them. Tonight, another Bearer will be gone.

"Come on," Jonas says, waving his hand over his shoulder. "Let's go to the main house." He leads us back the way we came. When we get to the split on the trail, Jonas says, "Go on ahead, I'm going to go clean up my place."

"I'll come with you and help," Anika offers.

I jump in and say, "Actually, Anika, why don't you come with Beth and me and let Brand go help clean up the mess. You know, guy time." Brand lets out a grunt. I continue. "We'll go see the other Bearers."

Jonas wraps his arm around Brand's shoulders. "Guy time! Yeah." *Thanks Calli.*

You're welcome.

We continue to the main house and enter the opened front doors. The atmosphere is solemn and serious.

Different Bearers stand in small groups, talking quietly, holding drinks. I'm reminded these people are all here in person, not bi-located.

Chuang sits on a couch, wearing a quartz blanket like a robe. The material shimmers beautifully in the sunlight streaming in through the window behind him. Chuang, however, looks ill. He's obviously not improving. I focus my mind on his injury and delve inside his body. The confusion powder seems to be conglomerated in one mass in his belly. Instead of dissolving and breaking down, the materials have merged together. If nothing else, the mass could be cut out and removed the old-fashioned way.

I wonder if I should offer my help to heal him?

As I near Chuang, our eyes meet, and his brows lower. He says to my mind, *If you had let Jie Wen go in with guns, I wouldn't be powerless right now. And here Crimson wants you in the leadership position. We'll all perish, given enough time.*

I'm sorry you feel that way, Chuang. I believe I could help you if you'd let me.

Not a chance!

Have it your way. I walk away figuring if I was able to detect the mass, some other Bearer will too, and he'll get the help he needs one way or the other.

I overhear mental communications. *Did she talk to you? What did she want?*

She said she could help me if I wanted her to.

Of all the nerve, thinking she can heal you when no one else can.

Exactly.

Huh. I guess I'm wrong about someone else helping him. I wonder if my enhanced healing ability is why I'm able to detect the mass. I walk into the next room and find Yeok Choo sitting among many vases of flowers. The whole scene reminds me of going to Anika's parent's funeral, only Yeok Choo is still alive and thanking people for coming.

Anika comes up behind me and says, "This is wrong."

"Why?" I ask without turning around.

"For one thing, it goes against nature's will to end your own life. Second, God's will. Third, suicide is against the law."

I turn and face her. Lowering my voice, I say, "Well, I'd recommend you keep your opinions to yourself today. As for the law, I don't know what the laws are for Bermuda or if this particular island even falls under their authority. Besides, Yeok Choo faked her death all those years ago. That's illegal too, when you think about it."

Anika makes a grunting sound but doesn't formulate any words.

I continue. "I plan on simply observing these amazing individuals and listening to their stories of great accomplishments. Then I'll join the others in celebrating the life and death of an influential person of history." I don't wait for Anika to respond. Instead, I walk into the kitchen.

Maetha and Crimson are seated at a small breakfast table, staring at each other. They must be having a mental conversation. Maetha looks my direction, then Crimson's head turns. I note the exhaustion on both their faces.

Crimson says, "Calli, good to see you." She stands from her seat and turns her head toward Maetha. "We'll talk later."

Maetha nods.

I protest. "You don't have to stop on my account."

Crimson smiles. "We're not." She walks out the back door and onto the wraparound porch, disappearing from view.

Maetha motions for me to sit in Crimson's vacant chair. I do. She says, "How did everything go with Clara?"

"Good. She's going to set up a meeting with the clans but thinks it will be a few months out."

"Yes. It won't be easy for her to make these arrangements, but she's had more than enough experience with the clans to know how to convince them to agree."

"Maetha, how old is Clara?"

She smiles slyly. "I was wondering when you'd clue into Clara. What was it that made you suspect her age?"

"Her antique collection—it's just like yours."

"Yes, she and I have similar taste."

"Are you going to tell me her age?"

"I will say she's older than Duncan, but that's all. She doesn't want anyone knowing her history and she's gone to great lengths to protect it."

I nod my head but add, "I can't help but feel let down to be kept in the dark."

Maetha says, "You know, she feels the same way about you."

"What do you mean?"

"She wonders why she's not being told everything."

"Why isn't she?"

"She's not a Bearer. And you're not a Spellcaster. Neither of you understand the complexities of the other, nor the catastrophic potential of merging the two."

I stare at Maetha. "But you're a Spellcaster *and* a Bearer."

"Yes, making me qualified to alert you to the dangers of associating too closely with any Spellcaster."

"You're confusing me."

"I know, but that's not my intention. I am hoping to impress upon your mind the reality of working with Spellcasters. They work alone for the most part."

"Clara told me quite a bit about them when I visited her."

"Well, I advise you to use caution when around any Spellcaster."

Does that include Maetha, I wonder.

We end our conversation and I walk back into the room with Yeok Choo. I need to offer up my condolences . . . or whatever this would be called. Fabian is speaking with her, so I wait by the wall. I overhear him talking about Yeok Choo's involvement with the early Chinese dynasties and the Silk Road with western countries. For a moment I imagine I'm in history class and am learning specifics I'll be tested on later.

Fabian moves on and I approach Yeok Choo. I've thought about what I'll say, but I still feel strange saying the words. "I want to thank you for your accomplishments in the history of the world. I wish I could have gotten to know you better."

She stares at me with vacant eyes and a dull expression. Her mind speaks to mine. *Marketa was my world. You took her from me.*

That's not what happened.

Leave me. The pain and harshness of her words hits right to my core.

I turn and walk from the house, feeling heavy and downtrodden. I miss Chris. I need him and his comfort. Walking along the pathway, I see the junction that leads to the beautiful beach. I look over my shoulder and head toward the sound of the waves and surf.

As dense foliage opens to beach, I stumble upon Brand and Beth having a heated discussion. Neither one of them sees me. I should turn around and leave but Beth's tone snags my attention.

She says, "No, Brand. *You* don't get it."

"What's there to get? I don't like fighting. So what if I repeat and keep you happy?"

"You've manipulated me to keep me happy. I feel like you've taken my choices away."

"Well, what if I'd let you fall on your face today when you got off the boat?"

"At least I would have known you didn't repeat."

"No. You would have been mad that I didn't repeat, knowing that I can."

"You don't know that."

"Yes. I do. That's why I repeated. You know Beth, I know you better than you know yourself. I've seen more sides of you, more reactions, all because I choose to repeat a situation or conversation until you're happy."

"Can't you hear yourself, Brand?"

"Yes. Very well, thank you."

"Don't you see anything wrong with manipulating me?"

"No. Do you want to know why I do what I do with you?"

"Enlighten me, please."

"Because . . . because I feel like what we have together is worth the effort. Because how I feel about you is worth working for. I love you, Beth. But you don't feel like you're worthy of being loved, so you push me away constantly."

"Are you seriously making this my fault?

"Come on, Beth."

"It sounds like you are."

"Listen, if I could get you to understand one thing, without repeating—which by the way I haven't done in this whole conversation—I'd want you to know you are in control of your own actions. I may have seen many more of your choices than you are aware of, but they've all been your choices. I'm not a bad guy. I'm not trying to take advantage of you. I only want you to have the opportunity to see how it feels to be loved and appreciated for your qualities. I can't make you see it. You have to allow it."

"So, it *is* my fault."

"No. It's the fault of everyone who has mistreated you and turned their backs on you your entire life. They are to blame."

"So, I'm screwed up? I can't let someone love me?"

"It's not your fault, Beth. But this is your life now; you choose who you allow in it. If you choose to push me away, thinking I'm trying to hurt you like everyone else has in the past, well, that's your choice. I'm hoping you'll see that I'm only acting in your best interests. I'll even promise to avoid repeating, if that will make you happy."

"How would I know if you are or aren't? How do I know you aren't right now?"

"I promise. I haven't repeated during this whole conversation."

"I don't believe you."

Brand says, "I'm sorry you can't see my intentions. I feel sorry for you in knowing you don't believe you should be happy or loved. I want you to know I love you, but maybe we need to take a break from one another while you sort out your feelings. If you find you want to be with me, with my promise to avoid repeating, please come find me. You already know what I want."

I hear footsteps approaching so I press my body behind the trunk of a big palm tree. Brand walks by and doesn't notice me. His head is hung low. I hear Beth crying softly and peek around the trunk to find her walking out onto the beach. I'm torn between which of the two I should go comfort. I should be a good friend to at least one of them.

I watch Brand walk a short distance on the path, then stop and reach his hand up to a low hanging branch of a juniper tree. He picks something up. I narrow my vision and focus on his hand. It's a quartz crystal. Could this be his Repeating quartz? With that thought, I enter his mind briefly and see he stashed his quartz in the crook of the tree as he and Beth walked toward the beach earlier. He really wasn't repeating with Beth. He couldn't.

Brand continues toward the main house. I turn and head to the beach.

I think I understand Beth's side of the situation a little better than Brand does. I find her sitting on the compact wet sand with her head in her hands. When she hears me, she sits up straight and wipes her eyes.

She says, "If he sent you to talk to me—"

"No. He doesn't know I'm here." I pause. "I overheard some of your conversation."

"You mean fight."

I don't respond to her words. Instead I say, "I know what it feels like to find out you've been manipulated by the Repeater power. Brand has used it on me on many occasions to try to get me to react a certain way. More recently, Chris secretly had a prism in his possession from August to January that he used on me several times."

"What? Did it make you mad to find out?"

"Oh yeah! At first I saw it as a violation. I'd been manipulated."

"I know, right?" she agrees and perks up.

"Then when I busted Chris, he said a lot of the same kinds of things Brand just said to you. 'I did it for us, I didn't want to lose you' and other things like that." I turn and face her. "I couldn't believe he felt so little of himself and was insecure about how I feel about him."

"Chris? Chris Harding feels inadequate? I guess his childhood and his father really messed up his mind and sense of self."

"Exactly."

"Did you two break up?"

"No. He promised he's not going to use the prism unless someone's life is in danger."

"You trust him?"

"Yes. I trust him because he was never trying to hurt me. He's a guy who has a hard time expressing his feelings without coming across too harsh. I also know from all the many repeats I've done with Brand I was always in control of my choices. Yes, Chris manipulated situations and conversations, but he never manipulated me. I still continued to choose him."

"Chris is quite serious. Not like Brand at all."

"That's the truth."

"I think what you're trying to do here is help me. But, our situations are a little different, Calli. Chris wanted to make sure he didn't say the wrong thing to you. Brand wanted to make sure I reacted in the way he wanted me to."

"Hmm, you have a point." I don't want to say anything else. I may have said too much already. Hopefully I've given her something to think about. "Well, if you ever want me to kick Brand's ass you just let me know." I smile and she gives me a hug.

"How sweet! You remembered me saying that to you about Chris."

"Of course. You're my friend, Beth. I want you to be happy. Brand is also my friend and I want him to be happy. Your futures may not end up being with each other, but maybe they will."

Beth looks off in the distance down the length of the beach. "Looks like Chris is here."

Excitement explodes in my body. I turn my head and see Chris standing on the bow of the yacht as it approaches the dock. The boat disappears behind the rocks in the distance as it nears its destination. I look back at Beth not wanting to leave her in this state, but also wanting to be with Chris.

She says, "It's all right, Calli. I'll be fine. Go." She nudges her shoulder against mine.

I stand and thank her, then run into the trees to the pathway. I hurry along to the dock and arrive just as people are walking down the ramp. Mary waves to me, then Chris comes into view. I can't wait any longer. Mary steps off the ramp and I run up it and right into Chris's arms. He's ready for me and catches my head with his hands, bringing his lips to mine. I wrap my arms up around his neck and let him take me away with his kisses.

"I've missed you," I say as I sigh into his mouth.

He intensifies the kiss and we stumble back against the wall. Pulling his head back, he says, "I've missed you, too. Bi-locating is such an empty feeling, not being able to touch you."

"I know."

"Excuse me," a voice nearby interrupts us. "We need to return to Bermuda. Are you on or off?"

Chris chuckles. "We're getting off." He takes my hand and leads me down the ramp to the dock. Once we are on solid ground, he wraps an arm around my shoulder and I slip my arm around his waist. I don't want to let him go. After witnessing Beth and Brand fight earlier, I feel closer to Chris and have a greater understanding of him and what he's been through.

We walk to the main house where Chris speaks with Yeok Choo. I remain at a distance, overhearing gentle conversations between Bearers. The overall mood in the house is somber. How could it be anything else? I feel a little guilty that such a sad event was responsible for bringing me such happiness at seeing Chris.

Crimson enters the room and walks to Yeok Choo. "It's time," she says with a heavy level of sadness. She extends her hand and Yeok Choo takes it. Together they walk to the door and exit the house. Everyone else follows in procession.

The sun is high in the sky and a gentle warm breeze ruffles the trees and bushes. We gather on the large grassy area behind the main house, forming a circle. Yeok Choo and Crimson stand in the center.

Crimson says, "I met Yeok Choo through Jie Wen during the orchestration of the overthrow of the Qin dynasty. This ushered in the Han dynasty and what became the golden age of Chinese history. I was impressed with her compassion, determination, and intense desire for progression. She became a Bearer through the process of eliminating the last of the Qin Healers and has been loyal and productive as a Bearer ever since. Her decision to surrender her diamond stems from her deep desire to aid progression." Crimson turns to Yeok Choo. "Do you have anything you'd like to say before your end?"

"Yes. I've had to evaluate my desires to continue as an agent of nature. Do I want to continue? Do I still have what it takes to make a difference? Am I still willing to help orchestrate events in the best interests of humanity? No. The moment Neema's diamond was removed by humans using obsidian and a weapon, I knew the Diamond Bearers' existence was forever changed." She points her finger toward Chris. "I'll never understand why he is a good candidate to become a Bearer after participating in Neema's death, or why so many young inexperienced Bearers have joined ranks. We've never brought on so many new Bearers at one time. Why now?" She turns to Crimson.

The crowd is silent. Crimson glances around the circle,

then says, "Maetha brought on six Bearers at one time in the beginning. She needed to set up a group of people she felt could do the job. People she felt would honor nature's will. Three of those six are still with us today. The young group is being assembled in much the same way as Maetha's original group. Not all will possess diamonds long term." Crimson leaves Yeok Coo's side and walks around the inside perimeter of the group while continuing to talk. "Neema knew she was on borrowed time ever since she and Maetha made Henry into a Bearer. I told her she would lose her diamond at a time when nature's will would be best suited. Losing her diamond was her punishment for going against me. Maetha has also been reprimanded for her involvement."

Out of the corner of my eye I see Jie Wen turn his head my direction. His voice enters my thoughts. *You must have her Blue Shard. She surrendered it to you, didn't she?*

What makes you think that?

Too many clues. Crimson is not going to tell the whole group, I assume.

Tell the whole group what? I keep up the pretense I don't have the Blue.

Crimson continues. "We mustn't forget Hasan. He was taken out by the female repeater without having gone against nature. Henry, Rolf, Neema, and Marketa were all examples of forgetting nature's will or misjudging what can happen if you go against it." She looks back to Yeok Choo. "You see a disturbing increase in young Bearers. I see a sharp decline in old Bearers wishing to continue following nature's will. One constant remains: the need to further humanity. The youth of the current generation are the future. They know the technology. Their minds are open and accepting to advancements and change. Too many of the Sanguine Bearers have hidden away, buried their heads over the last century, and are not up to performing what needs to happen. If you, Yeok Choo, have identified your inability and lack of desire to continue, then your willingness to surrender your diamond to someone who will be able to use it is the best choice. It is the only choice to best aid progression."

Yeok Choo nods. "That is my choice. I am grateful for the extended life I've been given, Crimson. I'm honored you believed in me enough to approve me as a Bearer. I respect your requirements of continuing to be a Bearer and know I no longer qualify. I am ready for my Surrendering."

"Very well." Crimson walks back to Yeok Choo and pulls out a small metal canister. She opens the lid and empties what looks like a necklace into her hand. The shine of the slim gold chain against the midday sun is offset by the small ominous black stone that can only be obsidian. A personal sized piece of power removing obsidian.

Crimson stands behind Yeok Choo and opens the clasp on the necklace. She reaches forward over Yeok Choo's head and places the necklace around her neck, securing the clasp at the back. I can no longer feel Yeok Choo's diamond. My pulse quickens with anticipation. I don't know how Crimson is going to remove the diamond. If it's anything like Marketa's removal, I don't want to watch.

Maetha walks toward Crimson holding a small tray. Crimson reaches and grasps onto a syringe from the tray, then turns to Yeok Choo who nods in approval and extends her arm toward Crimson.

Chris interweaves his fingers with mine and gently squeezes my hand. A subtle reminder he's supporting me, and I him.

As the thin needle of death punctures Yeok Choo's skin, she closes her eyes, points her chin to the sky, and takes a deep inhale. Crimson finishes injecting the serum and removes the needle. A small trickle of blood streaks down Yeok Choo's forearm as she lets her arm hang lifelessly.

Crimson places the syringe back on the tray, dismisses Maetha, and turns to face Yeok Choo. She takes hold of Yeok Choo's elbow and pauses.

My eyes dart right then left looking at the nearby faces of Bearers. Their expressions tell me they don't know any more than I do about what's happening. My attention is drawn back to Yeok Choo as she crumples sideways. Crimson catches her and eases her to the ground. Yeok Choo places a hand on top of Crimson's, then closes her eyes like she's going to sleep.

Crimson removes her hold on Yeok Choo's body and lays her all the way down on her back. She then straightens Yeok Choo's lifeless legs and arms. Lastly, she removes the obsidian from around Yeok Choo's neck.

The intense strumming of a diamond without an owner reverberates around the circle. I feel it as if my heart stopped momentarily then restarted. The sensation makes me cough and my eyes flood with tears.

Around the circle, I hear gasps, weeping, and whispering. I also see a few who have a complete lack of visible emotion on their faces.

Crimson addresses the group as she inserts the necklace back into the vial. "Yeok Choo personally asked for this method of death. Her body will now be carried up to the prepared pillar to be cremated."

Maetha steps into the circle carrying a lightweight frame with ornamental straps and what I assume are symbolic designs and pictures on them. Jie Wen, Kookju, Mary, and Avani step forward and together they help move Yeok Choo's body onto the frame. They pick up the four corners and begin following Crimson toward a trail at the edge of the grass. Everyone follows in procession.

Chris never lets go of my hand.

Chapter Eight - Changing of the Guard

Yeok Choo's willingness to surrender her diamond was not easy to watch, but it was quick and clean. However, her cremation set me on edge. I've never seen a body burned. I wish I could unsee and unsmell the whole event. The high amount of heat from the fire prevented us from being closer, thank God, but I'd rather not have seen it at all. Then again, I wish I never saw Marketa's chest blow open, or General Harding shot nearly in half, or Chris shot repeatedly, to name a few. This type of bloodshed might be commonplace among the older Bearers, but I'll never get used to it.

Something else I'll never get used to is discovering new abilities that Crimson possesses. She actually entered the fire area once Yeok Choo's body had burned away revealing her skeleton. Crimson reached into Yeok Choo's ribcage and took the diamond. As she moved in the flames, I noticed a force-field around her body, preventing her from being burned from the heat. I can only assume this was a display of the Elemental power of controlling fire.

A reminder of the upcoming blast I need to prepare for.

As Chris and I stand a little away from everyone else, I pick up on a hushed conversation between Anika and Ruth. Anika questions the correctness of choosing when to die versus letting nature dictate when our lives will end.

Ruth replies, "The rules, laws, and moral code you are

familiar with were not created with Immortals in mind."

"Well," Anika states, "I'm not sure I'm ready to toss aside everything I've ever known and believed."

"No one is going to force you to. No one forced me to give up my beliefs or spirituality."

"What? Are you a religious person?"

"In my own way. I find peace and fulfillment in following my heart and extending kindness to others. Anika, you are approved to become a Bearer, meaning you have the right state of mind and way of thinking to be able to properly handle the power associated with a diamond. This puts you on a higher level than many other people. You should be honored by the fact your good nature passes the strict qualifications of Crimson—a twelve-thousand-year-old human who has seen civilizations come and go."

"I am honored. But I don't think immortality is for me."

"You have your whole life to make that decision."

"I know."

Movement on the other side of the pyre draws my attention. Using my Hunter's vision, I see several Bearers digging in the ground. I squeeze Chris's hand.

"Come on. Let's go see what's going on over there." I pull him with me as we meander through the other Bearers.

Maetha directs the digging being performed by Amalgada and Avani. To the side of the plot are small headstones in the grass.

I let go of Chris's hand and walk over to get a better look. Many names are chiseled into many stones, some of which I recognize: Neema, Henry, Rolf, Gustave, and Hasan. Another rock lays atop the grass with Yeok Choo's name inscribed.

I turn to Maetha. "Is this the Diamond Bearers' cemetery?

"This is the Field of Remembrance. Not all headstones have bodies below."

"Is this where Gustave's diamond was harvested?"

"Yes." Maetha says with a grimace. "His removal was a bit bloodier than Yeok Choo's."

Chris steps forward. "Where are the unclaimed diamonds kept?"

Crimson joins us. "No diamond is unclaimed for long. But until it is, the diamond is kept in the securest place on Earth."

My mind swims back to a moment when Crimson referred to where she keeps the other pieces of the Grecian Blue diamond—inside her body. I guess she'd always know where the pieces are. Technically I should be able to feel those individual diamonds, but I can't. More mysteries about Crimson.

Other Bearers step up to take their turn in helping dig in the dirt. Even Chris and I take a turn in what feels like has evolved into a ceremony of its own. Yeok Choo's remains are put into a cloth bag and gently placed in the deep hole, then buried. Once Chuang positions the stone with her name on top of the mound, a feeling of completeness settles over me. I can't explain it any other way. I hardly think I'm the only one to feel the sensation.

With that, everyone turns and begins the trek back down to the main house. Yeok Choo's life is over and life in general is moving on. Harsh reality.

When we reach the house, Chris says, "Let's go walk on the beach and watch the sunset."

"I know the perfect one. I'll take you there." I lead him to the pathway that will take us to the beach Jonas showed earlier. As soon as we arrive at the edge of the sand, I'm taken back at the picture-perfect view spanning out in front of us. The setting sun casts oranges and yellows through the clouds that very well could be painted on the sky. They look that perfect. We are truly in a tropical paradise. Too bad it's not for a better occasion.

We kick off our shoes and start out onto the sand, walking for several minutes hand in hand in silence. Chris lets go and quickens his pace to get in front of me. He crouches down and picks something up.

"What's that?" I try to peek over his shoulder.

"A pebble." He stands and turns toward me. I look down at his hand. It looks like any other ordinary rock, oval, smooth, grey in color. Chris says, "Did you know that when a male penguin finds a female he wants to impress, he searches the whole beach for the perfect pebble to present to her? This can take some time, too." He steps a little closer to me and I can feel his heat. "When he finds the perfect one, he waddles up to the female and places the pebble at her feet. A proposal of sorts."

My heart begins to race and my voice drops involuntarily. "Are you going to give me a pebble?"

He looks me in the eye. "When I find the perfect one I will."

My cheeks heat up and I become flustered. I decide to joke my way around his serious hint at a proposal. "I'll only accept a pebble if you waddle first."

Chris tosses the tiny stone into the ocean. My eyes follow the pebble wishing I could have kept it. He says, studying my wistful gaze, "That one wasn't perfect."

We walk some more before he leads me up the beach where we sit on the sand cuddled in each other's arms. The sun is almost covered with water, or so it seems. Yeok Choo is gone, covered with dirt, resting among her comrades on Maetha's island of Immortals. What a crazy life I find myself in. Only a handful of years ago I was happy to people-watch at the mall with Suz, or travel with my parents to their medical conferences. Look at me now.

The last pixel of the sun sets and we get up from the sand to go back to the group. On the way, I say to Chris, "Have you tried to look into Chuang's body to see the powdered stuff?"

"No. I thought it can't be viewed."

"I saw it earlier. I think I could remove it, but he's obstinate."

"I'll go talk to him."

As we walk along the path through the thick greenery, I notice the transformed Shadow Demons are nearby, like they always are at night. I guess I thought maybe they couldn't travel over water or something.

Once we get to the group, I notice out at the perimeter of light and darkness other Shadow Demons, not the ones that usually follow me, lingering. I search the crowd for Crimson to ask her about their presence. I can't find her. I see Maetha and walk over to her.

"Maetha, why are there so many Shadow Demons here?"

"They seem to be attached to whichever Diamond Bearer used obsidian on them to alter their states of existence. Each Bearer who helped eradicate the Demons has told me of their herd of followers."

"Is that what they are now? Followers?"

"For lack of a better word, yes."

"Has anyone reported seeing any dangerous Demons?"

"No. They are all benign." She points to one near Duncan. "Do you recognize that one?"

I look at the eerie, not-quite-human, a hint of animal, skeletal frame hanging in the air just above the ground. "Is that Justin?"

"I believe it is."

I walk over to what might be Justin's form. It doesn't look at me. I walk directly toward it only to have it float out of my way. Now I'm standing amidst many other demons, my own demons join the mix. "Can any of you hear me?" I ask. No response. I walk out of the darkness, back to Maetha. "I haven't been in a situation where other Bearers' demons were present. When we're indoors, the demons aren't there. What can we do about them? Can we release them permanently, so they're not bound to us?"

Maetha says, "I don't know."

"Can we use them for good?"

"How?"

"I'm not sure."

"Let me view my future concerning them." She closes her eyes and concentrates for a minute or so. "All I find is a future without them."

I should look for my future too, but I see Chris talking with Chuang. I'll look for my future later. "Excuse me, Maetha." She nods and I walk away.

On the way over, I intensify my hearing to listen to Chris and Chuang.

Chris says to Chuang, "You don't know if that's true."

"Yes, I do."

I figure Chuang is telling Chris all about my leading them into death and destruction in China. I make sure I control my visual cues representing my emotions.

Chris replies to Chuang, "Do you want to?"

"No. Before this Surrendering began, I felt differently. Adamantly so. I even attacked Calli when she asked if I wanted her to help me. Now, I'm willing to try anything to stay alive."

"What made you change your mind?"

"Yeok Choo saying she knew she couldn't act in the

best interests of nature any longer. She'd gone through too many lives, searching for happiness, and when she finally found it with Marketa, she knew she'd be done if anything ever happened to her. I don't feel that way at all. I want to keep living, helping humanity, guiding progression, only now I have this powder preventing me." He flaps the quartz blanket that's draped over his shoulders. "And I have to keep this on at all times to have enough strength to move around."

Chris asks, "What if Calli can't help you?"

"I won't stop searching for a way to heal. I'm not done. I'm reinvigorated and fully accept my duty of being a Sanguine Diamond Bearer."

Chris sees me coming their direction. "Well, here's your chance to mend things with Calli."

I speak to Chris's mind. *You know, we've heard this type of speech before, from Marketa in Tennessee. She fooled us into believing she was dedicated to the Bearers. Do you think Chuang is doing the same thing?*

Ask him.

I approach them, pretending Chris and I haven't just spoken. "Chris, can I talk with you a moment?"

Chuang reaches out and touches my arm. "Calli. Earlier you offered to try to help me. Is the offer still open?"

"Of course." I keep my words professional. I am not going to walk blindly into another situation of life and death. "I'd prefer to attempt to heal you out here in public, though."

Chuang looks around the group and swallows a couple of times. "What if you can't heal me? Do you want everyone to see your weakness?"

"I prefer not to create an opportunity where any supporter of Marketa can try to finish what she started."

Chuang's eyes rush to my pointed stare. His voice lowers to a whisper. "I had no idea she was going to go that far. I certainly wouldn't have condoned it."

"Chuang, I will try to help you whether or not you decide to support me in the task that's been given me. I would be pleased to have you join in the cause, but I'd ask that you keep your opinions on methods used to yourself."

He nods.

"I think you should lie down on the ground in case my healing zaps your strength."

"All right." Chuang lowers to the ground, sits, then lays out flat, the quartz blanket still covering his body.

What are you doing, Chuang? Don't let her touch you!

I'm choosing Calli, Kookju.

Why?

I don't want to end up like Marketa and I certainly don't desire Yeok Choo's choice. I'm also curious to see what kind of power Calli has.

I'll be here to stop her if she hurts you.

I listen to these telepathic words between Chuang and Kookju, trying to keep up the guise I can't hear them. I decide to communicate on my own. I send my thoughts to Chris who still stands by my side. *Chris, watch Kookju. He might try to stop me.*

Shouldn't we get Maetha or Crimson?

Maetha's not far. Besides, you and I have the most power in this group.

I kneel by Chuang and hover my hands over his injured stomach. Once I've scanned his body, I say, "Your internal organs are healed and are in good working order."

"Yes, I know. But I can't use any powers on the substance."

By now, the crowd of Bearers has quieted and gathered around us. I sense Maetha has joined the group. I don't look up at anyone. Instead, I focus my mind on the mass inside him. The confusion powder is merged with natural fluid and minerals from his body. It has calcified. I use my powers on the minerals and fluid instead of the substance.

I say, "You know, Chuang, a modern x-ray would have revealed the powder had bound together. A skilled surgeon could have cut this out of you. Instead, I will." I look up and find Maetha. "Do you have a blade or scalpel on the island?"

"Yes. Give me a moment." She runs away in a flash.

Kookju kneels on the other side of Chuang. "Don't let her do this, Chuang."

I don't say anything. I keep my eyes on Chuang. If he's truly wanting me to heal him and he's being truthful with his words about recommitting himself to the Bearers, his reaction to Kookju will show it.

Maetha returns with a small medical kit and hands it to me.

"Chuang, listen to me!" Kookju pleads.

Chuang says to Kookju, "Would you heal me?"

"You know I can't."

"Calli says she can. I'm going to let her try. I trust her."

"She's a child!"

"And you're an old man who can't heal me. I'm tired of you encouraging me down paths of pain. You'd have me refuse her help and continue to live in misery."

"You'd live, though. She might kill you. None of us can see your future while you have the confusion substance inside you."

"Exactly why I want it removed. Move aside, Kookju." Chuang issues the order, then turns his head to me. "Proceed, Calli."

"All right. We need to take off the quartz blanket and expose your stomach. The blanket's power will try to heal my incision before I can complete what I need to do."

Chuang tosses the quartz blanket off and allows others to pull it out from under him. I push up his shirt and lay my hand on the side of his stomach. "I feel it."

Kookju swoops back in. "I want to feel what you feel." I move my hands away and Kookju takes over. "I don't feel anything."

I form a circle with my finger and thumb showing the approximate size of the one-inch lump I'm going to remove. "It's this big and is deep inside his belly." I hold up the scalpel and position it over Chuang's skin.

Kookju grunts in disproval.

Fabian declares, "Oh for the love of Odin! Would you get out of the way, Kookju, and let her work?" Other Bearers mutter their support of Fabian's declaration.

Kookju, obviously insulted by the majority siding with me, gets up and storms off.

I look at Chuang, the blade still hovering above his skin. "Okay?"

"Okay."

I push the blade into his skin and pull gently toward me, leaving a slit and gushing blood. Chuang cries out in pain. I use my healing powers and mentally pull the lump up through his body toward the opening I've created. A limit is reached. An obvious blocking or confusion of my powers. I close my eyes and focus on my diamond. I feel my heartbeat escalate and my heart heats up. Then my hand over his stomach begins burning intensely. With my eyes still shut, I hear the gasps and vocalized amazement from the group of what they're witnessing.

"How is she doing that?"

"What kind of power is she using?"

"I've never seen anything like it before."

Something touches my palm and I open my eyes. Through the blinding blue-green bright light emanating from my hand, I see a blood-covered ball. I close my fingers around it and drop it in the grass away from him. The bright light diminishes rapidly until I bring my hand back to his body and lay it flat against his stomach and incision. I close my eyes again and focus on my diamond. I desire to heal his injury, mend his cells, and strengthen his energy levels. My hand feels on fire again and I assume the bright light is back.

When no more injury is detectable, I remove my hand. All available energy drains from my body and I can no longer hold myself upright. My body slumps sideways uncontrollably. Chris catches me and wraps a comforting arm around my shoulders, rubbing my arm.

The questions and congratulations come from all directions. First and foremost from Chuang. I can't focus on his words, though. Everything seems to be fading to black.

Maetha says, "Chris, wrap her in the quartz blanket and help her to her bungalow. She's drained her energy."

I don't know how long I was asleep.

Maetha is by the right side of my bed. She says after meeting my gaze, "Calli, that was amazing. No question about it. However, don't do it again unless someone's life is threatened. Chuang could have been healed by someone else once you removed the mass."

"He and I both needed to prove we could trust each other." I pause. "I don't know why I couldn't feel my energy draining. I would have stopped if I had."

Someone touches my left arm, making me jump a little. I turn my head and find Chris. He takes my hand and brings it up to his mouth where he deposits soft kisses to the back of it.

Maetha clears her throat. "Well, I'll let you get back to doing that special healing thing you do. The sooner she's back on her feet the better."

"How long was I out?" I ask Chris.

"About an hour."

I pull my hand away from his mouth and wiggle over in the bed, lying on my side. I pat the bed like he's done to me in the past. I absolutely love the delighted grin he gives me as he moves to the bed. He lies down on his side facing me, takes my hand and intertwines our fingers.

He says, "You should have seen the faces of everyone else while you pulled the blob out of Chuang."

"Because of the blue glow?"

"No, well yes, but because of your ability to move the blob with your mind."

"I didn't want to go digging into his body, so I brought it to me."

"That's telekinesis, Calli."

"Oh. Yeah. I suppose it is."

"No one else can do it."

I think for a second, running the list of my abilities through my mind. He's right. But then I remember something. "Chris, when I cleared the poison out of Justin in the hotel room on the way to the Death Clan, I pulled the poison up his throat and out his mouth."

Chris props himself up on his elbow, excitement flashing in his eyes. "I remember. Only I didn't know that was as unusual as it really is. Everything you were doing back then was mind-blowing so it kind of got mixed in with everything else. But this isn't that simple, apparently."

I don't know exactly why I can do what I do. I glance down at our connected hands, then let my eyes travel up his arm, to his shoulder, and finally to his face resting in his palm. His blue eyes gaze at mine, searching for my thoughts, but not reading my mind. My body still feels heavy with exhaustion from healing Chuang yet being this near to Chris—mesmerizingly handsome Chris—I feel better with each passing second. I know a way I can recharge quicker.

I bring our connected hands to my mouth and kiss the back of his hand, then let go and reach forward, sliding my fingers along his neck and back into his thick hair. Exerting the smallest amount of pressure with my fingertips, I move him toward me.

He reacts as if he's been waiting for me to ask. His mouth descends to mine in urgency and his body moves next to mine seemingly on its own. We pick up the excitement where we left off New Year's Eve.

I feel light as air, yet heavy with yearning, absorbing his body heat. Time could stop right now, and I wouldn't have a problem with it. In fact, the world could end, and I wouldn't care because I'm in his arms, his strong caring arms. It's enough to make my head spin.

My mind is spinning a lot.

Devastating images from my nightmares and a few new ones fill my vision. I'm on top of the same building from my other dreams. I see panicked masses running through the streets. Explosions and fires burn the city. Is it an earthquake? I wonder in my mind. Then I see a few people walking through the streets in a group, six or seven men and women. The frightened crowd flees from them. The group members seem to be shooting lightning bolts out of their fingertips. Then one of the members, a woman, looks up at me. I realize Crimson is standing next to me, looking in the direction of the small group. She turns to me and says, "We must go." She grabs my waist, pulls me to her, and pushes off with her feet. My heart explodes with horror as she launches into the sky.

"Calli." Chris calls my name. I wish he'd save me from the nauseating experience Crimson is bent on giving me.

"Calli!"

I open my eyes and find Chris sitting on the bed next to me with both his hands on my shoulders. My body shakes uncontrollably. "What happened?"

"I'm not sure. But you're glowing bright blue." He relaxes his hold.

Sitting up next to him, I look at my hands. He's right.

"Did you have a vision?"

"Yes, about Portland."

"What made you scream?"

I screamed? "Probably the part where Crimson took me flying again. But there was something new, too. People were shooting lightning bolts from their fingers. What kind of power is that?"

"Maybe one of the Elementals?"

"I guess so. It was terrifying. We have to find a way to evacuate that city, Chris. Maybe we can prevent them from becoming empowered." I look down at my hands. They aren't glowing anymore.

Chris reaches forward and pushes my hair out of my eyes. His hand continues a gentle journey across my cheek and back behind my ear.

I press my cheek into his hand. "I'm sorry my vision ruined our moment."

"Don't be. A moment is all we have right now, and we made the most of it, believe me." He pulls my head forward and rests his forehead against mine. "I love you."

"I love you, too."

"I think you've earned the Bearers' respect by healing Chuang, both because they couldn't, and because he'd been so rude to you. Yet you helped him. You demonstrated unconditional compassion, something they lost long ago."

I pull back and look him in the eyes. "I don't ever want to lose it like them."

His eyes glisten with tears. I angle my head, trying to understand why this is emotional to him. He whispers, "I want to gain it. I need to."

I wrap my arms around him and pull him close. "You're not giving yourself enough credit, Chris." I issue comforting vibes to him, hoping I can help him realize how much I believe in him.

We continue to hold each other, absorbing each other's energy, for a few minutes. Then someone knocks on the door.

I let go of Chris. "Come in."

Jonas opens the door and enters the room, then diverts his eyes. "Sorry, I can come back."

Chris moves off the bed and sits in the nearby chair. "No, Jonas. What do you need?"

"I found something in the files. The company name you couldn't remember, Calli. Vorherrschaft. It's a Swiss-based manufacturing entity. They have ties to all the different aspects of what we've encountered so far: the power-removing machine, the obsidian bullets, quartz crystal growing operations, you name it. However, nothing in the files connects General Harding's operation with the operation in China. They are independent of each other. Well, with the one exception, they both had an employee named Agent Alpha."

"Freedom," I say on an exhale.

"From what I can tell, Freedom coordinated with Vorherrschaft and hired them to make his machine. He also helped set up the machine in China, but the two operations worked independently of each other."

"Toward what goal?" Chris asks.

"I don't know. Another similarity I found is a title used, one that we haven't mentioned or talked about: Power Reaper."

Chris rubs his face. "It sounds like a title for someone who reaps powers from people. Basically, harvesting powers, like my dad was doing."

Jonas lowers his voice. "Yes."

I try to change the subject, saying, "Any information about Vorherrschaft? Is there a business location?"

"I haven't found one yet, at least not one that actually exists. There are several addresses, but a quick Internet search revealed them to be fake. My idea is we check out the different manufacturing companies first, like the obsidian bullet plant in Missouri where Yellowstone obsidian has been sent.

"Thank you, Jonas. It's definitely worth checking into."

Jonas adds, "When you're feeling better, come to my bungalow and I'll give you more information. By the way, what you did for Chuang was . . . *awesome*!"

Chapter Nine - Brand on a Mission

After Jonas leaves the room, I get up and Chris and I head outside. My strength is full, and all my senses are on high. I find I'm able to zoom in on conversations with ease partly because these people are fellow Diamond Bearers and I'm connected to them in a different way than say Sarangerel and her parents.

I hear Chuang beating himself up for declining my offer to heal him before Yeok Choo died. He thinks if she'd been able to see his "poisoning" healed she might have changed her mind about surrendering her diamond. Chuang believes she was more scared of the future and the threats to the Bearers than she was missing Marketa.

Chuang's regrets remind me that no cosmic power includes being able to see what might have been. Brand's is the only one that comes close and even he has to actually experience the situation, then repeat back from it. Speculation is a pointless use of time, yet somehow we are all guilty of doing it.

I pick up on how the Bearers see me now as a strong leader, better than an equal. They understand why Crimson and Maetha chose me and they respect the decision. More than anything, though, they respect Crimson, and like Chuang, they want to continue to serve nature's will.

One of the biggest challenges I've faced was to unite the Bearers. I can't take all the credit for accomplishing that. Yeok Choo's decision to quit and Chuang's choice to remain and accept my help was highly influential. One thing I won't do is become comfortable. I will continue to move forward.

I spot Brand sitting on a chair amongst groups of conversation, but not participating. What's more is I can read his mind which means he isn't repeating at the moment. He's definitely feeling down about Beth.

I send my thoughts to Chris rather than speaking directly, even though he walks beside me. *Chris, I think Brand should be the one to investigate the Missouri obsidian plant. He needs a break from Denver.*

Don't you mean Beth?

Regardless, he'd be perfect for the undercover mission. Let's take him with us to Jonas's bungalow.

Good idea.

We approach him and I say, "Brand, would you come with us to Jonas's place?"

Brand grunts. "I already helped him clean it up. What are you gonna make me do now?"

"Just come on."

We arrive at Jonas's and knock on the door. Jonas lets us in. Anika is seated at the table with her hands wrapped around a mug full of steaming liquid. Jonas's bungalow is small and cozy, but the air crackles with tension.

After the door is closed, I say, "Brand, how would you like to go to Missouri to check out an obsidian plant Jonas found?"

"Me? Sure!"

Wow. I didn't think Brand would be so excited to get a task of his own.

I continue. "I'll find a Diamond Bearer to accompany you. The two of you will have to decide the best way to go about getting info. If at all possible, try to sabotage their operations."

Brand says, "I could do this on my own, you know."

"Yeah, but I wouldn't be able to communicate with

you. Having a Bearer with you gives me that connection."

Jonas says, "I wish I could go with you, Brand, but I'm supposed to avoid going to the States. I'm dead, remember?"

Chris turns to Jonas. "Why don't you change your appearance like Maetha?"

"I don't know how yet."

I consider that I've already altered my appearance to appear more like Chris's vision. Of course, I didn't know I was doing it, and I certainly didn't change my entire self the way Maetha can. Still, I've done a little of that.

"Why don't *you* come with me?" Brand asks, wiggling his eyebrows.

I don't even have to give this any thought. "No. I think it would help if we pair up with some of the older Bearers."

Brand is let down, but quickly recovers with the thought of having his first real assignment.

Chris says, "Jonas, why don't you tell us what you found and what you think is the best way to infiltrate the building."

"Sure."

As Jonas begins outlining his discovery, my mind wanders. I think about Beth, wondering where she is at the moment. She should be here with us. We're the younger Bearers and candidates.

I interrupt Jonas. "I'm going to step out and go find a Bearer to go with you to Missouri, Brand."

Chris says, "I'm going to stay, if that's okay. I think I might be able to use my government resources to help investigate this facility."

I nod and leave the bungalow.

Anika catches up with me down the pathway. "Calli, wait up. I wanted to talk to you about the Seer topaz you gave me."

"Did you use it?"

"Yes." She looks down at her feet. "I looked for my future and if Jonas was in it. All I saw was you."

"Me?"

"Yes. You and Jonas."

"What?" I cough and sputter.

Her eyes meet mine and I sense her hesitation to be completely honest with me. She blinks a couple times, then says, "I can't compete with you, Calli. Your name comes up in every conversation. And to see you in his future and not me was confirmation of what I've felt for a long time."

"I'm sorry Anika. But Jonas and I don't have anything going on."

"You don't now. Look, I hate to be the one to break this to you, but Chris isn't always going to be around."

I stop abruptly and take a deep cleansing breath to try to gain control of my rising anxiety. "Anika, I remember when I saw the future for the first time. I misinterpreted it. Perhaps you've done the same thing, not knowing how to look at small factors and jumping easily to conclusions."

Anika hands me the topaz. She says, "My conclusion is that being able to see the future is a gamble one way or the other. Knowing how things are going to work out is not healthy to the mind, body, or spirit. I'd rather be surprised. I'll leave the future divination up to others more qualified than me."

"Anika, I don't know what to say. I don't . . . Jonas and I are not . . . " I stumble over my words. "You don't have anything to worry about."

"You're right. I won't spend any more time worrying about him. His hands are full and his future even more so."

I haven't looked to Jonas's future. I try to make it a practice not to look at my friends' futures, especially potential relationships. I'm going to keep up with my practice.

Anika heads toward the main house after saying good night. I walk to the gathered Bearers, still mingling amongst themselves.

I send out vibrations with my diamond to the other diamonds to get everyone's attention. I'm a little surprised how well it works, but I hide my excitement. With everyone looking my direction, I say, "Jonas has located a facility that manufactures obsidian bullets in the state of Missouri. I'm sending Brand to investigate and need a Bearer to accompany him. Would any of you have time in your schedule for this task? I don't know how long it will take."

A couple seconds tick by, then Ruth speaks. "I could go with him."

"Excellent. He's being briefed in Jonas's bungalow. You can join him there."

She nods and leaves the group.

I send a message to Chris. *Ruth is coming to join you. She'll be going with Brand to Missouri. I'm going to my bungalow to rest.*

Okay. I'll tell Brand. Are you all right?

Yes. Just mentally exhausted.

Do you want me to come to you?

No, I need to meditate.

I'd be lying if I said that's fine.

I'm sorry, Chris. Please give me some time to sort out some . . . stuff.

I really want to be with you.

I want that, too, but you're too much of a distraction right now, Mr. Harding.

Well, you be sure to let me know if you decide you need to be distracted.

I meditated for a while after settling into my bed and apparently fell asleep because I just awoke from a terrible dream. I dreamt about the Portland blast—again. There were dead bodies piled upon dead bodies in mass graves. Critically ill people, mutations, cancer diagnoses, and the emergence of altered DNA. Obviously, an evacuation still didn't happen.

I need to learn who to contact in the city government. I'll do some research on the Internet and compile a list of names, titles, and addresses, starting with the mayor. Then possibly the chief of police. But what will I say to them?

My mind wanders to the events of yesterday: the Surrendering, Chuang's healing, Brand and Beth's re-lationship, Jonas and Anika's impending break-up, Chris handing me a pebble. I focus more on that memory than the rest. When the Portland blast hits, everything could go out the window. But if Chris is by my side I'll be fine. I know it.

Interestingly enough—and quite disturbing—I realize he's not in any of my visions of the blast. I don't want to read too much into it. This is probably because Chris won't be on top of the building with Crimson and me. He should be far away at that time. I don't want to consider any scenario in which Chris is no longer in the picture.

I start to feel overwhelmed, holding too many thoughts in my head at once, too many decisions.

I call to Chris with my mind. *Are you awake?*

Yes.

I could use your distraction for a little while.

You got it!

The next morning at breakfast in the main house Brand pulls me aside and asks, "Calli, can you get me an invisibility topaz."

"They don't work around cameras."

"I'm not worried about that. How long will it take?"

"I already have one charged. Just don't forget how quickly they lose their power."

"I won't, but I think it would be foolish not to have one in this situation. Ruth and I are leaving later this afternoon."

"Have you talked with Beth?"

"Why?"

"Does she know you're going on assignment?"

"No. She'll figure it out."

I'm shocked with his lackadaisical attitude. All I can say is, "Seriously?"

"Not your problem, Calli, so please back off."

"Okay." Somehow I know he repeated the conversation just now and found out I overheard them and talked with Beth. I feel I've overstepped my bounds with them. "I'm sorry, Brand. I didn't mean to interfere."

The door opens and Chris's uncle Don walks in. I think he's wearing the same clothing as when I saw him last. Maybe I'll suggest Merlin take Don shopping to update his wardrobe. Don's eyes scan the room and stop on Chris. "There's my favorite nephew!"

Chris gets up and gives Don a hug.

Don says, "I knew you were here yesterday and it just killed me to not be able to come visit with you, but you know, rules are rules. Speaking of rules, is Crimson here?"

"Don't you mean Jo Jo?"

Don shuffles his feet. "Yeah, 'Jo Jo' or whatever name

she's going by these days."

"She's gone, Uncle Don." Chris leads his uncle to a seat at our table. "I hear you're working on assembling a machine."

"That's correct. As soon as I get oatmeal in me I'll show you the progress."

After eating, we make our way upstairs in the main house. One of the many bedrooms is being used as a lab for the machine, although the machine is mostly loose parts lying around on the floor at this point.

Don walks over to the wall with a closet. "We'll have to knock out this wall to enlarge the room before we'll be able to properly use the thing. Well, that and install radiation containment seals and barriers. This thing is going to be hazardous."

Chris responds in more of a grumble, "If you build it right it won't kill anyone. I've been through one."

"You have? But that would mean . . . "

"Yeah, I lost my Runner power."

I look into Don's consciousness to determine just how much he knows about the Sanguine Diamond and Bearers and find he doesn't know much. In fact, not much at all. I have to figure that once he's completed the machine, Crimson will send him back home.

The information in his head is similar to what other workers and staff members know: just the basics of cosmic powers and the need for secrecy. They know the chain of command, enjoy being well taken care of financially, and honored to be a part of something bigger than themselves.

Don places a hand on Chris's shoulder. "If I build it right, you could get it back."

"No thanks."

I step closer. "Why would you think you could give him a power when the machine is designed to remove powers?"

Don walks over to a table with schematics spread out on top. "You see this one here? It is for what we're building. A remover." He shuffles through the papers and lifts one up. "But this one is for an infuser."

We walk over to Don and I take the paper from him, holding it with two hands. My eyes travel briskly over the page not really seeing the design, but rather looking for recognizable words. Then I locate a capital T and the number 19.

I nearly shriek. "Do you know what this is? This is how they made Brand."

Don says, "I don't follow."

Chris takes the plans out of my hands and looks them over. "How do you know?"

"T19. Project T19. Hans Lindlebauer." I toss out these fragments of information, thinking Chris will recognize them. He doesn't. I ask Don, "Does Maetha know about this?"

"Probably not. I only tell her what I know and I didn't know anything about a project. But the name Lindlebauer sounds familiar."

Chris asks me determinedly, "How do you know about this, Calli?"

I relay the experience of helping Maetha rescue Hans from the impending government capture last spring and how he informed us about the project.

"But if the project was canceled almost two decades ago," Don says, taking the plans from Chris and laying them back on the table, "why is this schematic dated just last year? Furthermore, why did the Chinese have the same schematics in their computer files?"

Is it possible there are other Repeaters roaming the earth? I rub my temples and close my eyes. I focus on

Crimson. *Can you hear me? Did you know about this? Are there more like Brand?*

No response. Not that I'm surprised.

Chris and I hike up to the highest point on the island, as per Jonas's directions. Maetha encouraged Jonas to come with us, but Chris said no. From the high vantage point we can see the Field of Remembrance, the beautiful beach, and the boat dock.

We spread out a blanket and have a small picnic, then lay back and stare at the endless blue sky. Not much time goes by before I see Crimson enter through the forcefield high above. I can tell she's using her invisibility to shield her arrival, which is probably a good idea because of all the non-powered people on the island. Seeing a flying human dangling in the sky doesn't fit into our normal range. I don't know why she entered from the top instead of coming in from the side like the boat. I draw the conclusion there must be an entrance at that exact point. Perhaps the boat knew the exact coordinates where to enter the force field.

I decide not to tell Chris what I've just seen. I make this decision to prevent distracting us from enjoying our time together.

"Chris, what's you biggest dream in life?"

He turns on his side, facing me. "Where's that question coming from?"

"I don't know. I just wondered, that's all."

"I'll have to think about it. What's yours?"

"I've wanted to be a doctor since I can remember. I like helping people feel better. Like with Chuang. I've seen my parent's patients after they've found relief from their pain or illnesses and I want to be able to help people feel that way. Now with my powers, I can do that and more."

"But . . . "

"But what?"

"Only up to a certain point. Otherwise you're going against nature's will."

"True, but I'll still be able to help many people. What about you?"

"I envy you being so sure of what you want. I haven't thought about it too much other than I want to make sure my mom is well taken care of."

"You're a great son."

"No. Any son would do the same."

"Are you sure about that?"

Chris reaches his hand out and traces my hairline with a feather touch. "There's only one thing I'm sure about and that's how I feel about you." He leans forward and brings his lips to mine, his hand travels down my neck and shoulder, pulling my body toward his.

Our intimate exchange deepens and reaches new levels. However, I can't help but feel uncomfortable knowing anyone could stumble upon us. I feel exposed and vulnerable, then panic sets in. I gently push Chris away.

"What is it?" he asks.

"We should get back." I don't feel like telling him about my panic attack.

"No one will be missing us. Besides, they can call us if they need." He taps his temple with his finger.

"That's the problem. We're never completely alone, you and I. We have no real privacy. Doesn't that bother you?" I ask.

"Well, do you constantly peek into other Bearers' minds to see what they're doing?"

"No."

"I don't think they do either."

"They don't have a Blue shard like I do."

"Oh, that. Yeah, that's a little different. I doubt she looks into your mind often."

"She doesn't have to. When Jonas and I shared the diamond, I always knew what he was doing. Crimson has the same connection with me. That's why I don't feel comfortable."

Chris sighs, but gives me a reassuring smile. "All right, let's head back."

When we arrive back at the main house, I find Crimson and ask, "May I have a word with you privately?"

"Of course."

I lead her up to the room with the machine pieces. Don sees her enter and becomes all flustered, then blushes with his fumblings. I wonder if he knows how long Crimson has been alive and that she doesn't share the same attraction to him.

"Don," I ask, "may we have privacy please?"

He nods and leaves the room, closing the door behind him.

I launch right in. "Didn't you hear me earlier? I tried calling for you."

"I told you I'm pulling back from you and your decisions. I have other things I'm dealing with right now. What did you need?"

"Are you trying to build a T19 machine?"

"Excuse me?"

"Are you having Don build a T19 machine?" I go to the table and pick up the schematic and show her, as if I need to. I hardly think she doesn't know already.

"When Brand and the other Repeaters surfaced, a new technology we weren't aware of was revealed. T19 is the name of the combination of settings and ingredients that results in Repeaters. There are other names of projects, but we don't know what power they create, if any at all. To stay competitive with the opposing forces, we must match if not exceed their knowledge." She takes the schematics and lays them back down on the table.

"So, that's a yes." I look all around the room at the disarray of parts and pieces lying everywhere. "We're behind, aren't we?"

"No. Right now they're trying to stay caught up with us. Maetha has already figured out how to heal DNA, like with Jonas, minus a bulky machine. She's worked on your family line's DNA resulting in your transformation and ability to withstand and recover quickly from injury. You healed faster than the others after being shot in China."

"Oh, I thought that was the greater healing power at work."

"That's part of it, and something the others don't have. The bigger and more important aspect is that your physical alterations make you able to capture the Elemental blast. That alone is what will bring success for humanity."

"Is that why I'm able to use telekinesis when no one else can? Or is it part of the Blue Diamond?"

"Not the Blue's power. Your alteration that Maetha brought about, coupled with the Sanguine Diamond's healing power is the reason. If you think about it, Healers manipulate cells and organs with their minds, moving and fixing them. You moved Chuang's mass right out of his body. That is a step beyond what Diamond Bearers can do."

"So, I'm Maetha's Brand. She created me by changing my DNA."

"Yes, you could look at it that way. If you do, consider then that she didn't have to build a machine to do it."

I pause, letting her words sink in. "What about Vorherrschaft? Do you know who or what that is?"

"No."

"Are there other Repeaters?"

"I don't know. It's difficult to locate a Repeater without the tell-tale signs of being afraid of the dark. Now that the Demons are gone, we'd have to sit and read every mind walking by us in search of a mind similar to Brand's. Where would we start?"

"Huh. I guess that's an unexpected consequence of eliminating the Demons' threat. We'll have to wait till we can identify someone who always gets their way, like Brand."

"Exactly. My bigger concern is the other possible powers that have been created we don't know about. Those are possibilities that could get in the way of you capturing the blast."

"Do you think Freedom was trying to mimic what Maetha was working on?"

"Who knows for sure? I think there were many factors that went into the creation of the technology, but the continuing of it has taken on a completely different goal." She stops for a moment, as if assessing something. "I must go now, Calli. I have pressing matters."

We leave the machine room and I join Chris downstairs. He informs me Jonas invited us to join him, Anika, Beth, and Sarangerel at his bungalow to discuss more possible links and connections from the files and data.

◇ ◇ ◇

Chris and I have an enjoyable evening with everyone—a nice reprieve from the stress of everything going on in the world. I don't think we'll ever be able to completely tune out the world, but for one evening we at least tried.

I found Sarangerel to be quite interesting to listen to. She is a great asset to the team here. Jonas and Anika acted as though nothing was amiss between them. Beth didn't seem affected whenever Brand's name was brought up.

As Chris walks me back to my bungalow, he says, "What do you think Brand will have to report tomorrow?"

"Hopefully he'll have information about the obsidian manufacturing."

"And the confusion powder?"

We arrive at my bungalow. "Yes, that too." The breeze rustles his hair and suddenly my stomach starts to flitter. Sometimes I forget how gorgeous he is. I chew on my bottom lip, then open the door. "Do you want to come in?"

His eyes light up, glinting in the moonlight. He grins and puts his hand on my waist, following behind me. His fingers rub under the edge of my shirt and my skin tingles at his touch.

I shut the door behind him, the light of the moon illuminating the room through the window, shining across his face. My heart races. All I can think of is he is leaving tomorrow and I want to feel more of his skin on mine.

I pull close to him, pressing my lips against his. He hesitates for a moment, but then his hands are in my hair, on my back, down around my hips. I dig my fingers into his shoulders, pulling him in tighter, sliding my hands along his neck and head. He smells so good, feels even better. My whole body lights up from the inside and I know that this is our moment.

I feel a strange sensation in my heart and pull back from Chris, breathless, only a moment before Ruth appears inside the room, having bi-located to us.

"Oh!" she says. A knowing smile spreads across her face.

Chris drops his hands to his side.

Ruth continues. "Sorry…um…Brand asked that we hold a gathering in the morning with the other Bearers on the island."

My face is flushed with embarrassment. "Of course," I mutter. "We will bi-locate to you in the morning."

"Okay. I'll let the others know. Have a good night." Ruth disappears, and with her, my mood.

I slap my hand to my forehead, then slide my fingers into my hair and grip my scalp. "I hate this sometimes. Everyone has free access to me, my brain, my location."

"I guess I thought you were overreacting a bit before about this. I'm sorry, Calli."

I look at him and sigh. "I'm sorry we got interrupted."

He smiles. "One day, we won't. One day it'll be just you and me. I promise." He kisses me softly, lingering for a few moments. "I'll see you in the morning. Good night."

After a rather sleepless night, I communicate with Chris and tell him I'll meet him at the main house after the gathering. Chris will be leaving the island in a couple hours to head back to Washington D.C. I don't want to see him go, but he has important work to do. Beth and Anika will be heading back to Denver at the same time. I've been assigned to remain here and help out with the different projects. I'm most interested in the power-removing machine, but I have a hunch Maetha is going to pair me up with Jonas instead.

I'm not too thrilled with the idea of being left on the island with Jonas. However, Chuang, Kookju and Jie Wen are also here along with Don.

I'm certainly not going to ask Chris what he thinks of the arrangement.

I sit in the lotus position on my bed and focus on Ruth's diamond. A room with two beds, obviously a hotel room, comes into view. Brand and Ruth are seated on the edge of one of the beds. Chris has already arrived, bi-located. Soon Maetha, Jonas, Chuang, Jie Wen, and Kookju show up.

"Good to see everyone," Brand says, rubbing h hands together. "Let's get started. We've found building and searched the public records for ownersh lien holders. The building is, not surprisingly, owr Vorherrschaft International. The contact informati dead end. Our nearest calculation is twenty peop the building every day, working two shifts. We been here very long, though."

I ask, "What about access to the building?"

Brand continues. "Locked down tight, lik Harding's compound . . . well, minus the obsidia guarded-gate entrance."

Maetha says, "Keep watching and docum you find."

Jonas adds, "Get some video of the peopl on plates if you can. Maybe some faces will be r my software."

I ask, "Have you tried to enter the facility?"

"No, I figured I'd wait on that. The topa only last so long."

"True."

Ruth says, "That's all for the report."

I end my connection feeling a little let down. The expectation to hear better findings only led to a bigger letdown.

A whole week has passed since Chris left the island. The evening sun hangs on the horizon just above the water. The magnificent view would be better shared, but Chris is busy tonight and can't bi-locate to me. Maetha had me work with Don, not on the machine but hauling and transporting supplies from another boat that arrived from the mainland. Don is still waiting for the arrival of a key component to move forward with the assembly.

I've helped with many day-to-day tasks in the last week from cleaning and yard work to inventorying food and supplies and helping with food prep. Maetha's island is a complex organization that doesn't operate on its own nor un magically. One could say it's like a secret resort. I've ined a newfound respect for her managerial side.

Chuang is all mended and relishing in his freedom n the quartz blanket. He shows me respect, but he n't go over the top in expressing gratitude. At least not muttering about me anymore. Chuang, Kookju, e Wen are often found strategizing what they believe xt move will be from the developers of the busted Their discussion is quite boring to me. The fact 't see the future concerning anything related to haft is distressing. Then again, neither can I.

tec has been preoccupied with the quartz blanket frien which has led to him and Tod becoming fast operat ween the two of them they'll have the machine Tod s soon as the last of the components arrive.

e, Mishell, is an incredibly intelligent scientist.

I overheard Jie Wen say she holds two PhDs, one in biological engineering and another in geophysics. I think she's going to be a tremendous asset with the coming Elemental blast. I've tried to get to know her better but she doesn't feel comfortable yet, mainly because of our language barrier. Sarangerel is helping her polish her language skills, though.

Yesterday, Jie Wen asked Maetha to put a Blue Mist secrecy circle around him and her so they could speak privately. When I heard him ask her, I panicked because she can't do that anymore. I have her blue shard. Her response was, "There's no need when we can speak telepathically." I don't know why Jie Wen feels the need to trick Maetha concerning the Blue shard. He already figured out, or at least he assumes, I have Maetha's shard. Perhaps he's trying to determine if there's more than one shard circulating, wondering if I have one as well as Maetha? That would make sense of his behavior.

A gust of salty air swirls my hair into my eyes. I push it away and wonder how Jonas handles living on the island. Aside from the beautiful sunsets, how does he not go insane with such a small space, small square footage, close quarters and ocean all around? I'm climbing the walls. Maybe that's the reason Maetha is keeping me so busy.

Calli, a voice sounds in my mind I identify as Ruth's.

Yes?

Please bi-locate to my diamond to speak with Brand.

I close my eyes and focus on her stone. Brand comes in to view sitting next to Ruth in their hotel room.

"Hey Calli. I used the invisibility topaz today to get inside the plant."

"How'd that go?"

"Just fine. I found out the employees work with many metals, rocks, and crystals. Any order arriving or being shipped with Yellowstone obsidian is handled by an armed guard. Several packages were shipped to Norway in the time I investigated."

"Did you get an address?"

"Who do you think you're dealing with? Of course I did. I already had Ruth give Jonas the address. He's investigating it."

"Okay."

Brand continues. "One room was producing quartz prisms, like from the machine. I think this is where they make them."

"Were any prisms shipped while you were there?"

"No. But further surveillance will get that info. My topaz is drained though."

"Did you get photographs?"

"I didn't feel safe. Being invisible doesn't make me undetectable. I'll keep watch and gather more info. It sure would be great to get another invisibility topaz. When mine ran out today I was almost caught. Good thing Ruth was there to help me get out in a hurry before the gates closed."

Ruth says, "The gates weren't about to close. There were several large trucks pulling in that we had to avoid, that's all."

"Yeah, well, it felt like we were about to get caught. Anyway, Calli, can you ask Crimson if I can get another topaz?"

"Yes. I'll ask. What about those trucks? Were they delivering or picking up?"

"I don't know. We watched from the building across the road for five hours. Nothing happened other than the drivers entered the building. We'll go down first thing in the morning."

I say, "I don't know how long it will take to get an invisibility topaz to you. I'll try to communicate with Crimson, but she doesn't always answer me, so . . . "

"Got it. All right."

"Good night, you two." I open my eyes and find the sun has completely set. I get up and make my way back to my bungalow and strap a topaz to my skin and begin charging it with Mind-Control for Brand.

The next morning, after cleaning up the breakfast dishes, I climb the stairs to check on Don and his progress. Midflight, Ruth appears beside me.

"Calli, the facility is empty, cleared out!"

"What?"

"Call for the others to join you so we can discuss this. Bi-locate to my diamond." With that, she vanishes.

I immediately send out a message to the nearest Bearers to go to Ruth. Then I sit on the step and close my eyes. When Ruth and Brand come into view, I see Jonas has already bi-located. Maetha, Jie Wen, Chuang, and Kookju arrive soon.

Brand rubs his temples. "I don't understand. It was there yesterday. Now it's just another abandoned warehouse."

"It's empty?" Jonas asks rather dumbfounded.

Brand continues. "I keep asking myself how could they load that much stuff in so short of a time?

I say, "I guess that's what the trucks were for, Brand."

"Yeah, we figured that too."

Jonas says, "I traced the address in Norway you gave me and was able to hack into the traffic grid there. Guess who my facial recognition program spotted—Max Corvus."

"So that's where the coward is hiding," Brand says.

Maetha says, "We need to get to Norway before they clear that facility too. I'll connect with the Bearers and find out who is closest and observe Max until more of us can arrive."

Crimson's voice enters my mine. She says, *You and I will go now.*

Now? Oh, no. Are we going to fly?

Of course.

I let out a whine like a toddler. "I really don't like flying."

Brand angles his head. "Huh? Do you have a better idea?"

"Sorry Brand, I was talking to Crimson. She and I are going to leave for Norway. Hopefully some other Bearers will be able to arrive as soon as they can."

Chapter Ten - Norway

We arrive after soaring through the skies over the Atlantic Ocean. Crimson did the "let go of the earth's gravity and let the world spin" thing, allowing us to travel remarkably fast. I was better prepared for the reentry jar to the system. We arrive near the building where Max was last seen. Large trucks are backed up to the docks, being loaded. Other trucks are waiting nearby.

I speak mentally. *They're already packing up. By the time anyone else gets here, there won't be anything left.*

Yes, but the difference is we can follow them and instruct the Bearers where to go.

Look, there's Max. I point. *Should we go grab him?*

No. We're outnumbered. Plus, we don't know what other kinds of weapons they might have. We'll observe and plan an attack once we are better prepared.

We pass the next few hours watching trucks being loaded with equipment and boxes. When the trucks begin to depart, Crimson says, *Let's follow them. Remain invisible.* She wraps her arms around me and together we rise into the sky, hovering above the slow moving caravan as it travels down the road.

I try to imagine I'm on a glass-bottomed boat or bridge to try to quell my fear of heights. Up ahead, the convoy turns right at an intersection. However, the last half of the trucks turns left—Max's truck included.

Uh oh, I send my concern to Crimson. *What do we do now?*

The ground begins to rise to our feet, or at least it feels

that way because I didn't get a "falling" sensation. Crimson says, *You follow Max; I'll follow the lead truck. Remain invisible and use your running power. If you're spotted, get away. Don't risk your neck over this.*

Okay.

My feet connect with the ground after our forward movement stops. The convoy of trucks zooms away from our stationary position. Crimson doesn't waste a second. She launches back into the air in pursuit of the lead trucks. I launch forward, running at full speed to catch up with the Max's truck. In no time at all, I'm positioned behind him.

I communicate with Jonas. *Jonas, can you hear me?*

Yeah, Calli.

Can you run a license plate from Norway? Do you have access to their system?

I'll do my best.

I give him the numbers and letters from the plate.

As I run behind Max's truck, I can't help but feel uncertain about being away from Crimson, mainly because the last time I saw Max, he shot me. Also, because I've never been in Norway before. What if I lose her? I don't have a passport, identification, money . . . nothing. I'm not even wearing appropriate clothing for the weather. I force myself to think about how to deal with each of those issues. I can keep my body warm with the healing power. I can control minds to avoid arrest or entanglements. I'm not stranded by any means.

Having boosted my mind with confidence, I feel better.

Max's truck arrives at a large warehouse in an industrial complex and drives inside the garage door. The other trucks are already inside.

Crimson, they've stopped.

Let the others know where you are. The trucks I'm following are still traveling.

Okay. I keep my distance from the building and decide not to enter, even though I could invisibly and with my superspeed running. I don't know if they have hidden obsidian in the building or security cameras and I don't want to risk my neck, as Crimson said.

The entrance door opens and a woman about thirty years old walks out holding a cell phone out in front of her. She pans slowly from left to right, her eyes focused on the screen in front of her. Dread weighs down my stomach as I know exactly what she's doing. She's looking for me or someone like me—someone only a camera can see. I hurry and hide behind a dumpster and peek over the top. She yells something in her native tongue and the door opens again. I see several others come out holding small boxes. The woman continues to pan slowly with her camera. The boxes are placed in a semi circle with five feet or so between boxes, enclosing the garage door and entrance door. Another person tosses what looks like confetti beyond the boxes.

The camera woman yells something else and I duck my head behind the dumpster. I can hear everyone communicating but can't tell what they're saying. I carefully move to the other edge of the dumpster to peek around. The woman is holding a different type of device, pointing it my direction.

Jonas speaks to my mind. *Calli, you need to run. They're going to find you.*

I don't wait to be told twice. I pour on all my running speed and run to the side of the nearest building to get out of sight. Then I keep running the way we came through the maze of roads in the industrial district. After several minutes, I stop and regroup my thoughts. I call for Jonas.

His voice sounds in my head. *Calli.*

How did you know I needed to run?

I connected with your diamond and viewed what you were seeing through your eyes. The second device was an infrared reader. They were looking for heat signatures.

I wonder if they saw me. I also wonder what the boxes were all about.

My guess is it's a security system. The sprinkles they tossed out are probably activators or alerting mechanisms of some kind. What's unfortunate is now that you're gone we don't know what else they're setting up as defenses.

Crimson connects with my mind and gives me instructions to stay put until she finds out where the other trucks are stopping. I warn her about the infrared detectors and hopes she has better luck than I did.

Several hours pass. I communicate with different Bearers, including Chris, about the situation. Jonas, Kookju, Jie Wen, and Chuang are almost to Norway via Maetha's plane. As luck would have it, no other Bearers are in Europe at the moment.

Crimson finds me after she's finished and together we go to an abandoned building to wait for the others.

I ask, "Where did the other trucks go?"

"They split up and went in a couple different directions. I wasn't able to follow each one. Most seemed to be headed to other countries in Europe. Unfortunately, I don't know for sure what was on the trucks, but I have a feeling the prize we're after is with Max."

Prize? "Perhaps Jonas can track the other trucks with his computer wizardry."

"Perhaps."

Once the others arrive, Crimson leads the discussion.

"Calli will take us to where Max and his trucks are parked. If we're able, we'll capture Max and collect any and all information from the location. I cannot see the outcome of this task, so be on guard."

And I thought it was unsettling to hear Maetha express uncertainty. Hearing Crimson say it is much worse.

I lead the group of Bearers to what I think is the location of Max and his trucks. But I can't seem to find the building. Maybe it's the lighting, or the fact that all the buildings look the same and dumpsters are located all over the place that makes it difficult to find the exact one.

"I know it's here somewhere."

Jonas tries to comfort me. "Maybe you're just confused. You were under a lot of stress and probably afraid."

"Yeah, but you saw the building through my eyes, Jonas. Don't you recognize anything?"

"No."

Chuang offers, "Maybe they changed the exterior of the building to throw you off."

I'm embarrassed and frustrated and the other Bearers can tell.

Kookju says, "Why don't you show us your memory of the building. Perhaps that will help."

I nod and close my eyes, trying to recall the memory of running behind the caravan and watching the trucks enter the building. But I can't. I open my eyes. "Maybe one of you should extract the memory. I can't seem to pull it up."

Crimson says, "I've already tried. Your memory shows a different building than what's in this vicinity. The longer we're here, we risk being spotted. Let's go back to the building to discuss this."

After arriving back at the abandoned warehouse, I plop down on the cement floor and rub my head. Jonas comes over and sits by me.

"Don't beat yourself up over this, Calli. You're in a foreign country—"

"I know you're trying to make me feel better, and I appreciate it, but please don't." I know there isn't anything else I could have done, but I still feel like I let everyone down.

He bumps his shoulder against mine. "Just trying to help a friend."

I let out a short breath then take in a slower one. "I know. Thanks."

Jie Wen says, "I think a war is coming our way."

I ask, "From who? Max Corvus or Vorherrschaft?"

"Does it matter? They are connected. They are our common enemy."

Jonas says, "We investigated their company's address and found nothing. It's a shell company."

Kookju chimes in. "Or is it?"

"What do you mean?" Jonas turns his head to Kookju.

"The contact information may lead nowhere, but the money has to go somewhere. Follow the money trail, the breadcrumbs."

I ask, "Jonas, were you able to run that license plate?"

"The results showed a rental company."

Kookju smiles and nods. "There you go. Someone rented it. Who? How did they pay? Is there surveillance footage?"

Jonas eyes Kookju curiously. "You're a regular detective, now aren't you? I didn't know that about you. How about you help me with this?"

Crimson says, "I don't think there's anything more we can do here. We don't know which building to watch and it would be wasting resources to try to watch multiple locations. We'll just have to wait until Max surfaces again."

◇ ◇ ◇

Before we left Norway, Jonas and Kookju tracked down the renter of the truck and found the credit card used was stolen. The rental company didn't have surveillance cameras, so there was no video to view for a face. Another dead end.

Kookju, Chuang, and Jie Wen choose not to go back to Maetha's island. They're returning to China. A couple natural disasters are coming that need to be prepared for—meaning someone of importance needs to be protected.

My mind is focused on the reason why I couldn't find Max's building. I don't have an answer. I became more confused the longer I tried to search for the spot, almost a physically sick feeling.

Crimson had me fly in Maetha's plane with Jonas back to the island. The difference of several hours flight-time verses the speed at which Crimson was able to cover the distance is pretty remarkable, really. As much as I hate flying with her, I find myself dreading being stuck in an airplane for six hours. It seems like such a waste of time.

Once Jonas and I are on the transport boat headed to the island, Chris bi-locates to us.

Chris smiles broadly when his eyes meet mine. "Good to see you, Calli."

I smile back.

Jonas clears his throat. Chris turns and recognizes him. "Jonas."

"Yeah, good to see you too, Chris. What's up?"

Chris looks back at me. "Max called me."

"What?" Jonas and I exclaim together.

"He wanted money."

"Was he demanding it?" I ask.

"No, more like begging."

"What did you say?"

"I asked him what he needed it for. He wouldn't tell me. I asked where he was, but he wouldn't say."

Jonas says, "I wish your phone was on my tracking system. I could have located Max or at least his general area."

"Yeah, but," I say, "that would only show us the general area we just searched, Jonas."

Chris shakes his head. "Maybe I should just give him some, you know, to keep him calling."

"I don't know if that's a good idea." I try to look to the future to see, to no avail.

"I'll talk to Maetha and ask her opinion. I've got to go, Calli. But first, I've scheduled some time off for the last weekend in April so we can go to Portland."

"Great! I'll try to figure out what to say to get the officials to believe me."

After goodbyes, Chris vanishes, leaving me with Jonas and awkward silence as our boat slices through the Pacific toward the endless sea, or what seems to be. I know the island isn't too far now even though I can't see it.

I'm excited to spend some quality time with Chris in two months. Eight weeks—such a long wait.

After two weeks of working closely with Jonas trying to locate Max—and getting nowhere—I figured my time may be better spent off the Island. So, with Maetha's permission, for the last six weeks I've been traveling around the United States and Canada with Mary.

I was incredibly thrilled to discover Mary ditched her pastel robe for some slim fitting camouflage fatigues. Her robe made her stand out in a crowd of regular people in a way that brought unwanted attention. Nothing quite like appearing as if you're wearing your bathrobe in public. Her fatigues, however, drew a different kind of attention: one of respect and having authority. Because we were headed to my parents' house first, I hoped her appearance and strong presence would help allay their desire for me to have a bodyguard.

Yep, I was spot on with that assumption. No bathrobe would have had the same reaction.

After visiting my parents, Mary and I traveled to Denver. We found Anika and Beth hosting Fabian and Amenemhet who were passing through while chasing down leads related to Vorherrschaft. So far, the Bearers haven't been able to pin down any solid information. I know I'm not the only one perplexed about the difficulty in locating *anything* about this mysterious company.

Another thing I work on is what I'm going to say to Portland's officials. I can't just say they need to evacuate a major city without good cause. But I'm not sure "a bunch of people are going to die because of cosmic rays no one can see hitting the sky" is the best route to take. I practice a few things, using Jonas or Mary as sounding boards, until I feel as confident as I can get. Even though I'm sure it'll still sound crazy.

Yesterday I called Clara to see if she had an update about the Clan Meeting. She did. The meeting will take place late June at the Hunters' forest.

Now today has finally arrived and I get to meet Chris and fly to Portland, Oregon. I feel so silly, but I can't stop smiling. Even Jonas caught me humming and teased me about it. All I keep thinking about it the last time we were together, how good he felt in my bungalow, and what might happen now that we will have some time by ourselves.

The plane ride felt like days instead of hours and I've already unbuckled my seatbelt even before Captain Rutherfield expertly landed the plane in Washington D.C. to pick up Chris and drop off Mary.

I squint my eyes against the morning sunlight as I scour the area out the window, searching for Chris. When I finally spot him I rush to the door waiting for the captain to open it.

Chris seems like he's just as anxious to be with me. He's waiting outside the plane when the the stairs lower. In a single bound, he leaps up into the plane and into my arms. His hands cup my face as his lips meet mine with such intensity that I'm knocked off balance in a good way. I cling to him. He holds me steady. Good thing, too, because I'm melting against him.

Chris whispers in my ear after breaking our kiss, "I can't believe it's been eight weeks since we last held each other."

"Good to see you, Mr. Harding," Captain Rutherfield says, patting Chris on the shoulder as he walks by. "We'll be taking off soon. Please find your seats."

I didn't even notice Mary deplaned and Rodger closed the door. The world kind of ceases to exist when I'm in Chris's arms. Well, until I realize we're putting on a display. Then I come to my senses.

We take our seats and buckle up for a non-stop seven-hour flight. This is one time I'm glad to not be flying with Crimson. I have a feeling the next several hours will sail by all too fast. But I plan to use every last second being immersed within Chris's bubble.

"Welcome to Portland," Captain Rutherfield says,

ending our long stretch of thoroughly enjoyable personal physical contact. "I hope you brought an umbrella."

After de-boarding and renting a car, Chris drives to our hotel, windshield wipers pushing aside the sprinkled raindrops.

I remember the last time we were here, there was a man named James at the front desk. He's not here this time, but I recall seeing his future and discovering he will be affected by the coming blast.

After leaving our bags in our rooms, we walk the streets of downtown Portland heading toward City Hall. The rain has stopped, leaving puddles that we try to avoid as we walk. Street vendors, pan handlers, business professionals, and tourists from many ethnicities crowd the wet sidewalks. I dampen my Hunter's senses and try not to look too many people in the eye, so I won't hear their thoughts or see their futures. I really need to work on blocking them unless I want to look. However, I do detect some people with powers in the crowd. Nothing noteworthy, though, just interesting.

Inside the building, we approach the reception desk. "We'd like to speak to the mayor."

"Do you have an appointment?" the woman asks.

"No."

"He's in meetings. You'll have to make an appointment."

"Naturally," Chris mutters.

I ask, "When is his first availability?"

The receptionist examines the schedule. "Well, actually, he has an opening in about an hour."

Nodding, I say, "We'll take it."

To kill time, Chris and I wander around the nearby streets, checking out the unique shops and small businesses. My mind is on high alert for anything unusual or odd. Being Portland, Oregon, unusual seems to be the norm.

Once we get into the mayor's office, he looks at us and places his hands on the desk clasping his fingers together. He is not a person with powers and that's too bad. Perhaps our meeting would work better if he understood the cosmic blasts at all. He says, "What can I help you with?"

Throwing a here-goes-nothing glance at Chris, I say, "Well, sir, we have information about a danger to the Greater Portland area."

"Is this environmental?" he asks, not sounding too concerned.

"Yes, but also dangerous to individuals, to the citizens."

"What is this danger? And do we need to involve the head of Emergency Management?"

"We know of an, um, energy blast that will hit Portland next year in August. A lot of people could be harmed if they're nearby."

The mayor doesn't move. His eyes slowly move to Chris, then back to me. "Who are you, exactly?"

"I'm Calli Courtnae."

"Okay, and you are?" he says to Chris.

"Chris Harding."

"Are you military or special forces?" His eyes move between us again.

Chris responds, "No."

"NASA?"

"No."

"Terrorists?"

I wish I could view the future in a quicker fashion. Better yet, I wish Brand were here to help me tailor the conversation. I hardly think Chris's ability to repeat ten seconds would help at this point. I continue. "No. Please listen to what I'm saying. Many people will be harmed if they are still in the city when the blast hits. They need to be evacuated prior to the blast."

"Who's planning the blast? How do you know about it?"

"No one is planning it; the blast will hit because of planetary alignment to the source. This only happens once every couple of millennia."

He leans forward and lowers his voice. "Get out."

"Sir, please."

He picks up his phone and hovers his fingers over the keypad. "I'll call security if you don't leave now."

Chris stands. "All right."

As we vacate the office, I hear the mayor give direction to the receptionist to alert security to notify the police if we "wackos" come back.

Once outside, Chris leans his back up against the building. "Yeah, that went as well as I thought it would."

"All my practicing was for nothing. I knew this would be hard, but I at least thought we'd be kind of successful. Maybe we need to talk to the Emergency Management person he mentioned?"

"I agree."

We walk to the building next to the police headquarters and into the foyer. The directory displays the suite number for the Director of EM. We get in the elevator.

Chris asks, "Want to bet on how many seconds we're able to talk before we're threatened or arrested?"

"I have a different idea. Just follow my lead."

We go through the standard procedure of waiting to see the woman in charge. Once we're in her office, I say, "I'm writing a novel about a disaster set in a big city. I want to make the evacuation plan believable and I'm wondering if I could base my novel off Portland's mass evacuation plan?"

"We don't have a mass evacuation plan."

I literally choke and cough. "I'm sorry. I didn't expect you to say that."

Chris angles his head to the side. "Why don't you have a plan?"

"Well, what kind of event would necessitate an evacuation of that magnitude?" she quizzes us.

I ask, "Earthquake?"

"We recommend sheltering in place."

"Flood?"

"That would not require a mass evac."

Chris offers up, "What about a biohazard spill?"

"Localized evac."

"Or a terrorist attack?"

"Localized evac."

"Nuclear bomb!" He's losing his cool.

She leans forward in her chair and rests her arms on the desk. *Uh oh. I think we're about to get the boot.* "What kind of a book are you writing?"

I clear my throat. "A thriller suspense."

"What is the disaster in your book?"

"Irradiation blast from outer space."

She sits back in her chair. "So, it's a fantasy book. What's it called?"

"Uh, I haven't named it yet."

"Are there any terrorists in your 'book'?" She uses air quotes.

"No."

"Listen. Any Portland evacuation plans are online. You can find what you need there. Good day."

We leave the office and go back to the hotel to lick our wounds, so to speak.

"Chris," I say, powering up my laptop computer. "I'm going to check out what evac plans they do have."

"Good idea. We probably should have done that before we arrived. Could have saved some embarrassment."

I'm not sure I'll find anything more than what we were just told, but maybe I'll get a better grasp of what the officials are prepared to do in emergencies.

Chris asks, "Calli, when you have visions of the blast, are you in a particular location in the city?"

"On top of a building, a high rise. I don't know which one. It's on the west side of the Willamette River, though. I always see the river and the west hills are behind me."

"Okay, that narrows it down. Is it taller than the other buildings?"

I contemplate for a second. "I'm not sure. I'll try to pay better attention next nightmare." I type on the keypad and start my search. Chris places a call for food delivery, then comes over and pulls up a chair beside me.

The evening wears on as we search page after page, site after site, trying to formulate a better plan to evacuate the greater Portland area. After several hours we remove the bedspread and lie down in each other's arms, my head on his chest, and continue to hash out possible scenarios. I feel at peace in his arms, empowered, like I can accomplish anything. I close my eyes and listen to his voice, and his heartbeat.

I hear a man's voice. "C'mon, he went this way."

I'm in a forest with him, the middle of fall with brown and yellow leaves on the ground and a grey overcast sky above us. The man and I are hunting. I recognize him as James the hotel clerk. He leads me forward into an area where rocks, twigs, and small branches are suspended in the air, gently floating about. We walk carefully, trying not to disturb our surroundings.

A shot rings out and splinters of wood from a nearby tree hit my face. We duck for cover. I hear male and female voices yelling indiscernibly in the distance. Before I can zero in on their words, the rocks and branches hanging in the air begin to circle around us as a strong gust of wind picks up speed. Soon we are engulfed in a storm of debris, which scratches my face.

James cries out to me. "Calli, do something!"

I reach out with my consciousness and feel the fragments in the air. My mind connects with every object, then I feel a link to the energy controlling the rocks and twigs. I will the air around us to halt. My energy clashes with the energy of the one controlling the storm, pushing against it in a telekinetic tug of war. Everything stands still, trying to move against my will.

I scream, "James, now!"

James bolts forward and a deafening crack of lightning erupts from his palm. The thundering boom resonates through my entire body. My ears ring, muffling the sounds around me. My shoulder explodes in pain at the same time as I hear gunshots. My powers dim. Two more bullets enter my stomach and I cry out in agony. My powers are completely gone. As I collapse on the ground the debris storm picks up again. A heavy rock smashes my head, and all goes black.

My eyes pop open. I'm in my bed, sweat pouring down my face, my heart racing against my ribs. It was just a dream. My mind is blown with what we are up against with the Elemental powers. This vision showed yet another example of harnessing lightning bolts. Clearly James the clerk is going to be affected with that particular ability, and he'll be fighting on our side against . . . who or what. One thing's for sure, the energy I felt associated with the debris storm wasn't human.

For the first time, I consider for a moment that we should involve the U.S. government in helping to evacuate the city. The fewer amounts of people affected by the blast the better. The question remains: how do we get anyone to listen to us?

I roll over to cuddle with Chris but realize he isn't there.

"Calli, are you all right?" his voice sounds from across the room.

Sitting up, I turn to face him. He's standing by the door. "I thought maybe you'd left."

"I was just in the bathroom, but I could hear you were restless. Was it a vision?"

I look down at my tightly clasped hands. "It was horrible. We're in big trouble with this blast."

He sits beside me and puts his arm around my shoulders, pulling me close to him. "What did you see?"

"The hotel clerk James will be able to shoot lightning bolts from his hands. He seemed to be on our side, fighting against a force . . . I'm not sure what we were fighting against. It wasn't human. Here, let me show you." I place my palms against his temples and project the vision I had into his mind.

After it's over, Chris reaches up with shaking hands, gently takes hold of my wrists and brings my hands down from his head. His worried eyes meet mine. "What else have you seen?"

"The visions change all the time. This was the first one of this sort. Usually I'm on top of the building looking down over the city."

"I'm sorry you have to go through this, Calli." He

pulls me into his arms and holds me close.

I don't know how to respond. It's not like I chose this path or willingly signed up for the job. Everything was thrust upon me before I was ever conceived. Maetha's DNA experiments weren't designed for me, necessarily. I just happened to be the one who became strong enough to complete the task. Knowing what I know, it's not like I'm going to feel sorry for myself and walk away from everything. No.

I pull back a little and look Chris in his beautiful blue eyes. "Don't feel sorry for me. Be my support. We're here, we're in this together, and we're smart. We'll figure this thing out."

"I worry about you, Calli. I can't help that. I know you're more than able to take care of yourself. I also know you can take care of me. I guess I worry about the emotional toll all this will have on you. How can I help you with that?"

"You're helping right now. Your kisses help even more."

His expression has a flash of intrigue as he quickly acts upon my suggestion. The temperature of his lips against mine warms my whole body and any ill feelings remaining from the vision vanish. Healing kisses. And yet, I feel myself hesitating to allow our moment to evolve.

He must sense my mood change because he pulls back. "You're worried about being interrupted, aren't you?"

"A little. Okay, a lot."

He hugs me tenderly. "I don't want to be interrupted either. Maybe we'll just need to inform everyone to give us our privacy."

"That won't work with Crimson. The shard connects her to my mind in a way that cannot be blocked."

"Well, that's a dilemma." He tightens his embrace. "Just being near you is enough for now."

◇ ◇ ◇

After leaving Portland with Chris, I'm dropped off in Denver. Chris is headed back to Washington D.C. Our time in Oregon was wonderful, if you don't count the embarrassing encounters with the city officials. Chris and I did a little sight-seeing and explored the area further, using the time both for ourselves and to check out possible evacuation routes. We drove west to the Pacific Ocean and walked along the beach. Definitely a different experience walking that beach compared to the one on Maetha's island. Oregon's coastline is cold, yet strikingly beautiful.

We concluded that an attempt to evacuate the Portland area by sending people west wasn't a good idea. The two-lane highways would undoubtedly jam up tight and prevent an evacuation. The city would need to focus evacuations to the north, east, and south, following the main highways.

Arriving at the Denver house, I find Brand, Anika, Crimson, and Don. We exchange greetings and catch up on the happenings of everyone. I don't want to ask where Beth is and I don't want to pry into anyone's mind to find out.

I'm finding I value privacy highly.

Brand talks about his quests of tracking down leads from the Missouri obsidian plant. He's only hit dead ends. Don is here to hunt for clues regarding the power-removing machine he's trying to build on the island. His brother, Stan—being the paranoid, conspiracy theorist that he was—left behind loads of information and research about items that might be helpful in Don's quest. I guess it's a good thing we never cleared the whole house out. Anika is helping Don and charging a Healer topaz for him.

I find a moment when Brand and I are alone to ask him some questions.

"Brand, what's your biggest hang up about becoming a Bearer?"

He grunts and dramatically scrunches his eyes closed. "The repeating and future visions. I need the quartz stabilized before I try to use a diamond."

"So, you will try?"

"Only if my body accepts the quartz."

"Brand, this is where you're confused, in my opinion. A diamond would help you prevent losing your quartz. With an eye on the future, you could foresee any event that might harm you or possibly kill you. You could avoid those situations versus thinking you can always repeat out of them."

He looks at me as though I've spoken magic words. "Huh. I hadn't thought of that."

"I'm pretty sure I told you that already, maybe not in those exact words, but I'm glad you're hearing me now. Besides, holding a diamond and learning how to use the powers doesn't lock you into becoming a Bearer."

He chuckles, then says, "With the way things have been going lately, having a diamond in your body doesn't necessarily keep you alive anymore."

Crimson comes in the room. "Brand, I'd like you to come with me on a task. I need you to help me talk with some special people."

"*You* need *me*?"

"Yes. We're going to go check in with some individuals who have naturally occurring Mind-Control power."

I'd heard Crimson talk about these people before and

how she keeps tabs on them to make sure they're not misusing their power.

Crimson continues, including me in the conversation. "I need Brand to be able to repeat the conversations, so we can get the message across in as little time as possible."

"Oh goody!" He rubs his hands together. "Do I get to fly with you?"

"No. That would kill you. Well, let me clarify that answer. Flying with you would kill you, Hovering wouldn't. But that's not a preferred form of travel."

Chapter Eleven - Clan Meeting Woes

Two months have passed since Brand left with Crimson. I hear from Brand every now and then. He doesn't tell me much, probably because Crimson is present and he has to watch what he says. I look over Brand's list of addresses gathered from the Missouri plant. I found out later Ruth extracted his memory of what he'd seen while inside the building and wrote it all down. This ended up being as good as a photograph. Unfortunately, all the addresses I've checked on have been dead ends.

Chris and I were able to meet up in rural West Virginia for another date. We didn't want to risk him being seen with me, even though Max Corvus has dropped off the map, so we chose an out-of-way restaurant for dinner. I wonder when we'll ever be able to openly be a couple. How could we get married if we have to keep our relationship a secret? These are questions I have no answers for.

For now, I'm on my way to the local airport where I'll join Clara and Beth on Maetha's plane. We're heading to South Carolina to attend the clan gathering Clara organized. To say I'm nervous would be an understatement. These people still don't know the whole story of what happened when Justin tried to reunite the amulet shards. The whole event seems like a lifetime ago to me, but to the clans, they've harbored a boat-load of anger over the deaths of their leaders and the loss of the amulets.

Good thing we're bringing the quartz prisms to warm our welcome.

On the plane, I ask Beth, "Have you thought about

whether you're going to become a Bearer?"

She says, "I don't know yet. I'm not Unaltered so that would have to change first. I want to be able to be in my little brother's life. If I'm a Bearer that may not be possible."

"Understandable."

Beth pauses for a moment, then asks, "How's Brand doing?"

"He's functioning. I don't know exactly how he's doing, though. How are you doing?"

"Functioning."

I make an impulsive decision to tell Beth something, without viewing the future to see how she'll handle it. "You know, Beth, on Maetha's Island when I overheard some of your conversation, I saw Brand grab something from a tree after he left you. It was his quartz."

"Why would he put it in a tree?"

"My guess is to have an honest conversation with you."

"Why didn't you tell me earlier?"

"I didn't know if I should. I still don't know. Why? Would it have made a difference?"

She doesn't answer. Instead turns her head and looks out the window.

I sure hope I didn't just do a bad thing. There's no time to ponder further. Our plane descends to land at the Greenville-Spartanburg airport in South Carolina.

Once on the ground, Clara rents a car and soon we are on our way, heading to a town called Rocky Bottom, in the heart of Jocassee Gorges Wilderness Area in the Smokey Mountains.

"This place is beautiful," I state, more to myself than anyone else. The lush greenery, ferns, and moss remind me of Portland, OR, along with the humidity levels.

Beth says, "Yeah, I can see why they call these the Smokey Mountains. The low clouds and mist make them look that way."

Once we reach the small community of Rocky Bottom, Clara turns the car off the main street onto Horse Pasture Road. We drive the windy road for a few minutes till we reach a pullout where a couple of cars are already parked.

"Is this it?" I ask.

"No. We will walk from here."

We all exit the car and Clara opens the trunk. I can smell the aromas of nature's sweet, piney, fertile soil. The hanging mist makes me wonder if we're going to be rained on.

Beth asks Clara, "Are you sure this is safe? I mean, these are Hunters."

Clara chuckles. "Beth, leaders of all the clans are coming too. If this wasn't a safe place, do you think they'd put themselves in danger?"

"A simple yes would have done fine," Beth mutters.

I say to Clara, "Are we being watched?"

"Probably. This location is heavily guarded."

Beth asks, "Do people die in this forest?"

"Many people 'get lost' and return from where they came. In fact, if you tried to find this location without me, you'd fail."

"That's just freaky."

"Beth, you'll carry these," Clara hands her the cloth bag of prisms from the power-removing machine. "Calli, you and I will carry the others. You're not supposed to have contact with the prisms."

Clara locks the car and we walk toward the trees. She leads us to a trail that is probably more for animals than hikers. Much of it is uneven, with roots creating tripping hazards, and slippery moss-covered rocks. We follow the trail for a half hour.

Clara stops and looks all around, for what, I don't know. Then she moves off the trail. She pulls out a peculiar rock from her bag and holds it in front of her. She says, "Stay close to me."

Beth's wide eyes meet mine.

Clara leads us through the thick bushes and evergreens at a brisk pace, turning this way and that, making it difficult to stay close. The incredible stench of Hunters hits my nose. I mentally reduce my olfactory receptors, so I don't dry heave.

"Why does it suddenly stink?" Beth asks, her hand to her nose.

"Hunters," Clara says. "Don't worry. You'll adjust soon enough, and it won't smell so bad." She stops walking and raises the rock above her head. Astonishingly, the air in front of us parts like living-room curtains, enough for us to walk through.

After entering through the "doorway," I turn around to see the opening merging back together like oil spots on water joining together, similar to the opening we went through on our way to Maetha's island.

Beth looks at me and I read her mind. She's also likening the experience to Maetha's island.

Clara says, "We've entered the Hunters' Forest. Now that we're inside, you don't have to follow close anymore.

I ask, looking over my shoulder, "Clara, what was that?"

She smiles. "The whole camp is surrounded by a magical bubble."

I point to her hand. "What does the rock do?"

"It's a key. If anyone accidentally bumps into the boundary without a key," she holds up the rock, "they'll be rendered confused and disoriented."

I want to discuss this more, however my nervous jitters flare up, reminding me of the reason we're here. I'll have to put the bubble/rock topic on my mental shelf for now.

We walk for another ten minutes and come over a ridge where down below is a village populated with small log cabins, tents, and rudimentary huts. People move about with purpose, carrying armfuls of firewood, buckets of water, baskets of berries and other edibles. Children run and play as if they haven't a care in the world. The whole scene makes me think we just passed through a portal and have gone back in time.

A tall woman with dark skin and long flowing brown hair approaches us. She wears clothing made of tanned leather, like what old trappers might wear, with a bow and quiver full of arrows strapped to her back.

Clara introduces us. "Huntress, this is Calli Courtnae and Beth Hammond."

I extend my hand in courtesy, but she doesn't reciprocate. She says, "Pardon my hesitation, Ms. Courtnae. I'll reserve my welcome until I feel like welcoming you. Dominic was my brother and didn't deserve to die."

Beth tries to stifle a protest, which only draws Huntress' attention.

Huntress says, "Ms. Hammond, please accept my condolences for the loss of your parents."

"Uh, yeah, well, thank you." Beth clears her throat and asks, "Is your name really Huntress?"

"I am the leader of the Hunters. Anyone wishing to address me must do so using the name Huntress. Come with me."

Some children run past us, giggling as they go. *They're so dirty.* It seems Hunters are more 'primitive' in their lifestyle and actions. As we walk and approach other adults, they bow their heads when they see Huntress and step aside. I get the idea that if this were a pack of wolves, she'd be the alpha wolf.

Clara asks, "Is your food and water supply holding out, Huntress?"

"Yes. We manage our resources well, along with our population."

Beth points to a child. "Are the children Hunters as well?"

"No. They are born here in the forest to mated Hunters. They are learning the ways of the Hunters. They know nothing else of the world outside."

"Do they have cosmic abilities?" Beth asks.

"The electromagnetic disruption of the dome prevents that from happening."

I deduce that the words dome and bubble are referring to the same thing. I glance around at the children and feel for their powers. Huntress is right. They have no cosmic abilities, yet they are not Unaltereds either. So, some DNA alteration has occurred even with the electromagnetic disruption. Interesting.

A shrill whistle interrupts our conversation. Huntress looks beyond us. She says, "The others are arriving. Follow me and I'll take you to a safe place."

Beth glares at Clara as we follow Huntress. "What does that mean?" she whispers.

Clara says, "The other clan leaders still believe Calli murdered their leaders. We can't risk vigilante justice being carried out before Calli has a chance to clear her name."

My own alarm bells go off and I quickly look for my future. I see myself in a hotel room. That's all it takes for me to know nothing fatal will happen to me here in the Hunters' forest.

Huntress leads us to a small cabin. "Wait in here. I'll come get you when we're ready."

The old-fashioned cabin is dark and rustic, with wooden furniture and cupboards. The sound of an igniting match pulls my attention to Clara who lights an oil lantern on the wooden table. Beth wanders around the room investigating the grimy environment.

"Why is everything so dirty? Don't they ever clean?"

Clara doesn't answer.

I sit on one of the chairs and close my eyes.

Beth and Clara carry on a conversation about how the bubble works concerning the electromagnetic interference properties. Satellites cannot see or detect the camp because of the disruption in radio waves and visual clarity. Heat sensing devices don't work against the dome. Animals can walk through, allowing Hunters food. However, humans who come too close to the bubble without a key will pass out, at which point Hunters will carry them back to the trail they came from.

Huntress comes to our cabin. She seems distressed. "It's time. I'll escort you."

I follow directly behind her and can't help but feel I'm heading to the electric chair or some other doomed place. My heart thuds nervously and my insides twist around.

To get my mind off the impending grilling, I focus on the bow and arrows on her back. One of the arrows is upside down with the tip pointing up. On the very point is a black triangular piece. I narrow my vision and study it. It's obsidian, I'm positive. I say to Huntress, "Those are interesting arrows you have in your quiver. Did you make them?"

"No. I found them next to a skeleton of a Native American during my explorations of the Badlands. I reported the skeleton to the local tribe, so a proper burial could take place. Because I did so, the chief awarded me with the arrows. The arrowheads take away cosmic powers when stabbed. I carry them as a symbol of my leadership, knowing I can disable anyone in a flash, including anyone in my forest."

Beth throws a wary glance my way.

"When did you find the skeleton?" I ask.

"Two years ago."

"Too bad you didn't have those when the Death Clan was running amok," Beth adds.

Voices and murmurings reach my ears as we near the group. We stop beside a cabin. The group must be around the corner. I can't see anyone, but their angry energy heightens all my senses.

Huntress turns to me. "I suggest you be open and truthful. We all deserve to know what happened."

I nod, trying to swallow against my dry mouth.

She leads us around the corner to a wood plank platform overlooking the gathered crowd. As she tries to calm the increasingly agitated group, I scan faces for familiar people. I see some I recognize, those I assumed would be present. Huntress motions for me to step forward and begin.

My hands are cold and clammy. I want to wipe them on my jacket, but I don't want to reveal I'm nervous. I clear my throat and say, "Many of you were at the clearing where the Death Clan was destroyed. I was injured in the blast. A piece of the diamond lodged itself inside my heart."

Arthur Stiles, the Seers' leader asks, "Why weren't we told about that?"

Grant Winbush, looking exactly like he did when I met him at the hotel the night before the Death Clan meeting, says "How are you still alive?"

"I don't know the answers to those questions, Arthur

and Grant. But Clara and the Healers can confirm my story."

Heads swivel to the Healers, Andrew Stuart and Robert Yates, who look shocked I would call them out like this.

Arthur asks, "Is this true?"

Both Andrew and Robert nod. Then Andrew says, "We were ordered to secrecy by the Spellcaster Maetha."

An older woman asks Clara, "You knew all this time she had a diamond piece? Why did you keep that a secret, especially after Charles died?"

I scan the woman's mind and find she is Charles Rhondell's wife, Irene, who was one of the kidnapped victims of the Death Clan. She saw the diamond explode on my chest.

Clara says, "I was also ordered to silence. Calli has more to tell you. Please save your questions till the end."

I continue, "Thank you, Clara. The abduction of the amulet wearers for the Readers, Seers, and Hunters was orchestrated by an ex-Runner named Justin Macintyre. He wanted to reunite the shards for himself. I showed up at the Healers' compound with Brand Safferson, who possesses a new power, to introduce him to the different clans. One element of Brand's power is he can experience what's going to happen and make changes to the present to avoid or alter the outcome." I direct my next words to the Healers. "Right after you relinquished your amulet to me, Brand could tell you were about to die, not from the drug-laced food, but from Justin who was about to shoot you. Brand told me if we ran away at that moment, the lives of everyone in the room would be spared. I ran with your clan's amulet to save your lives, not to steal it."

Andrew Stuart says, "Was Justin responsible for the drugging too?"

"Yes."

A woman I identify as a Healer shouts out, "It's a little too convenient that you and your friend arrived at the same time as our food had been tampered with. How do we know you weren't working with Justin?"

Someone else asks, "What is the new power? Is it like the Seer power?"

Beth steps forward and raises her hands toward the crowd. "Let her finish talking."

I thank Beth, then say, "I'll tell you more about the new power in a minute. After Brand and I fled the Healers' compound, we were kidnapped by Justin and taken captive, the same as Charles Rhondell, Curtis Schultz, and Chris Harding. Dominic the Hunter was delivered the next day." I skip over the details and move to the reuniting of the shards. "Justin didn't know he'd been misled about the diamond shards. He didn't know reuniting the shards would kill him. He died a bloody death. However, Justin wasn't working alone. Another man named Henry from a secret government organization arrived right after Justin died. Henry carried a black rock that we now know is Yellowstone obsidian. It disabled our powers. Henry ordered the guards to kill everyone. We fought back, but unfortunately only Chris and I escaped. I was able to grab the diamond before fleeing. Henry was responsible for the deaths of Charles, Dominic, and Curtis. He misled Justin into believing he could become all powerful.

Andrew asks, "Where's the diamond now?"

"Inside my heart. The whole Sanguine Diamond is inside me."

Heads turn back and forth while whispers and mumblings fill the air. "How is that possible?", "Where is Henry?", and "He should be punished."

I state clearly, "Henry is dead. The important thing to

remember is I follow nature's will. I use these multiple powers for the betterment of humanity."

The grumblings and whispers grow in volume, laced with doubt.

Beth jumps forward, obviously alarmed by the growing hesitation in the crowd. "Hey! I was assigned to find Calli and bring her in. When I caught her, I learned the man she talked about was behind the deaths of the amulet wearers—your friends."

Irene asks, "And you believed her?"

"No. Not at first. But then I was shown proof. The proof was compelling enough for me to join Calli in the battle to keep Henry from getting the diamond."

"What proof?"

"Henry confessed everything directly to me."

Grant shouts, "You should have brought Calli to us."

"Time was of the essence. Look, if any of you doubt Calli or her intentions, you should know the Shadow Demons are gone because of her. She and Brand experimented with the demons to find out how to get rid of them."

The crowd silences, riveted by Beth's words.

I feel the need to correct her. "They're not gone entirely, they're just not a threat anymore. Does anyone have more questions about the clan leaders' cause of death?"

No one speaks for a moment, then Huntress surprises me with a question. "Will there be more demons?"

"I don't know. I've designed Pulse Emitter devices that offer protection in the rare case we missed one or if new ones come about."

She asks, "How did you get rid of them?"

"I used obsidian to remove their powers."

Arthur Stiles asks, "What can you tell us about all the

nonsense concerning obsidian going around on the Internet?"

"I recommend you don't buy any offered online. It's a scam. Not all obsidian will negate powers, only the kind from the Yellowstone National Park outcropping."

"But what if we need to defend ourselves from someone like the Death Clan?"

Someone else in the crowd shouts, "Yeah! It sounds like a piece of obsidian would have protected lives and prevented them from killing with their thoughts."

I speak over the crowd's growing questions. "Obsidian removes *your* power too. Besides, we didn't know about it when the Death Clan was a problem." My brain runs through the different scenarios where obsidian doesn't work, like what if the Death Clan had charged Imperial topaz on their bodies, or what if their power had been removed and stored in a quartz crystal and they had that on their person? The crowd doesn't know about these things yet. Instead, I say, "The moment we identified the black rock as obsidian, we began looking for a way to counteract it. What we didn't know was the secret government facility in Denver, CO, was already two steps ahead of us. They've been running experiments on people with powers. They've also been trying to create synthesized powers. Brand Safferson's new power is actually not natural. It's human-made. His power was created in the government facility twenty years ago."

The crowd murmurs and shuffles.

"We're still sifting through data recovered from the Denver compound, and more recently, a similar compound located in China. The clans need to unite and coordinate. You're too disorganized, relying on yourselves, being picked off one by one."

"What do you suggest we do?" Grant Winbush asks.

"Well, for one," I say, "you need to have meetings like this more often. Come together and fight this enemy as one strong unit."

Unknown people ask, "But won't that bring unwanted attention?" and "Like from the government?"

Huntress says, "We've kept our location off the government's radar for over fifty years. I for one don't want to bring attention to the Hunters."

I reply, "All meetings don't have to take place here. They can be revolving. There are a couple reasons why you must unite together. Evil forces, whom we call Reapers, are using cosmic powers to enhance their technology, and they're taking the powers directly from you." I point to the crowd. "Clara was almost a victim of this a year ago." She nods. "Reapers want your power. They will take it and transfer it into one of these pieces of quartz using a special machine." I hold up a bag. "These belonged to Healers. Some of you may know someone who has lost their power."

I set the bag down and motion for Beth to hold up a prism for all to see. "Clans choosing to unite with me will receive one of these quartz prisms containing all the powers, just like the diamond amulets. However, these prisms are not deadly to the touch. For example, Beth is a Runner and she can hold the quartz with her bare hands."

Irene asks, "What is expected from the clans that choose to unite?"

"They will help with a pressing issue; a foreseen cosmic blast will hit in a little over one year, containing a power so disastrous that if precautions are not taken, the world as you know it will end in a century and a half." I hear several people's thoughts, wondering what the power will be. I say, "The power will bring the ability to harness the elements: fire, wind, water, and ground. We're calling it the Elemental power."

Arthur says, "How do you know this? I'm a Seer and I don't foresee this."

"I have a stronger power than you from the Sanguine Diamond. Leading up to the blast date, we need to organize an evacuation of pregnant women in Portland, Oregon, those who will be in the stage of alteration. The more individuals we can prevent being hit with this power the better. That will be one less person with powers the Reapers can extract."

"But if we get involved, it will expose our powers."

How can I say this better, so they'll understand? "I don't think that can be helped at this point. In the aftermath of the cosmic blast, and when the alteration matures, the whole world will know about cosmic powers. We could at least be viewed as people who want to help and protect, rather than as—"

Beth cuts me off. "Don't say what you're about to say. They don't like it."

I look down at her hand and see the prism she's still holding. "Thanks," I say. I'm glad she stopped me from calling them "cowards who can't admit the world is changing." I know I'm losing my patience. I need to get them to see my intentions are good. I take a deep breath and say, "Look, if a clan wants to unite with the group to prepare for and fight against the Elemental power, they will receive a multi-powered prism. Regardless of whether or not the clans unite together, each clan will be given these quartz crystals corresponding to their clan's power," I point to the bags of quartz, "as each one represents a member of their clan who lost their power and these belong back with them.

Andrew Stuart speaks up. "Are you saying those quartz will give healing power back to our members who've lost it?"

"Yes."

"I know of at least five people from our clan who were taken against their will, held for a time, then released, powerless." He turns and motions for a woman to come forward.

A middle-aged female emerges from the crowd. I can tell in an instant she's Unaltered because of her aura. She bows her head slightly; her long hair falls in front of her face. "Ms. Courtnae, my name is Rhonda. I was a Healer until I was taken and run through the machine."

"I'm sorry this happened to you, Rhonda." I feel like the crowd needs to hear one person's experience to appreciate the full scope of what's going on. I say, "Would you tell us what happened?"

"The abductors came to my house and grabbed me when I opened the door. They put a cloth over my nose and mouth that had some kind of powder on it. I wasn't knocked out, but I couldn't use my powers anymore. I felt a strange confusion about how to use my power even though I still had it. They also put a bag over my head so I couldn't see where they were taking me."

I remember hearing from Chuang how it felt to have the powder in the body. Not-quite-obsidian.

She continues. "They drove a short while, then took off the bag and led me to a building with black rocks cemented to the outside. Once inside, they took me to a room and performed medical type tests. They told me I was being relieved of my power. I begged them not to take it, but they didn't listen. Afterward, they loaded me in a van with eight other people I didn't know and drove us to a deserted parking lot where they dropped us off."

I ask, "Were the others in the van Healers as well?"

"I don't know. We didn't talk to each other that much.

Before getting in the van, they told me I was the only person with powers from the group. I figured the regular people would think I was crazy if I complained about losing my healing ability."

I shake my head. "They probably told the others the exact same thing. The fear of being discovered and ridiculed, or worse, was a powerful tool to use against you."

"Once we were dropped off, we walked to a gas station and called the police. The nine of us were transported to the station where we made our statements. Of the nine, I had the shortest abduction time of less than twenty-four hours. Some of the others had been missing for several days."

"You must live in Denver, then."

"Denver, no. I live in Charlotte, N.C."

"What? Not Colorado? When did this happen to you?"

"Three weeks ago."

A sudden coldness chills my entire body. "You lost your power only three weeks ago?"

"That's right."

I look over at Beth and don't need to read her mind to know she's aware of what this means: there's another active power-removing machine in the U.S. This whole situation just escalated by leaps and bounds.

"Rhonda," I say, placing my hand on her arm, "thank you for sharing your experience." I open the bag with Healer quartz and remove one. "Here. I hope this works as well as the power that was taken from you."

She takes the quartz and smiles brightly, then rejoins the crowd. Those near her huddle around her, asking questions.

I raise my voice and say, "Rhonda's story reveals a new threat: an additional machine we didn't know about. We have to assume there's probably more, too. I know it's hard to imagine the new cosmic power but try for a second to visualize what would happen if the Reapers got hold of the Elemental power. The impending cosmic blast needs preventative measures taken and follow-up action after it hits. We must unite for our own safety, for the safety of your children, and for our future."

Robert Yates asks, "How are we supposed to fight against these Reapers?"

I say, "We pull together and form a network, sharing updates and warnings. We put our best minds together and strategize on how to handle upcoming situations. And," I say, glancing over at Beth, then at the prisms. She holds one up high again. "We fight against the Reapers with these. Unite with me! One person from each clan will have all the powers plus Brand's new ability to experience ten seconds of time before it happens. This is enough time to avoid being killed, or to prevent someone's death."

Andrew Stuart says, "The Healers will join you, Ms. Courtnae."

"Thank you. Would you be willing to host the new cosmic powers in your compound? You'd need to expand your buildings."

Andrew and Robert talk quietly amongst themselves, then Andrew says, "We are willing to accommodate, but we'll need financial assistance to make the renovations. How much renovating are we talking about and how much time do we have?"

"I'm sure the financial end will be taken care of. But for now, I don't have the answers to your other questions." I glance around at the other clan leaders. I turn to Beth. "Would you give a prism to the Healers and instruct them how to use the Repeating power." She nods. "Will anyone else unite with us?"

Steven says, "The Readers will have to contemplate on the decision. Can we have time to think?"

"Yes."

Irene asks, "Who exactly are you talking about when you say 'we'?"

I'm caught off guard by the question. "What do you mean?"

She adds, pointing to Clara and Beth, "Are you three the leaders? Are we joining the Runners to prepare for the coming cosmic power?"

Other voices in the crowd join in. "What about Maetha?"

Another, "I read on the Internet there are two with diamonds. Is that true?"

I raise my hands in front of me to quell the questions. "Irene, when I say 'we' I'm talking about Beth, Clara, Maetha, and more. If you want to know who else, you'll just have to join up and help us save humanity. And yes, there is another person with a diamond."

Arthur asks Clara, "Do you have a diamond?"

"No. But I am joining with Calli to minimize the fallout of the Portland blast. The Runners are joining the cause. Will the Seers join, Arthur?"

"I need to discuss it further with my clan leaders."

People begin talking over each other, asking questions about the second diamond like who has it, where did it come from, and does it hold the same powers as the Sanguine Diamond.

I respond with, "The answers to these questions will only be shared with those who choose to help with the upcoming cosmic blast. Join me and I'll answer as many of questions as I can."

Huntress steps forward and takes charge. "This meeting is adjourned." Huntress leads me off the platform and down to the crowd. Beth remains at my side ready to defend if needed. The group spreads out a little, talking in small circles. The Healers experiment with the prism, and Clara is given one for the Runners' clan.

I feel thrilled that the meeting went as well as it did. As I observe the others, an unfamiliar constricting sensation twinges in my chest. I notice Rhonda the Healer walking toward me.

"Calli, can I talk with you a moment?"

"Sure."

Beth moves closer to my side.

Rhonda says, "I think I can feel your diamond."

"Really?"

Beth jumps in. "Let's move this conversation away from the group." Beth leads us around the corner of a nearby cabin, then asks Rhonda, "Are you sure you're not just imaging Calli's diamond? I mean, you already know she has one."

Rhonda focuses on my body. Again, the slight constricting sensation moves up my body in correlation with Rhonda's eyes—the same feeling I felt moments ago. Why haven't I felt this before when Crimson or Maetha healed me? Perhaps because I was too busy writhing in pain from injuries to notice the subtle sensation I'm feeling right now.

"No," Rhonda responds to Beth. "Her body feels different than yours. You are definitely a Runner. Calli's body holds no cosmic power, just an emanating force coming from her heart."

Beth asks, "Have you tried to feel inside your own body?"

"Oh, Healers can't heal themselves."

"Have you tried with the quartz?"

Rhonda shakes her head, closes her eyes, and pauses.

A subtle smile begins to form. "Yes. Yes! I can feel *my own* heart." She opens her eyes wide. "How is this possible?"

Beth turns to Rhonda. "Would you let me hold your quartz to see if the powers work with me?"

Rhonda hands the quartz to Beth and Beth focuses on me. I'm quite nervous. Not to have Beth feel my diamond, but to find out if both Unaltered and Altered humans are affected the same way with the quartz.

The same gentle constricting feeling moves through my body. My eyes meet Beth's. I don't know whose eyes are wider, hers or mine. Beth hands the quartz back to Rhonda.

Rhonda says, "Thank you so much, Calli, for giving me this stone. I'll treasure and protect it."

I force a smile, and say to Beth, "Would you take Rhonda and give her more information about the quartz?"

"Sure."

They leave and I walk away from the crowd, away from the buildings, and sit down on the forest floor. I realize just how bad this situation really is. The Reapers aren't merely taking powers from people, they are making those powers immortal and resistant to obsidian, but for what purpose? More importantly is the fact that both Rhonda and Beth can sense my diamond with the quartz. That means any Reaper with a Healer quartz could do the same thing. Is it possible the Diamond Bearers might be targeted and taken out? I'm thinking the obsidian bullets, grenades, and the mysterious powder were designed specifically for rounding up Diamond Bearers.

I try to communicate with Chris. *I need to talk to you.* I wait for his response. Nothing. I try to bi-locate to him but can't push my energy past the ceiling of the bubble. This place feels like a fortress . . . or a prison. An intense need to get out blasts through my system. I no longer feel comfortable. I can't tell if it's my imagination or if I'm having a premonition.

I don't feel safe.

I stand and hustle back to where I last saw Clara.

Chapter Twelve - Bullseye on his Back

After a quick request to leave the bubble, Clara leads me outside the perimeter.

Clara asks, "Are you all right?"

I take a deep breath. "I'm just a little panicked. I need to meditate. Would you stay near me?"

"I have to or else you'll be affected by the confusion enchantment."

"The what?"

Before she can respond, Chris's voice enters my mind.

Calli, what's happening?

"Confusion enchantment," Clara continues.

I rub my forehead. Too many things all at once to address. "Hang on Clara. I need to meditate."

I walk over to a tree and sit with my back against the trunk. Clara sits as well. I close my eyes and focus on Chris's diamond.

Chris! Oh you don't know how relieved I am to hear your voice.

Don't come to me. I'm not in a secure place.

Okay, I won't. However, I have some distressing information, Chris.

So do I. What's yours?

There's an active power-removing machine on the East Coast.

What?

A former Healer was abducted three weeks ago, zapped of her power, and released in under a day. Today, I gave her a Healer quartz. I pause a moment. *Chris, she was able to detect my diamond using the quartz.*

Oh no. That's not good.

I know. Beth tried it and could feel my diamond too. You are at risk of being discovered, Chris. Keep a sharp eye on your future. I hope no one with a Healer's quartz realizes they can detect us. All Bearers are going to have to be extra vigilant scanning their futures. What's your news?

I almost don't want to tell you, but I'd better. Max has resurfaced on the Internet.

Oh, great! I push my head back against the tree trunk. *What's he talking about now?*

The diamonds.

Did he name me and Jonas?

No. He's trying to get some bigger entities to pay him for his knowledge.

The government?

No. Vorherrschaft.

But, I thought he was already working for them.

Apparently not.

Chris, I think they want the diamonds, all the diamonds. We've got to find Max and shut him up. I'm so frustrated I lost his location in Norway.

Jonas is on it. He's the one who found the new material on Max's site yesterday.

Yesterday? Why didn't you tell me?

You had the big gathering to prepare for. I didn't want to burden you with this. Besides, there wasn't anything more you could do that we couldn't.

I'm going to get the others and head back to the hotel so we can look up the website.

Okay. Let me know when you're there. I love you, Calli.

I love you, too.

Our connection ends and I open my eyes. My senses return, bringing the peaceful sounds of the forest around me.

I jump to my feet and look down at Clara who seems alarmed at my sudden movements. "Clara, when we arrived here, you used a rock to get through the bubble. You said the rock was a key."

"Yes."

"A moment ago, you used the words 'confusion enchantment.' How does the bubble work, exactly?"

"This bubble was designed by a Spellcaster. I don't know the exact mechanics of the enchantment. I only know how one is set up."

"I think there's a bubble around Max's hideout. When I tried to take people there, I couldn't find it and became confused and disoriented. Is it possible to break through a bubble?"

"No." Clara stands and takes me by the arm and leads me further away from the bubble. She speaks softly and with great care. "Let us take a walk."

I feel restless, but her tone makes me believe she will tell me something important.

We make our way into the trees. Clara points to one and tells me its name and what the bark is used for. She does the same for a bush. I try to pay attention, but my thoughts are on Max and how he's making my job extremely difficult.

We stop walking. Clara plucks a wild flower and turns to me. "Look at the flower as if I'm talking about it." I do as she instructs. She continues. "I didn't want to have a sensitive conversation too close to the boundary. They are Hunters after all."

I nod, knowing that Hunters have enhanced senses for tracking, including hearing.

Clara continues. "The placement of the perimeter rocks around the bubble is important. Bubbles curve up, connecting side-to-side and at the apex. It doesn't go down into the ground unless the rocks are buried, in which case the bubble begins further down, but still rises and curves to the center. If Max is in a building and the rocks are on the ground, a tunnel underneath, like the sewer system or duct work, could get you under the protection."

"What about making a key?"

"Without knowing exactly what the Spellcaster used to make the bubble, I wouldn't dare."

"Wait. Does that mean Max has a Spellcaster working with him?"

"Maybe, or it just means one set it up for him and has nothing to do with his actions."

I pause a moment, then say, "We need to get back to the hotel. Max is working his blog again."

"Oh dear. All right. Let's go excuse ourselves. I'll tell the clan leaders to communicate with me when they make their decision."

"While you're doing that, I'll speak with Huntress."

We enter the bubble again and return to the gathered group.

I pull Huntress aside. "Thank you for opening your home to us, but we must leave. I hope you'll consider joining us in this cause. If so, please let Clara know. By the way, those arrowheads you wear with confidence will not work on Reapers other than to injure them. Reapers have quartz, which is immune to obsidian. Your defenses are outdated, Huntress. You need to unite with us so you can have a prism to help protect your clan." I don't wait for her response as I have more-pressing issues to deal with and I need to get back to the hotel.

◇ ◇ ◇

Once we get back to the hotel, I turn on my computer and start the masked Internet browser. I sure don't want our location tracked by Max. After the browser opens, I type in Max's website address.

A solid black background pops up. Then an animation of hundreds of loose diamonds tumble from the top of the screen to the bottom. The words, "They Are Among Us" flashes after the diamonds are gone. A video box begins to play. Max is filming himself, his actual face, with his full name posted across the bottom of the video.

Beth says, "This guy is absolutely nuts! He just put a huge bullseye on his back."

"My name is Max Corvus. I am a U.S. Army soldier and I'm at war. This war is one that most of you will never see—you should hope and pray you never see what I've seen. But you can believe me when I say there are individuals around you that have unimaginable super-powers. Dangerous powers. You'd be wise to examine my website closely to learn the identifying traits and signs of this enemy so you can spot them, because we are all at war, war against nature and the Diamond People."

Clara's eyes meet mine. "We can only hope someone takes him out quick."

Max continues. "I had to drop off the radar for a little while after my failed attempt to expose the Diamond People. My information and archives were stolen which almost discouraged me entirely from starting back up again. I no longer had any proof to support my claims. Well, now I have new proof."

The video cuts to black and white surveillance footage of what looks like a manufacturing floor. The camera position is up high, capturing mostly the tops of heads, not faces. Boxes move down conveyer belts, passing workers who inspect the contents. I instantly spot Brand walking carefully between workers. Even though I can't see his face, his body shape, the way he moves, and his hair style is recognizable. The footage must have been taken at the Missouri facility where Brand investigated the obsidian bullet factory.

"See this person here," Max points with his finger. "The workers said they didn't see him on the floor that day. Now watch this next screen. These two employees are walking right toward him. Normally people will shift and turn when they pass someone else to avoid running into them. But this person is the only one who moves. The other two didn't even know he was there."

The frame switches to a different angle of an empty hallway. Brand comes walking around the corner, but his face is digitally blurred out. The shot freezes mid step. Max says, "Here he is again. I've hidden his identity not to protect him, but to encourage bidders. Who wants to know who the Invisible Man is? And how badly do you want to know? But wait, there's more."

The screen switches to a different video. The filming is bumpy and dark, and at first it's hard to tell what I'm looking at. Then the focus changes and reveals the filming is taking place inside a moving vehicle. The camera faces the side mirror out the passenger window, displaying the area behind the truck.

Beth says, "What are we supposed to be seeing?"

"I don't know."

The camera zooms in on the mirror, blurs a little, then focuses.

Beth points to the screen and exclaims, "Is that you, Calli?"

Oh no! "Yes, I think it is."

The camera pans to the left and focuses on the speedometer: 70.

"You're running 70mph?"

"No. That's kilometers. It's around 45mph."

Max narrates the video. "What you're seeing here is one of them running behind our truck. We're traveling at 70kph and the individual is not having any trouble keeping up. But what you can't see in this video is the fact that when I looked in the mirror without the camera, I couldn't see the runner. Not only can this person run at superhuman speeds, they can do so invisible to the human eye. But not to a camera lens."

I say, "He's not gendering me."

"What do you mean?"

"No pronouns like she or her. Instead, he says person, runner, they, and them."

Max continues. "My driver couldn't see them in the mirror, but I could with the camera." The screen switches back to Max. He looks as though he's drank way too much coffee. His eyes are opened more than normal, his hands shake, and his neck arteries bulge as he talks. "This footage isn't fake. I didn't doctor it. What's more is I know these two people. I know where they live—"

"Is he threatening you?" Clara asks.

Blood rushes from my head, pooling in my gut. I feel sick.

"—I feel adequately protected to put my own face and name on the line to expose these individuals. I no longer worry about being killed for my knowledge because if I am, I've put measures in place to ensure my information and secrets will be spilled worldwide."

I feel the overwhelming need to call my parents. I must warn them.

Chris speaks to my mind. *Take a deep breath, Calli. Max isn't going to do anything to your parents. They're safe.*

How do you know?

I've already moved them to safety, to Bermuda.

Max continues in a wild, losing his mind kind of way. "If you could see what I'm dealing with, you'd know it is true. Several governments are hunting me down. They don't want me scaring the citizens. Why would they want me to shut up if it wasn't true? But I'm here to tell you, t*hey do exist!*"

The video ends. Beth scrolls down the page to begin looking at the comments.

Chris bi-locates to my side. "Sorry, I had to get to my apartment before I could come to you."

I say, "Chris, will you alert the Bearers to a Gathering? Have them connect to my diamond."

"Yes. When do you want this to take place?"

"As soon as possible."

"Okay."

Clara walks over to us. "Chris? How are you doing this?" She reaches out and sticks her hand right through him. "Are you a Bearer, Chris?"

Chris and I exchange worried glances. Neither of us realized Clara didn't know. She was at General Harding's compound when everything went down, she just wasn't included in exactly what happened.

I suppose I'd better catch her up to speed. Maetha's cautionary words surface in my mind about Bearers and Spellcasters. I don't feel in my gut that involving Clara in the current situation is a bad thing. She is the Runners' leader, after all, plus she already knows quite a bit already.

"Clara, we're about to have a Diamond Bearer Gathering. You're welcome to stay and observe if you like. If you do, you'll be expected to respect the secrecy of the group."

She says, "I understand, explicitly, Calli."

"Well, part of that secret keeping obligation would

include not divulging who carries a diamond." I motion to Chris.

Her eyes widen and she nods.

One by one, the Bearers begin appearing in the small hotel room. Crimson speaks to my mind telling me she's on her way to attend. She arrives just before the last Bearers appear. The fact that Crimson is in person brings a heightened level of importance to the topics to be discussed.

I speak to her mind, *Where's Brand?*

He's in Texas at a hotel.

Were you able to meet with the individuals you needed to?

Yes. They're safe now.

I hope it's okay I let Clara stay for the Gathering.

You don't need my approval, Calli. However, I would appreciate it if you referred to me as a Bearer around Clara.

I note that all the Bearers are present. I say to the group, "Thank you for coming so quickly. Most of you know about Max's website, I'm sure. He needs to be shut down. Jonas, is there anything that can be done?"

"I'm working on it. Without an exact location I can't take down servers."

I say, "About that, I think he's using an enchanted bubble to confuse intruders."

Chris asks, "How does that work?"

Maetha speaks up. "It's the same concept as the electromagnetic disruption dome that protects my island from detection. The enchantment for the island was set up using the existing rock below the water line."

I ask, "Who created or designed it?"

"A Spellcaster named Vita. She specializes in this area."

Clara says. "I know Vita. She also set up the Hunters' bubble." I'll ask her if she helped Max."

"Good luck," Maetha says. "She won't talk to me anymore."

Jonas says, "Calli, if I may interject, any Bearers using phones need to turn them off and if you can, take the battery out right now. We don't know what kind of partnerships Max has made or what kind of technology he has access to. I'll get new phones for everyone, and we will be changing them out regularly."

Beth and I reach for our phones and turn them off. Maetha, Duncan, and Aernoud vanish from the gathering. They return soon, I assume having just disabled their phones like Beth and me.

I catch Maetha's eye and she says, "I told you I don't like those things."

Jonas continues. "I know there are new mobile phone monitoring devices in existence that allow the user to identify your exact location, obtaining any contacts, pictures, video, and saved docs on the phone. The devices are controversial, violating civil rights, but they're still being used."

I ask, "If you could get one of those things, could you use it to spy on Max?"

"Well, yeah, but I wouldn't be able to get one very easily. I have other methods to do basically the same thing. I need his phone number, though."

Chris speaks up. "I have a number he's used to call me. I don't know if he's still using it."

"Have you tried calling him back?" Beth asks.

"No. I didn't think of that."

Jonas says, "Don't call yet. Let me help you so we can attempt to see where the call gets routed."

Avani says, "What difference does it make if we find out where he is? We can't get to him if he's in an enchanted bubble."

Chuang says, "We could bomb the area where Calli last saw him. I think that would break the bubble."

Ruth says, "Why? If he's not there anymore we end up with more trouble than before we started."

"Not to mention innocent casualties," Chris says.

"That's part of the game, unfortunately," Chuang says.

I clear my throat. "Jonas, Chris tells me my parents have been relocated to the island."

Jonas says, "Yes. They are here. So is Brand's mother and older brother."

"What about your mother, Jonas?"

"I requested she be left alone. Her future doesn't show any danger at this time," Jonas says.

I ask, "Did my parents or Brand's family have negative futures?"

"Yes."

I'm relieved to hear others were looking out for my parents and Brand's, but I make a mental note to point this out to Brand. The fact he doesn't have a diamond yet prevents him from taking part in this gathering.

I say, "Another issue to be addressed: I don't think we should depend upon invisibility topaz any longer. The recorded footage of Brand and me on Max's website will have everyone on high alert. Does everyone agree with me?"

Yes's and head nods confirm my suggestion. I add, "I'm not sure if anyone else has figured this out yet, but Healer quartz allows the user to detect diamonds."

"What?" several Bearers exclaim. Other Bearers grumble to each other, but all listen intently when I speak.

I explain what happened with the Healer Rhonda and how she was able to feel my diamond.

Amalgada asks, "Is she going to tell others about this?"

Fabian follows with, "Did you instruct her to keep that a secret?"

I answer, "No, I didn't."

Duncan cuts at me. "What were you thinking? We must all do everything we can to protect the lives of the Bearers."

Clara speaks up. "I'll find her and tell her to keep quiet."

I say, "There's more. This woman who received the Healer quartz had her power removed only three weeks ago in South Carolina. There is an active machine here in the U.S."

"Where?"

"We don't know exactly."

Jonas says, "I'll monitor power usage spikes in that area to see if we can detect the surge needed to operate the machine."

"Good," I say.

Jie Wen asks, "Were you able to unite the clans?"

"The Runners and Healers are on board. I expect the others to join once they realize the magnitude of the situation: both with the power-removing machine and the upcoming blast."

Jie Wen presses, "How did you fair in Portland? Did you get the officials to listen to you?"

"Uh, well, not exactly. They listened and then tossed us out." Jie Wen's smug expression is entirely unwanted by me. "I'll figure out something else. We still have a year left."

"Calli," Avani says, "I've scanned the Portland area and found several inventive intelligent minds that should be preserved. They should have top priority once evacuations take place."

"Thank you. The Healers agreed to house those

affected with the Elemental blast at their facility in California. I'm going to Norway with Clara and hopefully Brand to try to find Max again. Everyone should remain on high alert when you're around Unaltereds, or if you feel a constricting sensation in your chest. It may indicate someone is sensing your diamond. Does anyone have questions?" I look around the group. No one speaks up. "Okay. We're done for now."

Bearers vanish one by one, except for Jonas who remains and moves near Clara.

"Hi Clara. Do you remember me?"

She looks him over. "If I didn't know better, I'd say you're Jonas Flemming. But he died."

Jonas smiles broadly. "Not exactly. I mean, I would have. Technically I did, for legalities, but Maetha healed me. Now I'm a Bearer like Calli."

"I don't know what to say," Clara says, her eyes traveling over Jonas. "I didn't know Maetha could perform a healing on that level." She smiles. "I'm happy you're alive."

After everyone leaves, Crimson heads back to Brand, leaving Beth and Clara with me.

I ask Clara, "What did you think of the Bearers?"

"I didn't know there were so many. I've actually met a couple of them in my travels, but I didn't know of their significance. Like with the woman who drove you and Beth to meet me and Nate."

I look over to Beth who seems to know better than to explain who Crimson really is.

Clara says, "We should go to Norway to the place you feel Max is located. Maybe we can find him somehow."

"Okay, but Brand should come too. You know, just in case we need a do over."

"I agree."

"Only problem is he's in Texas right now," I say.

"That's only a technicality. A little arranging and he can be set on his way to us."

It's taken a week to get all the arrangements pulled together so Clara, Brand, Jonas, and I can travel to Norway. Our plane is currently descending to the airport.

In the last few days, Chris was able to call Max on the phone. Jonas helped to trace the call. They didn't come up with anything other than Max is somewhere in Norway. At least we know he's still there.

Chris told me about his call with Max. He asked Max why he thinks he has exclusive intel that no one else knows. Chris then told Max he knows everything Max knows and if he started spouting details Max's info would lose value real quick. So Max offered to cut Chris in on the profits—whatever that means.

I'm proud of Chris for approaching Max in that way. I only wish I could have been a fly on the wall to see Max's reaction to Chris's threats. And better yet, Chris was able to keep up the pretenses he's against the Diamond People, as Max calls us.

After Captain Rutherfield completes the landing and brings the plane to a halt outside a maintenance hangar, the four of us exit and make our way to rent a car. I muse to myself that if we were with Maetha, she'd have a car waiting for us. Now that I've had the opportunity to fly with Crimson and avoid all the little time-consuming details of everyday human life, I find myself feeling impatient to be slowed down like this. Three of us have the Runner's ability, but Brand doesn't and can't be handed the power now because he's an Unaltered. He really needs his diamond. I suppose I could let him use my necklace with the Runners topaz and that way we could bypass the rental car all together, but eventually the topaz will deplete and we'll be in the middle of nowhere without a car. So, on to the rental agency.

Brand and Jonas sit in the backseat as Clara drives following my instructions to the industrial complex area of town.

I say, "Slow down, Clara. We should park here and walk the rest of the way just in case Max is watching for suspicious vehicles."

Brand announces, "We're not going to run into trouble."

"Really?" Clara says, arching an eyebrow while eyeing Brand in the mirror.

"Yeah. The building is empty. You don't have to park here. Keep driving."

Clara looks at me for reassurance. I forget she's not as familiar with Brand's power. I tell her it's okay and she keeps driving. She turns one more corner and I recognize the building immediately.

"There it is. I can't believe this place was here all along, but I couldn't see it."

Clara says, "That's the power of the confusion enchantment." She stops the car and turns it off.

We get out and begin walking around the building. We never leave each other's sight, though. The warehouse is empty with no evidence remaining to indicate what they were doing. We walk all around the perimeter of the building. Clara carefully inspects the ground, picking up tiny shimmery bits of what looks like discarded gum foil.

She extends her hand to me. "These are enchanted."

Brand leans in for a better look. "What is that?"

"I'm not sure." She angles her hand right and left,

allowing the light to reflect off the surface of the bits.

I say, "Those are the confetti bits they tossed outside the door." I look to the ground and find another one. I stoop to pick it up. Just before I touch it, I feel a similar sensation enter my body—confusion. "If these are what caused my earlier confusion, why aren't they as strong as before? Do they lose power over time?"

Clara says, "I would suppose those were a component of a system. Without the other parts nearby, the enchantment isn't as strong

The shimmer of the fleck is like what the quartz blankets display. I face Jonas. "I want you to show these to Tod and have him analyze them to see if they contain quartz."

"Okay," Jonas says.

Brand announces, "There's nothing more to see here. This has been a huge waste of time."

"Oh, I don't know, Brand," Clara says. "We now have some of the elements Max used to hide with. These can be reverse-engineered to create a key that could enter another hideout, if he uses the same material. Given how most of the substance is gone, I believe he will."

Jonas's eyes widen. "You're smart, Ms. Winter."

"Why thank you, Jonas."

Clara says, "We should get back to the plane so we can determine our next move."

Back on the plane, Chris bi-locates to me.

I say, "I found the warehouse, but Max was already gone."

Brand sits down by me and bumps his shoulder into mine. "It's *because* Max was gone that you found it, Calli.

The bubble was gone."

Chris's displeased glare lands on Brand and stays there.

I stand and move across the aisle and sit down. "Chris," I pull his attention to me, "can you try to call Max again so we can see if he's in Norway?"

Jonas interrupts our conversation. "I can't track a call without my computer, so it wouldn't matter unless you can get Max to admit where he is."

Chris rubs his chin. "I don't think I could ask a question like that without making him suspicious."

Clara says, "He'll be well protected, wherever he is." She holds up a piece of the confetti. "We need to study the material we found and see if we can design a key. The Hunter's key allows me to see the perimeter of the bubble. I think if I could create a key with this I could see the bubble it corresponds with. We can only research that on Maetha's island.

"I guess that's where we're headed then," Jonas says rather excitedly.

Captain Rutherfield turns in his seat and says, "We have a twelve-hour delay."

Chris looks at Jonas and Brand, then me. "I wish I was there with you."

"Me too," I answer.

He switches to telepathic speak. *I feel so helpless, Calli.*

You don't need to worry about me, Chris.

But I do.

Is this about Brand and Jonas?

No. I want to be with you. I don't feel like I'm doing anything of value here in D.C. I'd rather be where the action is.

Well, my future shows I'll be heading back to Denver to do boring Denver stuff. Honestly, Chris, I think you have more consistent action than I do. Maybe I should come hang out with you.

💎 💎 💎

"Calli," Clara says as she stands on the Denver house porch after I open the door. "I've heard from the Hunters, Readers, and Seers clans. They want to join up because of Max's blog and prepare for the Portland blast and the ensuing exposure of the clans."

"They are all in?" I can hardly contain my excitement.

"May I come in?"

I step out of the way. "Of course. Sorry."

Clara continues. "The leaders are. I can't speak for the members of all clans."

Beth comes in from the kitchen, having obviously overheard, and says, "You did it, Calli! You convinced them to join."

"I don't know," I shake my head. "I think the pat on the back should go to Max."

"No, you got them thinking at the Hunter's forest," Beth reaffirms. "Prior to that, I think a lot of people discounted Max, and I bet there were others who didn't even know about the blog. You raised awareness of Vorherrschaft, the Reapers, and Max."

Clara continues. "I've given the prisms to the clans and I've heard several stories about the use of the prism's Repeater power. They all seem to be pleased to have such a powerful stone. I know I am."

Beth says, "Well that's the best news we've heard all month! It's been quiet around here, except for the neighborhood backyard bar-b-que parties that seem to happen every night."

The front door opens and Brand enters. "What? Did I hear someone say bar-b-que?"

Amenemhet follows Brand inside the front room. "Calli," he says, nodding at me. I smile back.

Beth seems a bit rattled with Brand's sudden appearance. "What are you doing here?"

"Good to see you too, Beth. Amenemhet is going to insert my quartz."

I say, "I thought Maetha was going to do that."

"She doesn't have time. She recommended Amenemhet because he's worked with mummification in his human life. He knows all the gaps and empty spaces inside the head and face."

Beth looks up at Brand with a sneaky smile. "And between the ears."

"That's rude," he barks.

"I was kidding, Brand. You're the smartest guy I know."

Brand relaxes his ridged stance and shrugs his shoulders. "Thanks."

My eyes move back and forth between them considering the possibility that Beth may be holding a prism or maybe she's just really happy to see Brand.

Beth says, "I hope everything works out and you heal quickly."

Amenemhet says in his formal military-style manner, "It will either work or it won't. Maetha feels things have settled sufficiently for Brand to be out of commission for a little while."

"Yeah, with Max basically having gone underground again, and no word on any missing clansmen or recently removed powers, perhaps we can get this done before anything new surfaces."

"Where is this going to happen?" I ask.

"Here."

"Oh." My eyebrows rise involuntarily. "When?"

"In a few days. I have some supplies to round up before we start."

Clara moves closer to Amenemhet. “So, you’ve worked with mummification. May I be of assistance? I’m a Spellcaster.”

“I’m aware of who you are. You’ve obviously forgotten me, though.”

“Excuse me?” she asks.

Calli, Chris’s voice enters my mind. *Calli, I’m ready to have my diamond inserted.*

Chapter Thirteen - Birthday Surprises

I'm torn between wanting to hear how Amenemhet and Clara know each other and wanting to talk with Chris. I excuse myself and go into the kitchen, sit at the table, and close my eyes.

You are, Chris? You're not going to wait till after the Elemental blast, like Crimson recommended?

No. After you showed me the vision while we were in Portland, I realized I could help you better if my diamond was inside me. I don't have access to all the powers any other way.

Okay. Have you told Maetha of your plans?

No. I don't want her to know.

Why?

Why does she need to know? Why does anyone need to know? This will be a very personal experience for both of us and I really don't want anyone else involved. Are you all right with that?

Okay. I guess. I wonder why he's a bit on the defensive side. *When do you want to do this?*

Next Saturday is your birthday and we'll be together on Maetha's island. How about then?

That's soon, but perfect. My parents will want to celebrate with me, too.

I'm sure we can figure out how to divide the time so everyone's happy.

We end our mental communications and I'm left feeling incredibly nervous and worried to insert Chris's diamond. What if he doesn't heal or if his body rejects it like mine did after Justin died. Technically, he is the second person to receive a diamond who went through the power-removing machine, the first being his father. I don't know if I'll be strong enough to remove it and heal his heart if he's not able to heal. I can't even look to his future to see if it will be successful because his future ends when the diamond stops his heart. The greater healing power I'm able to wield should theoretically help me heal him, but I shouldn't count on that.

I've tried looking at my own future, asking when I'll see Chris again. The only vision I get is the one of me walking toward him on Maetha's island. I can't tell if I'm just remembering the vision, or if the same future is still in place, meaning Chris will survive the insertion. The vision of my grandchildren running toward me doesn't surface when I look to the future. Does that mean the future is different now? Or does that mean I'm not searching correctly? I don't know. At least we'll be on the island with other Diamond Bearers, including Maetha, who can come help, if need be.

Long ago, when Freedom tried to get me to part with the diamond, he warned me of the pain I'd experience watching my loved ones die. He didn't say how much it would hurt to have to be the one to end a life, like with Chris, then be responsible for hopefully bringing him back. Of course, Freedom wouldn't have foreseen that future back then. Chris wasn't an Unaltered yet.

I know Chris has mastered the powers of the diamond. He can hold the diamond in his hand, outside of the pouch, and control the powers. He can heal using the diamond. All signs point to him being able to heal himself. I'm really only there as backup in case he can't. But that's what stresses me out. What if *I* can't?

◇ ◇ ◇

We arrive at the airport and make our way to the docks where we board the boat specially outfitted with the "key" to travel through the bubble around the island. I fully understand now how it works. There aren't doorways. There is only a substance that parts the barrier in a small way, creating an entry point. Crimson must also have a key and that's how she enters and leaves.

Arriving at the island, we head directly to see my parents at their private bungalow away from the main house. We don't stay long because we'll see them again at dinner, but I give them both big hugs, happy that they're safe.

Then we stop by Jonas's place. The door is open, so we peek our heads inside. Sarangerel is working on a laptop at the table. Jonas sits at his desk surrounded by several computer screens displaying different things. When he looks our way, he jumps up out of his chair and comes over to welcome us.

He gives me a quick hug and says, "Hey there. Happy Birthday, Calli." He slaps Chris on the shoulder and invites us inside.

We make idle chitchat, but I'm anxious to settle in. Before we leave, Jonas says, "They put you in the beach bungalow."

"Really?" I say.

"Yeah, kind of a birthday present, but also private."

Chris says, "Well, that's convenient."

Sarangerel comes over and asks Chris a question. Jonas uses the moment to pull me aside, to say, "Calli, I just want you to know if there's anything you need, anything, I'm happy to help."

"Uh, okay. Where's that coming from?"

Jonas wrings his hands. "Nowhere. I'm sort of sensing tension and I wanted you to know you can talk to me about anything."

"Thanks, Jonas. I appreciate that. I am a little stressed right now, but I think things will be better in a while." Things will be sooo much better once Chris's diamond is safely inside his heart and he's alive and kicking. I change the subject. "Any news on the investigation of the bubble material from Norway?"

"Not yet. Tod and Don are working on it."

We leave Jonas's place and head to the main house where we find Maetha and Crimson. I don't think I've ever had such a big birthday bash as what's shaping up to happen tonight. I'm not crazy about this much attention. Never have been.

I say, "I didn't know you both would be here this weekend."

Crimson smiles tersely. "Your birthday is going to be one to remember. Besides, I would have been here anyway. A few Bearers are arriving tomorrow to discuss the happenings at the International Climate Summit."

Chris asks, "Who is involved with the global warming issue?"

"Everyone, in essence. But right now the focused Bearers are Avani, Kookju, Amalgada, Ruth, and Aernoud."

Chris turns to Crimson. "Can't you see the future concerning global warming?"

"Of course. However, the more pressing issues, like the Elemental blast, need my focus. For tonight, let's concentrate on Calli becoming another year wiser and not talk about cosmic blasts, diamonds, or climate changes."

Chris and I walk on the beach, hand in hand, in a similar setting as we did in February following Yeok Choo's surrendering. The sun hangs just above the horizon, reflecting warm colors everywhere. Chris's skin appears golden. I want to touch him to make sure he's real and this is not a dream.

The whole night feels like a blur. Almost all the important people in my life were at my birthday dinner. Music, good food, and a rule to not talk about anything related to diamonds or upcoming blasts made for a welcoming break. And now a stroll on the beach with Chris. I can't imagine anything better.

Chris takes my hand and gently squeezes. Yep, he's really here, not a dream, and not bi-located either. He asks, "What did you wish for when you blew out your candles?"

"I can't tell you or it won't come true." My response is knee-jerk. Everyone knows the rules about blowing out candles. Besides, I'm nervous to tell Chris I desperately wished to be able to heal him with the secret diamond insertion we're about to do. I don't want him to know how much this worries me. However, now that I know Crimson is on the island, I can let go of some of my concerns. Nothing is truly secret around her.

"Silly superstitions," Chris mutters, then drops my hand and hurries in front of me. He squats down and picks something up off the sand.

I try to peek over his shoulder. "Another pebble?"

"There's only one perfect stone for my perfect girl." He swivels around and reaches his clasped hand toward my feet."

I wonder what the pebble will look like, this perfect stone as he calls it.

He removes his hand and I look down at the sand. I don't see anything at first. I guess I thought I'd see a grey rock. Instead, I catch a sparkle of white and silver. I bend down to get a better look and see what looks like a small clear crystal sitting on the sand. I lower myself so that Chris and I are face to face. I take a closer look at the round crystal and excitement jitters speed through my body as I admire the intense light refraction, the kind that only comes from a diamond. Carefully taking the diamond between my thumb and first finger, I lift it off the sand. I soon realize the diamond is attached to a buried ring. My heart flutters excitedly against my ribs, my eyes are wide open.

Is Chris about to—

Is this where he—

I can't breathe enough air to satisfy my racing heart.

Chris rises so that he's on one knee. He reaches out and helps me stand. On bended knee he looks up and says, "Calli, will you be my better half, my partner, my inspiration? Will you marry me?"

Tears burst out of nowhere and a mile-wide smile erupts. "Yes! Of course." I fling my arms around him as he stands, embracing his body with mine.

He hugs me back and then takes my head in his hands and kisses me to seal the proposal. I love the feelings and sensations I get when I'm in his arms and I imagine our auras are shining brightly, but I don't want to open my eyes to see.

Chris pulls back a little and asks, "Did you know I was going to propose?"

"No. I didn't have a clue."

"So, you didn't try to read my mind?"

"No."

He smiles and leads me up the beach to the bungalow where we retrieve a blanket from the closet. I see that my bags have been delivered already and are sitting on the floor.

"Wait," I blurt out. "You didn't waddle."

"Should I do it all over again?"

"Nah."

We walk out the door and spread a blanket down on the sand up where the greenery ends and the beach begins. We sit down next to each other facing the setting sun. Chris puts his arm around me.

I look down at my engagement ring and admire the brilliant shimmers and sharp glints of light as I move my finger around. "I love this ring, Chris. You have great taste in jewelry."

"The diamond is a family heirloom, once belonged to royalty. I chose the setting. Platinum. The band is extra special, but you can't see it till the wedding."

"And when are you thinking of getting married?"

"I'd like to be married before the Portland blast. What do you think?"

"Before? I don't think we'll have time to pull that off. Besides, I'd like to be engaged to you for a little while to decide if I want to keep you."

"You haven't figured that out yet?"

I press my shoulder further against his body. "Just trying to keep you on your toes."

"Do you want a big wedding?" he asks, caressing my arm.

"Actually, no." I think about how wonderful this night was with my birthday and everyone around me. "A simple ceremony here on the island would be perfect for me."

"Mary told me the Bearers call getting married a 'Coupling.' She said some of the Bearers have paired off and coupled over time."

"I believe it." I smile and snuggle closer. "When you asked me to come to the island to give you your diamond, you actually meant that you could give me one. Am I right?"

"No. I do want to insert my diamond as well. I just wanted *your* diamond to be a surprise."

"That it was."

Chris pulls the Sanguine Diamond from his pocket and lays it beside the blanket, then lies back. I join him.

"Are you ready for this?" I ask.

"Not yet. I want to relax with you for a bit first." He pulls me into an embrace and kisses my head.

My head rests on his chest, his heart thuds loudly under my ear. Is this the last time I'll hear his heart? What if I can't save him? I scrunch my eyes tight and take a deep breath. I need to stop stressing myself out. My head needs to be clear to help him the best.

He says, "I remember when I walked into Clara's office and saw you there. You were so young, so new to the world of powers. You didn't even know what Shadow Demons were yet. And then I flipped you upside down with my unblocked mind. But you handled the situation so maturely, so impressively . . . and then you died on the stone altar." I turn my head and look at him. He says, "I still have traumatic dreams of that moment."

"I didn't know that."

"But not so much since I became Unaltered. Or maybe the dreams slowed down because of the diamond. I'm not sure."

I say, "My dreams stopped once I got the diamond in the pouch. However, they've come back now."

"Really? What do you relive in your dreams?"

"The Portland blast. I see it over and over again. Each time in a little more disturbing detail."

"Calli, those are visions, not dreams."

"I'm not so sure. I feel like my mind is creating

possible outcomes, not necessarily the actual outcome."

"Well, you've been through some pretty terrible things in the last four and a half years. You've seen things you can't unsee. Do those things haunt your dreams?"

"The many times I've watched you die never seem to leave my mind. Even though Brand repeated you back, I still remember it."

"Too bad Brand couldn't be here today to see if I'll make it through the insertion."

"Healing takes longer than two minutes. Brand wouldn't be any help in this situation. He wasn't able to tell me for sure if I'd make it through my own insertion."

Chris whispers, "I'm a little hesitant to do this."

I lift my head and rest on my elbow. Looking him in the eye, I say, "You don't have to, you know."

"I need to. I can't fully help you if I don't have the diamond inside me."

"Well, you're able to hold the diamond on your bare skin and use the healing power, so you should be able to heal yourself. If for whatever reason you're unable to heal after the insertion, I'll do everything in my power to help you survive." I playfully poke my finger against his chest. "You and I have a world to save, mister." I lean forward and kiss him.

He kisses me back, then pulls me back into the embrace and caresses my hair. "I'm just trying to get up my courage to slam a magical rock into my chest."

"You?" I prop up on my elbow. "No. I'll do it."

"No, actually, I'm going to. If my body doesn't accept it, you can pull it out and heal my injury. We are, after all, two Bearers in love, right? The healing power is stronger between us. I remember watching Maetha pull the diamond out of your heart at Lake Patoka when you weren't able to heal yourself." He sits up and takes off his shirt.

I feel like reminding him of Maetha and Crimson's instructions concerning his insertion, but decide against it. I sit up beside him and look to his future. Nothing has changed from what I've viewed in the past. The diamond will stop his heart like it did with mine. The future beyond that cannot be seen, other than the wishful thinking that someday he and I will meet up on this beach. When I carried the diamond the first time, my future couldn't be seen beyond my heart stopping because technically that's when I ceased being human Calli and became Bearer Calli. The same will happen with Chris. I hope. Deep down, I know help is a few steps away.

He picks up the diamond and lies back down. With his hand holding the diamond raised straight upward toward the sky above his chest, he takes a deep breath, looks me in the eye, winks, then slams the diamond down against his sternum.

The ensuing blast nearly blows me over. Panicked, I regain my balance just before the strumming sensation of a diamond without an owner rocks my world more than I thought possible. Chris is technically dead. I look at his chest. Through the blood and exposed bone, I see his heart and the diamond. It's partially sticking out, not completely inside the muscle. His heart isn't pumping. Is this normal? I look at his face. His eyes are open, his gaze paused and slightly askew, his mouth opened a crack.

"Come on, Chris! You can do this. Think healing."

The fact the diamond isn't all the way inside his heart concerns me, not to mention the amount of blood loss. How can his heart heal? I decide to push the diamond in further, and if healing doesn't begin, I'm going to work on him.

I poke my finger into the hole in his chest and come in contact with his still-warm heart. I push the diamond in more and gently pull the muscle over the edges as much as I can. I straddle his waist and place my hands over his open wound. Closing my eyes, I reach deep within myself and access the healing power of my diamond. My hands begin to tremble and heat up, but I don't stop what I'm doing. I don't open my eyes. I connect with his body, his muscle tissue, fibers, fascia, and ribs, healing as I go.

Why isn't he breathing yet? Why isn't his heart beating?

I open my eyes to see the brilliant blue-green glow emanating from my hands. Most of his chest is healed. I decide to focus on his diamond instead of his body. I close my eyes and connect my diamond with his, willing his to exude healing power. My hands feel like they're on fire from the intense heat, yet his chest isn't moving, his heart isn't beating.

This is my worst nightmare! My eyes sting with tears. I try to think of what else I can do, short of cursing Crimson and Maetha. They're on the island, literally seconds away. Surely, they've sensed his diamond doesn't have an owner anymore. Why aren't they coming to help? I refocus on Chris. Maybe I need to dig the diamond out and go from there. His brain has been without oxygen for a few minutes now. But the skin on his chest is completely healed. To dig the diamond out would mean opening him up again.

I move to his side and begin chest compressions. Regular old CPR. This is what I've resorted to. I'm trying to bring Chris back from the dead with regular human methods. I tilt his head back and pull his chin down and give him life-saving breaths of air. I resume chest compressions, counting out loud and calling out his name, hoping I'm not damaging his heart even more with each compression. More breaths of air. I feel completely devastated that I can't bring him back.

I whisper, because my throat is too constricted with emotion to speak, "Come back to me, Chris."

I start more compressions, then I feel movement. I stop abruptly and connect my diamond with his. His heart is quivering. My medical knowledge tells me he needs a shock of electricity to regulate the heart. I close my eyes and imagine feeling all the energy I possess, and the static in the air around me, then send all the healing energy I can in one big jolt. His body contracts as if he's been shocked with a defibulator. I feel for his diamond again and find his heart struggling to beat. I give him more breaths of air. My hands hurt and burn like I've dipped them in scalding water. My ring finger burns more intensely than the rest.

I plead, "Chris, you can do it. Heal yourself. Activate your healing power and heal yourself."

I place my hands on his chest again and without any help from me, my hands produce bright blue-green light. My power is being drawn from me and into Chris. I'm filled with immeasurable hope as I realize he's accessing our combined intense healing power.

"That's it, Chris. Keep going. You're doing it."

But he's still not breathing on his own. Keeping one hand over his heart, I give him more breaths of oxygen and caress his forehead. His heart is strengthening, each beat moving his blood further. I give him more breaths of air. Then I see his eyes blink.

Tears stream down my face. "You're strong, you can do this."

He takes his first breath in what feels like ten minutes. I lay my hand on his chest and feel his heart beating stronger than before. He breathes in and out at a regular pace. Finally!

I wipe my eyes with my forearms because the backs of my hands are hot to the touch. Then I run my hands over his chest, feeling for any broken ribs or anything else that still needs to mend. I can tell he's still healing himself, so that's good. But he's not all the way conscious yet.

My emotional floodgates burst and I cry. I cry hard. I press my cheek against Chris's shoulder and sob my guts out. I just watched my best friend kill himself. He chose to do this. In reality, Chris Harding is now dead. Chris the Bearer is born.

My strength seems to drain out of me with every tear that falls down my cheeks. I lay down on my right side next to Chris and lay my left hand over his heart. Deep blues and greens reflect in the diamond on my finger, bringing on a whole new wave of emotion.

He proposed to me.

We're engaged.

I almost lost him.

My eyelids become heavy and my vision blurs. The last thing I see is Chris's chest rising and falling with his breathing.

"Calli, you did it!"

I open my eyes and try to focus on the surroundings. I'm laying on a hard surface. Pushing myself up, I stand and look around. This isn't the beach. Where's Chris? It appears I'm up high on top of a building with radio antennas. As I walk to the edge I see mountains in the distance, other high rise buildings, lush green forests and a river down below crossed by several bridges. I'm in Portland, Oregon. I look down to the streets. Everything seems to be abandoned. Across the river, the I-5 freeway is completely empty.

My hand hurts like it's burned. I look down and see my fist clutched, holding something. My engagement ring glows emerald green. Opening my hand, I find a Sanguine Diamond glowing in the center with the same deep intensity of green as my ring. My finger still burns so I take the diamond into my right hand and then try to wiggle the engagement ring off my finger. It's stuck. Panic consumes me and my pulse races. I pull and yank. Nothing. I have to get this off.

"You captured the Elemental blast." Crimson approaches from behind. "I'm sorry, Calli. But it had to be this way."

"What do you mean?" I say, still yanking violently on the ring.

"I couldn't stop it from happening, so I kept you from knowing it would."

"Stop what? Know what?"

Chris's voice calls to me.

I ask Crimson again, "Stop what? Know what?"

Chris calls my name. "Calli, wake up."

I open my eyes and find Chris sitting shirtless next to me on the blanket in the sand. A soft breeze blows his hair around a little. Ocean waves gently lap against the shore nearby letting me know I've just had a dream and I'm not in Portland, Oregon.

I sit up and rub my eyes. My hands feel fine and don't burn any longer. I grasp the ring and easily remove it, then slide it back on my finger. I examine my hands closely. There's no blood on them. Was it *all* a dream? I reach out and touch Chris's bare chest. No blood here either. I feel his heart beating and can tell he has a diamond inside. Then I remember when he and I accessed the deep healing power together on New Year's Eve, all the blood on my skin disappeared that time as well.

"It worked?" I raise my eyes to his.

"Yeah." He smiles. "You healed me."

"No, you healed you." I pull my hand back and rub my head, trying to recall the dream.

"Are you all right?"

"Yes. I'm drained of energy, that's all. That was horrible, Chris. I felt so helpless."

"I know exactly how you feel. I watched you slam a diamond into yourself from a helpless position, too. Not only that, I had to pretend I wasn't bothered or upset so my father would continue to keep me in the compound. I was devastated, well, until you began to heal yourself. Then I had a whole new admiration for you."

"No one came to help, Chris."

"Did you think they would?"

"Well, yeah, kind of. You were dead for many minutes while I healed you. Your diamond didn't have an owner and they would have known that. But no one came. I gave you CPR, Chris. *CPR.* Then I shocked your heart."

He loosens his hold on me and moves back a little. He looks me in the eye. "With what?"

"My hands."

"How?"

"I don't know. It must be part of the greater healing ability."

His tense lines around his eyes and mouth relax. "I'm really glad it worked, Calli." He pulls me back into a hug.

I can't help but be reminded of when he saved me on the river bank on the way to the Death Clan. He performed CPR on me and started my heart, too. Then I healed his water-soaked lungs. And then the whole misunderstanding about a "witch" came up when I told him I'd seen a vision. His reaction then was similar to his reaction now when I said I shocked his heart. Of course, we both know a whole lot more now than we did. And he's hugging me instead of stalking off into the night.

Chris drops his hold, picks his shirt up, and shakes the sand off. He puts it on and says, "Let's go tell the others."

He helps me stand. I'm feeling much better now. My energy levels are back to normal. We walk together on the dimly lit path to the main house. Jonas, and Sarangerel are sitting at an outdoor table.

As soon as Jonas sees us coming, he jumps up and rushes to Chris. At first, he seems confused. "What happened? I sensed your death."

My first thought is: why didn't you come try to help? What happened to "if you need anything, I'm here for you"?

Chris states, "I'm a Bearer now."

Jonas's mouth falls open and he utters, "But . . . I thought . . . "

Behind him, Maetha and Crimson come out of the house. Maetha cuts Jonas off, saying, "We sensed your insertion, Chris. It looks as though everything is healed properly." Her eyes are directed to his chest. "I sensed you struggled with healing yourself."

Chris says, "Um, yeah."

I step forward, my angry thoughts becoming words. "If you sensed Chris was struggling, why didn't you come help me heal him?"

Maetha says, "Help you? Chris is the one who would have needed help healing himself, and you were there to assist him."

"Chris was dead! I had to finish inserting his diamond for him and then start his heart so he could heal himself."

Jonas runs his fingers through his hair and asks with a tone of disbelief, "You had to start his heart? How'd you do that?"

"I shocked him," I nearly shout, while motioning with my hands as if I'm holding paddles.

Maetha looks at Crimson, then back to Chris and says, "Did you put your own diamond in your heart?"

"Yes."

Crimson lowers one eyebrow and raises the other, then looks at Maetha. "Didn't we give instructions for Calli to insert his diamond?"

"Yes." Maetha looks at Chris. "Why on earth would you do that?"

Crimson turns to me. "Why didn't you follow my instructions?" Her stern tone sets my hair on end as goosebumps spring up all over my body.

Jonas hurries over to Sarangerel and ushers her inside the house to give the four of us privacy. *Thank you, Jonas.*

I'm about to respond but Chris answers, "I didn't want Calli to—"

Crimson's voice lowers, like my father's when he's serious. "The instructions were for Calli to insert the diamond and then for you to heal yourself. I'm surprised you are alive at all!"

Chris takes a defensive stance. "Well, Calli shoved her own diamond in herself. I figured it would work for me, too."

"Yes, but she already had a shard to prevent her from dying."

"What about my dad? He shoved the diamond in his own chest and didn't die."

"He had an unusual inclination for harnessing the healing ability," Crimson says. "Pure luck on his part. I thought he'd die."

Maetha says to me, "Why didn't you follow Crimson's instructions? Didn't *you* look to his future?"

"Yes! And he was going to die. Which is what I was told would happen. Why would I think I was seeing something dangerously wrong?"

"The instruction also included removing his diamond and healing his heart if he wasn't strong enough to do it himself."

"You're treating me like I've done something wrong. If it was so important for this to go a certain way, why didn't you come help?"

"We didn't know he was going to insert his diamond today."

"Really? That's your answer?" I ask.

Maetha puts her hand in front of her and pats the air. "Calm down, Calli."

Anger boils in my stomach. "No, I won't. Not yet. I've never been so afraid or scared to death in my life, but I thought 'hey, these thousands-years-old wise women wouldn't let me do this by myself if there was anything to be worried about.' Boy, was I wrong!"

"We didn't know."

"You didn't know?" My voice cracks.

"We didn't know Chris was receiving his diamond today."

"Well you certainly knew the moment his diamond no longer had an owner. You could have come at that point. Why didn't you?"

Chris puts his arm around me. "We've had a little too much order-giving, consequences-be-damned for the night. We're going to go take a break from you two and have some privacy." Chris guides my shoulders to the opposite direction and I gladly let him lead me away from Maetha and Crimson.

As more distance is put between us, I relax a bit and my emotions calm down.

Chris says, "I wouldn't have ever thought Jo Jo would stand by and let me die."

I look over at his stony profile. "You haven't called her by that name for a really long time."

"In my mind there's the all-knowing, all-controlling

Crimson and there's the sweet woman down the block who fed me lemonade and cookies and taught me how to ride a motorcycle. Tonight, she seemed more human, more like Jo Jo, more like someone who makes mistakes. At least, I want to think she made a mistake."

We arrive at the bungalow, go inside and drop down on the couch.

Chris says, with a hitch in his voice, "I'm tired of being a puppet."

I nod. "I'm tired of not being told the whole story but being expected to know it anyway." I retrieve my bag from the floor by my feet and dig deep for the small metal container I brought with me. "You know, Chris, you and I are now the two most powerful Bearers in the world. This is our world, our time." I clasp the container after locating it, but don't remove it from the bag. I put a finger to my mouth signaling him to be quiet, then I pull out my other hand.

Chris's eyes widen at the sight of the metal tin and he sits up straight. "Is that—?"

"Shhh." I open the tin, revealing large obsidian inside. My powers rush from my body.

"What are you doing?" Chris asks, his voice unsteady.

I dump the stone out into my hand and reach forward, laying it on the table where it can affect both of us. "I want total concealment."

"Don't you think they'll sense obsidian and come running?" He points at the wall in the direction of the main house.

"No. You told them we needed a break and privacy. It's possible they might come check on us to make sure we're all right. But I don't even think they'll do that, given how mad we became."

"Why exactly do you have that out then?"

"I told you. I want total privacy." I tap my head to indicate how Crimson can hear my thoughts even when I'm in a Blue mist circle. I pause for a second to gather my words, then say, "Crimson just said a couple things that made me stop and think. When you referred to me slamming the diamond into my own heart at your father's compound, she acted as though she already knew I wouldn't die because I had the shard. More recently, I was instructed to insert your diamond and if you couldn't heal, I was to remove the diamond and heal you. I think, just as Crimson knew I would heal myself, she knew you wouldn't be able to. I think she thought we'd return with the diamond in your hand, not in your heart."

"Or that I wouldn't return at all. She seemed quite surprised I wasn't dead. That really upset me."

"Me too. Crimson and Maetha both seemed a little too upset that I didn't insert your diamond, not so much because you put yourself at risk, but because we didn't follow the plan."

"I think they want to run the show. They tell me I need to make the choices and bring the clans and Bearers together, but they want to actually be in charge. I don't see how that can happen and be successful. It makes me wonder what they're using you and me for. Again."

He doesn't respond. His eyebrows lower and his jaw sets.

I continue. "Given what I've learned about Crimson, she could have taken Freedom out at any time. She could have used her invisibility to sneak into the compound and kill him. But she didn't. I think she kept him alive for a different reason. I haven't figured that one out yet. What I do know is she's not telling me everything." I lean forward, feeling daring and rebellious, but also feeling like I'm backed into a corner. "Chris, let's take charge of the future of *our* world. No more relying on getting our information from those two. They clearly have their own agenda. Sure, they want the best outcome, but who exactly is it best for? Us? Or them?"

"What do you propose to do?"

His use of the word "propose" reminds me I'm now engaged to him. If he hadn't survived, I wouldn't be. I become all the madder. I say, "Concerning the Portland blast, I think I've figured out how to get the city officials to listen to us."

"How?"

"We need to go to the U.S. government for help."

"Excuse me?"

"Think about it. Max is this huge threat to the continued secrecy of the Bearers and people with powers. I think Crimson could do something about this, but she chooses not to."

"What, like kill Max?"

"Perhaps. But the question is, why hasn't she done anything to shut him up . . . unless she knows the secret is not going to be safe any longer anyway. Why expose herself over something that will resolve itself. Max's efforts to expose people with powers and Diamond Bearers will become old news once the blast hits and the world finds out about cosmic powers. I'm thinking if we do the unexpected and go to the government for help now, long before the blast, we'll save the most amount of lives."

"Calli, you don't know the government like I do. They'll freak out, lock us up, and throw away the key."

"I hope that won't happen. But all the same, Max's blog wouldn't carry as much of a threat if we 'out' ourselves."

"No, but we'd have targets nailed to our backs. Besides, Max dropped off the map again. His blog is gone."

"What? When?"

"A few days ago."

"Did he get a buyer?"

"Who knows? His phone number is disconnected too." Chris points to the obsidian in my hand. "We can't even view our own futures to know if going to the Feds is a good idea."

"That's true, but think about the future of the thousands of people who will most likely die if we don't try somehow to save them. This is our future, this is our present. This is our time. Let's take charge."

Chris says, "Perhaps we should just use Mind-Control for the Portland evacuation."

"I know you're still trying to figure out a way to keep the powers secret yet save lives. Mind-Control would work on one or two officials, but not a whole population. The citizens need to agree they should leave. If they are forced, thinking their leaders have gone mad, well, there will be a lot of resistance."

"We could call in a terrorist threat. Create mass evacuation."

"Remember, they don't have a mass evac plan."

"I know. That just means one needs to be explored and developed. We need to give them a reason to develop one."

"I'm afraid they'll have us arrested if we show up again."

"We have one year to figure it out."

"Not quite, Chris. We have one year till the blast hits. We need to make the preparations now. Where will all those people go? And for how long? What about the ones who don't own a vehicle? Or the homeless transients? What about food? Lodging? Basic necessities? We need help. We should include the government in this."

"But that will expose everything we've tried to keep secret."

"Chris, the future after the blast is going to expose the existence of unimaginable powers. The five clans and their individual powers could be viewed as the 'police' who will help protect the citizens without powers. If we set this up right, the government could turn to us for help. Shouldn't we open a direct line of communication now and sand off all the rough edges prior to the blast?"

His voice quivers. "You do have a valid point. What will the other Bearers think of your idea?"

"They won't like it. They wouldn't go to the government for help. But don't you see? This may be the one thing I do differently that others wouldn't do, resulting in a positive outcome."

"Should we tell Maetha or Crimson what we're going to do?"

"No. That's why I'm using this." I point to the obsidian.

"When should we go?"

"Now."

"How?"

"We run and/or swim."

"And the bubble? How do we get through it?"

I rub my chin. "We'll have to go to the boat and take the key."

"Why don't we just take the boat?"

"Oh. I didn't think of that."

Chris takes me gently by the hand. "Calli, let's take a breath. I agree that we should go to the government, but I don't think we should go tonight. Logically, first, if you think Crimson and Maetha aren't going to be watching us tonight, you're mistaken. Plus, Crimson would be waiting for us at the dock in Bermuda, because, you know, she can fly. Not to mention, in order to swim or run we have to put away the obsidian, revealing our location. Second, strategically, which is my specialty by the way, we need to plan this out a little better. We're trying to fool an Immortal, whose range of abilities we don't fully understand. We need to be stealthy."

"Stealthy?"

"Act like a spy, think like one too. Block your mind, keep your desires buried. Don't let on to your intentions."

"That's kind of hard for me to do, Chris. I have a Blue shard that connects Crimson to me.

"Exactly. That's why we need to act as though nothing is up. We continue acting as though nothing is wrong or as though we don't have any outside intentions. That way we don't draw attention our way. Don't even think about it until we're back in D.C. In fact, it helps to focus your thoughts on something entirely different to throw them off if they read your mind."

"Should we keep the obsidian open longer?"

"Yes. But I think we should go out and walk on the beach so we can be seen visually. That will rest their minds and confirm that we are using obsidian for privacy. Then, tomorrow, we'll leave on the boat, a little early, but not raising any alarms. We don't want any of the other Bearers knowing what we're up to either. We aren't only outing ourselves, we're revealing an entire underground group and clans of superpowers to the very source that has hunted us down relentlessly."

"Yes. Things are going to change."

Chapter Fourteen - The Backup Guy

We keep the obsidian open and walk down to the beach together. The moonlight illuminates the white surf, giving the illusion the water glows. The closer we get to the other buildings the more ambient lighting reflects our way.

I fidget with my ring and realize this wonderful night has completely changed. It started with a birthday party and well wishes, then a proposal and diamond insertion, and now a plot against my superiors . . . so to speak. All this in a matter of hours. I haven't even shared the news about our engagement with anyone.

"Chris, let's go tell my parents about our engagement."

"Good idea."

We walk along the lighted pathways and approach my parents' bungalow. They are sitting outside at a patio table.

My father says, "Well, there's the birthday girl." They both stand and welcome us with open arms. I consider that they have no clue what I've been through tonight since dinner.

"Oh look, Allan, she's wearing the ring!" Beaming ear to ear, my mother reaches out and takes my hand, angling my fingers to get a better look.

I look down at my hand, then back to my mom. "Did you already know I'd be getting a ring this weekend?" I say.

"I hoped you would."

My father pats Chris on the back as my mother admires the ring.

My mother asks, "Were you surprised, Calli?"

"Yes."

"He asked for your hand a while ago," my father says. "I've been waiting to hear he proposed."

I glance over to Chris who has a sheepish grin. "How did you keep me from finding out what you were about to do? I didn't sense it in your behavior or actions at all."

Chris winks at me and replies, "I purposefully never thought about proposing in case you read my thoughts. Sometimes it's necessary to not think about something to succeed at completing the task."

I know he's giving me a hint about how to close off my mind. Because the obsidian is still open, I haven't had to close off my thoughts yet. But soon, we'll have to put it away. I'd better put all my focus on the engagement and the ring so when Crimson is able to connect with my mind, she won't be aware of our intentions to betray her.

We stay with my parents for a little while longer, then begin walking back to my bungalow.

"We're going to have to put the obsidian away at some point, Calli," Chris says.

"I know," I say, wondering if I'll be able to keep my mind clear enough to throw off the others from knowing our intentions.

"Besides, I miss my powers." Chris squeezes my hand.

Jonas pops out of the bushes intercepting our path. "I need to talk to you two," he whispers, then motions for us to follow him. He leads us to my bungalow. All along the way, I consider how using the obsidian prevented us from knowing he was nearby. Should we be alarmed?

Reaching my bungalow and the illumination from the light by the front door, Jonas faces us. He extends his hand revealing he's holding what looks like obsidian. Of course, I can't tell for sure because I currently have obsidian sucking out my powers.

Jonas says, "I don't know how to say this carefully, so

I'm just going to blurt it out. I was told you two were going to have a fight and breakup tonight."

"Huh?" I say, but it comes out as just a sound, not a word. I glance at Chris. "Do you know what he's talking about?"

Chris doesn't respond.

Jonas continues. "You two were supposedly going to fight tonight and break up. I was told earlier today to be ready because Calli would need comforting."

"What?" I squawk, trying to keep my voice down. My mind fills with Jonas's awkward offer of support earlier. I turn to Chris and ask, "Why would they think that?"

Chris lets out an exhale, rubs the back of his neck and says, "Probably because all day I've kept an issue at the front of my mind and stewed on it as if it's really bothering me and that I was going to talk to you about it tonight. If I had, you and I would have fought."

"What issue?" I ask, feeling confused and worried at the same time.

"Uh, no. I'm not going to say because it's not really an issue. I only treated it like one to trick you in case you tried peeking into my mind. I didn't want you to see my plans to propose to you. I'm sure you've noticed, but it's hard to surprise a Diamond Bearer. That's why I proposed before the diamond insertion."

Jonas adds, "Well, you certainly surprised Maetha and Crimson."

Relief sweeps over me. "You had the jump on me, too." And yet, I'm a little bothered by his mention of a "not really an issue" issue.

"Wait!" Jonas shakes his head, then points to Chris. "Did you just say you proposed to her?"

"Yeah."

I hold up my left hand. Jonas opens his eyes wide as

he admires the ring. I ask, "So, who told you we were going to fight?"

"Maetha. The future showed you'd be distraught and I'd comfort you."

"I bet," Chris scoffs. I'm pretty sure I can hear his eyes roll.

"As a friend, of course," Jonas adds, speaking directly to Chris. "But . . . well, there's more. When you two left the group after dinner, before well, you know, I overheard Maetha say Calli had at least achieved the desired level of healing needed for the task, and that whatever happened between you and Calli tonight didn't matter. Then after a while, your diamond sent out the message you'd died, and I wanted to come to you, but they stopped me." He turns to me and says, "That's why I didn't come help, Calli. They said it was nature's will." He looks at Chris. "The power removing machine must have affected you in such a way that you couldn't heal yourself, that's what they said. But I could tell they were absolutely confused about your diamond being inserted instead of you two having the fight they foresaw."

"Are you saying they stopped you from coming to help and they chose not to help either?" My heart races against my ribs as I become angrier than I've ever been. *I truly was all alone in saving Chris!* Anger turns to tears and I say to Chris, "I almost lost you thinking they'd come help." I head toward the beach, my throat constricting and tears burning my eyes.

"Calli," Chris calls. I hear him approaching. "Calli. Stop, please." He puts a gentle hand on my shoulder.

I stop and turn into his embrace. Tears overflow for the second time in a matter of hours. This is so not like me. I'm usually in control of my emotions, level-headed, and thinking clearly. But not today. I can't access my healing ability, perhaps that's why I'm a wreck right now.

"I'm sorry, Calli. I shouldn't have messed with the natural order of things."

I wipe my eyes and look up at him.

He adds. "I screwed up."

"Why are you blaming yourself?"

"I didn't let you insert the diamond. I put you in a situation that was almost devastating. I should have let you insert it."

Jonas arrives at our side, having overheard, obviously. "That wouldn't have mattered Chris. When your diamond strummed without an owner, they thought Calli *had* inserted it, not you. When you showed up, alive, and a full Bearer, Crimson froze my tongue so I couldn't question you further."

Chris says, "I don't understand. They thought Calli inserted the diamond but they figured I would die?"

"That's what I'm saying."

He drops his hold on my body and steps back. The moonlight casts blue-grey shadows under his cheekbones giving him a stern look. I wish I could read his mind.

Jonas points to Chris. "You changed the future."

"Good or bad?" I ask.

"They didn't say. But they weren't happy. So, I guess that means bad."

Chris says, "They're upset I became a full Bearer."

Jonas swallows hard, looks at me, then Chris. "No. You're not hearing me, Chris. They're upset because you *lived*."

My eyes fly between Jonas and Chris, my gut twists painfully wondering what Chris is thinking.

"I was *supposed* to die?"

"Yeah, but, you didn't, thanks to Calli. Which, by the way, really freaked Maetha and Crimson out. You should have heard them squabble after you guys left, and then when you went dark with obsidian—wow. They came unglued. They said things . . . " he pauses, chews on his bottom lip for a second while he looks at me. "Anyway, I grabbed my obsidian from my hut and went dark too. I needed to think some things through without them in my head."

Chris's mouth pinches tight, his eyebrows scrunch. "What did they say?"

Jonas looks at his feet and shoves his hands into his pockets. His voice drops to barely more than a whisper. "Calli harnessed electricity and shocked you back to life. That was what bothered them the most."

I gasp, "Why?"

"Probably because you changed the future, too. Apparently, you weren't supposed to be able to bring him back."

Chris asks Jonas, "Was it going to matter when the diamond was inserted or would it have made a difference?"

"No."

I say, "So, if I'd inserted his diamond, like they wanted, I wouldn't have been able to save his life." I rub my face hard, then turn to Chris. "But you inserted your own diamond and I healed you instead."

Chris asks, "How long have you known about this, Jonas?"

Jonas hesitates. "For a while now."

"What?" Chris and I say together.

He puts his hands up in front of him. "Before you go getting all mad that I didn't say anything, remember what I'm doing right now."

"Did they actually *tell* you I'd die?"

"Yes. I should tell you both, they've been grooming me to take Chris's place."

Chris's eyes meet mine. He gives me the look of "I told you so."

"Grooming?" I ask.

"You know, preparing me to be with you. When the Elemental blast hits, you need to have a love interest in your life to give you the will to survive."

Chris walks a few steps away, cursing and throwing his hands in the air. "That's right! I'm just a 'love interest' to them. How could I forget that?"

Jonas continues. "Then, last week, something changed. The future showed something different. You two were going to fight and break up. Calli wouldn't have to insert your diamond and you wouldn't die. This had them worried for all new reasons." He looks at me. "They came to me again and let me know you'd be distraught on your birthday evening following a breakup. I needed to be prepared. But then tonight you both came to the house, together, and Chris is a Bearer."

Chris turns his head and stares out to the breaking waves. "A week ago is when I decided to propose on Calli's birthday."

I look the other direction to the distant lights of the main house. "Are they watching us right now?"

"No. At least, I don't think so. After you two left, and after they hashed things out, Crimson left the island. Maetha went into her room, I assume to meditate or bi-locate."

I say, "All this time they've instructed me to avoid looking at my future, to only look for my impending death. I've obeyed, for the most part."

Chris looks back at me. "Good thing you didn't try to look or you would have seen our fight."

Right, the "issue." I can't worry about that right now. I ask Jonas, "Why are you turning on them and telling us everything?"

"What do you mean? You're my friends."

"Yeah," Chris jumps in. "But you said you've known for a while."

"I thought it was nature's will. I've always been a firm believer and dedicated follower of nature's will. Calli, you knew I was going to die when we transported the diamond to the Death Clan and you offered me a chance to be healed. I chose to follow nature's will instead of being tempted to live longer. I even donated my body to science, well, Maetha's science, and you know how that turned out. I remember one particular moment after I was healed. Maetha was speaking to someone outside my room. I think it was Crimson, but I'm not sure. It could have been any other female Bearer. But I heard her say, 'I was able to save the boy. She cares deeply for him.' The other female said, 'She must not know he's alive until it will best suit nature's will.' Well, tonight, I realized there's only Crimson's will and she's using you two."

I reach my hand forward and touch his arm. "Jonas, she's using you as well."

He fidgets, clearly affected by my touch. He chuckles nervously. "Well, when she finds out I betrayed her, I'll probably get Marketa's fate."

I want to tell him he'll be fine, but honestly, I don't know. Instead, I say, "Then let's make sure she doesn't find out."

Jonas moves back a step, breaking our contact. "You know that's not possible. I'm going to level with her the first chance I get, mainly because I want answers. I probably won't get them, but I'm still going to ask. I'm technically already dead. So, if she decides to reclaim my diamond—which by the way they didn't foresee me getting—then so be it."

Chris says, "I hope she'll decide she still needs you and your computer wizardry."

"She has Sarangerel now. I'm an old, clunky DOS computer next to her. I don't have much to offer anymore."

"That's not true, Jonas," Chris says. "You and Sarangerel make a great team. You both have strengths." Jonas's chin drops to his chest. Chris continues in a more serious tone. "I don't have any magic words to make you feel better other than I'm not mad at you for keeping the secret about my death. You probably kept quiet more for Calli's sake than mine, which only makes me respect you more. We've all kept secrets in the past. Secrets will continue to be kept. Hopefully our friendships can remain intact."

Jonas's Adam's apple bobs up and down, then he launches himself at Chris for a big brotherly hug. "Thank you, Chris!"

I let the two of them hug it out for a bit. Once they separate, I ask Chris, "So where exactly do we stand? We changed the future, first with you slamming your own diamond, and second with me shocking you back to life. Should we put the obsidian away to see what the outcome will be?" I stop short of revealing our plans in front of Jonas of going to the government. More secrets.

"Not yet." Chris shakes his head. "I don't have my thoughts under control."

"Here," Jonas digs in his pocket, then extends his hand to me. "Take these topazes. They're charged with Seer power."

I take the three stones and focus on one of them and look to the future of the Portland Elemental blast, hoping to see the images from my dream. Shapes and dull forms fly through my mind, but nothing discernible. The topaz drains after only a few minutes. I hand it back to Jonas. "That one was pretty weak."

"What? It's Imperial Topaz."

"Who charged it?"

"I did. What were you trying to look for?"

"The Portland blast."

"Sheez, I can't even see that with the full diamond's power. Try looking for something easier, like will you be alive tomorrow?"

I close my eyes, focus on the second topaz, and think about my future for the morning. I see myself eating breakfast with Chris, Maetha stands across the room. Yes, I'll be alive. I focus on my future for tomorrow evening. A scene opens where I'm in Chris's apartment in D.C. He's smiling at me, so I guess we'll both be alive tomorrow night. I open my eyes and sense the topaz in my hand is depleted.

"Here, this one is drained."

"Well, what's the verdict?"

"Chris and I will be alive tomorrow night and in D.C."

Jonas lets out a heavy sigh. "You're going back already? I thought you two were going to stay a couple days. You just got engaged. You should be celebrating."

Chris shrugs one shoulder. "Yeah, we should."

Jonas kicks the sand and tilts his head to the side. "Happy Birthday, Calli."

I reply, "Thanks, but I can't tell if you're being genuine or sarcastic."

"You should know by now I'm always genuinely sarcastic." Jonas grins and wiggles his dark brows.

I open my arms and give him a hug to which he hugs me back, sort of. I step away, noting his hesitation toward me. Maybe he worries what Chris will think of him being too affectionate. I stop short of overanalyzing his behavior.

"Jonas, thank you for telling us what you know. I hope everything works out for the best when you talk to Maetha and Crimson, but can you wait till we leave tomorrow? Actually, can you wait till later on tomorrow?"

"I'll do my best. I'm going to go and let you two enjoy what's left of the night."

We say our goodbyes and he walks away. I can't imagine Crimson taking his diamond for being honest. Marketa tried to kill me. That was different. Jonas is trying to help. But part of me doesn't know anymore. If Crimson and Maetha were willing to let Chris die, who knows what they might do to preserve their perception of nature's will.

Chris takes me by the hand. "Come on."

We walk back to my bungalow and go inside. I sit on the couch and lay my head back, closing my eyes. Images flash behind my eyelids of events that happened tonight. I don't want to think about what almost came to be. Then I remember the intense heat and bright blue-green light emanating from my hands. I lift my head and look at my engagement ring.

Chris strikes a match and lights the candles on the kitchen table, then he comes and sits next to me. "What are you thinking about?"

I twist the ring with my other hand and experience a twinge of pain on my finger. I wince and examine my finger a little closer. Sliding the ring over my knuckle, I see a red burn circling where the band was. Images of the vision I had invade my mind of not being able to remove the ring after the upcoming blast.

"What's the matter?" Chris asks, sitting down next to me.

My eyes meet Chris's. "When I healed you, my hands heated up and I guess the ring did as well."

"Are you burned?"

"I think so. It doesn't hurt that much. Once we put the obsidian away I'll heal it."

"I'm sorry you had to go through that, but I'm glad you were able to bring me back."

"I wonder how long they've known or at least believed you would die when you inserted your diamond?"

"I don't know. Perhaps it was right after I held onto the two prisms."

"I think the more likely answer is the time she spoke with us in the hotel before Anika's parents' funeral. Crimson said something that seemed odd, something about you possibly choosing to never have your diamond inserted. I wondered what she meant. Maybe she was worried I wouldn't be interested enough in Jonas."

"But why wouldn't they tell me I was going to die from the diamond insertion? What purpose did that serve?"

I think for a second and am hit with a sickening thought. "I bet they knew I wasn't interested in Jonas. If I inserted your diamond and you died, I might be so distraught that I'd find comfort with Jonas as a friend. They probably hoped that over time I'd warm up to him." I slide my ring back into position, "One thing's for sure, I won't ever figure one of them is going to come bail me or you out again. We're on our own."

"I don't think that's entirely accurate, Calli. Crimson would bail *you* out of a dangerous situation. Me, not so much."

I hear the dejection in his voice and can't help but feel angry at Crimson. How could she nurture him all these years, then turn her back on him? I say, "Those two got this train rolling and now they're going to have to hang on for the ride."

Chris makes a strange face and rubs his chest.

"Are you okay?"

"I don't know. My heart kind of… hurts."

I immediately try to heal him, but remember the obsidian is blocking me.

I take his hand and we head inside. I tuck the obsidian back into its case. Immediately my powers rush back into me. I hear Chris sigh, knowing that he felt the same thing.

"I'm okay," he says, taking some deep breaths. "I can heal myself. This is so incredible." He pauses and looks at the small box. "So much for our privacy."

"We can have it again, just in small batches until your heart heals." My eyes tear up and I walk over to him, putting my head against his chest, listening to his heartbeat. He wraps his arms around me and holds me tight. Tears spill down my cheeks.

He pulls me away and brushes them from my face. "We will figure this out. I promise." He rubs the top of my engagement ring. "We're in this together from now on."

The flickering flames of the candles glimmer on the facets of the center stone on my ring. I move my finger back and forth, up and down, to admire the beauty of the diamond. "You said the diamond is an heirloom. What is its history?"

"It belonged to royalty from India centuries ago. One of my ancestors was paid for their services with this diamond. Back then the diamond was bigger. When technology improved, the stone was cut with more facets to display its beauty. Several women have worn the diamond either in a necklace or ring through the centuries, including my grandmother who wore it in a broach. Before she died, she gave it to my mother who gave it to me. My mother said it's a lucky diamond—this coming from a woman who struggled to accept I had been altered by cosmic energy."

"What do you mean lucky?"

"I don't know. I checked it out and found it doesn't hold powers like the Sanguine Diamond, so I don't think it has anything of significance."

"Well, I was wearing it when I saved your life, so I guess it is a lucky diamond." I smile.

Sunlight streams through the curtains, shining on Chris's profile as he lies beside me on the bed. I barely remember falling asleep. As soon as we laid down, I wanted to stay awake forever and stare at him, but the day's stress and emotional toll won out. The only thing I remember is the steady sound of his beating heart, alive, and containing a diamond.

I study his features, admiring his perfect proportions and bone structure. My hand rests on his chest, the lucky diamond glimmering in the morning light.

"Good morning, handsome," I say in Chris's ear.

His eyes crack open a bit and he turns his head to look at me. A satisfied smile spreads on his face. "Morning."

"How do you feel?"

"Hungry."

"After everything you've been through you are only concerned with your empty stomach?" I tease.

"What can I say? In all seriousness, though, my heart is developing scar tissue. That's what I sensed last night when I healed it. Did yours do that?"

"No. But our situations are different."

"True. Well, let's get this day underway."

"Should we keep the obsidian open to prevent mind reads? I don't know if I can block my thoughts well enough yet."

"I think so. Once we're on the airplane, we can close it. If I need to heal my heart, I'll leave its presence. Let's go to the main house and find out when the boat is leaving . . . and get something to eat."

I get up and change into some fresh clothing and we leave the bungalow. I bring my bags with me so we can leave the island without delay.

Once inside the dining room of the main house, Jonas approaches us. "Are you guys all right?"

"Yes. Are you?"

"Still breathing." Jonas tries to sound optimistic though his smile seems forced. "Let me have a look at that ring in the daylight." He points to my hand and I raise it up. He doesn't touch me, but peers closely.

My eyes move between Jonas and Chris. As Jonas admires my ring, Chris watches Jonas, but not with jealousy this time. If I had to label the expression on Chris's face it would be appreciation.

Jonas says, "That's the prettiest color of green I've seen. It matches your eyes."

"Green?" I ask, angling my hand to get a better look at my ring. "It doesn't look green to me."

Chris reaches over and takes my hand. He leans in to look at the ring. While he does this, I look up at Jonas and find him staring at me. He smiles ever so slightly, then says, "I hope to see you again someday."

I don't know how to react. I'm remembering a time when Crimson told me neither Chris nor Jonas are good Diamond Bearer candidates. They were never pre-approved to become Bearers. I'm genuinely worried for Jonas.

Chris says, letting go of my hand, "Jonas, they're not going to punish you."

"I know. I'm not going to give them the chance."

Sarangerel enters the room and comes over and we quickly change the subject. After she offers up congratulations and well wishes, we dish up some breakfast.

Maetha remains at a distance due to the exposed obsidian. "How are you two today?" she asks.

"Good," I answer.

"I see you are wearing a beautiful ring. I assume you celebrated the evening's successful diamond insertion by becoming engaged to marry."

Chris says with a heavy sting in his tone, "I proposed to her before the insertion. We never had the opportunity to share our news with you last night."

Maetha takes a step closer, then steps backs. "You were wearing the ring when you healed Chris? May I see it?"

"Why?" I ask.

"I'm curious."

I'm not sure if I want to leave the obsidian's blocking power. She might detect our plans. I say, "Come take a look." I slide the ring off my finger and hold it out to her. She doesn't move, instead her eyes narrow as she looks at the ring.

She says, "Your finger is injured."

"Yes, just a mild burn from when my hands heated up during the healing." It's obvious she's not going to come see the ring, so I put it back on my finger.

"Chris and I are going back to D.C. today."

"Well, I hope you have an enjoyable time together. Please be cautious. You have obsidian in your future."

"Obviously," Chris picks up the chunk from the table and sets it down.

I ask her, "Are you searching my future with a topaz?"

"Yes."

Chris takes my hand. "We'll keep an eye on our own

futures."

"I'll let the boat captain know you'll be departing today. The boat will leave in one hour to head to Bermuda to pick up the Bearers we talked about yesterday."

"We'll be ready," Chris says.

We finish our breakfast and stop by my parents' bungalow on our way to the boat dock.

My father asks, "Calli, how much longer do you think we'll need to stay in hiding?"

"I'm not sure, Dad. That's not something I can see right now."

"She'll let us know as soon as she knows, Allan."

We give hugs and love you's, then Chris and I leave Maetha's island.

Once we're on the plane and in the air, Chris says, "I think you can put that away now." He points to the obsidian.

I put the piece inside the metal tin and close the lid. At once my powers rush back into my body. I notice Chris's breathing increases and his hold on the armrests tightens.

"Are you all right?"

"I will be," he says breathlessly.

I scan his heart and find he's healing scar tissue within the muscle. I say, "Your body seems to be rejecting the diamond."

"Only when I'm around obsidian. Otherwise I'm able to use the healing ability to stay in top form."

"I'm worried about you, Chris. This shouldn't be happening."

"Well, the queens were right when they figured my body was negatively affected by the power removing machine. I'll just need to be more vigilant about caring for my heart than other Bearers."

Queens? "I think it's because I had to push the diamond in the rest of the way."

"You did?"

"We haven't really talked about this and I'm not sure I want to relive that experience yet. I'd let you extract my memories, but that would weaken you and we can't have that."

"Once we're in a better position, I do want to see what happened."

"Okay."

"Let's talk wedding plans to keep our minds occupied."

"That's a good idea. I need to keep focused." I worry it might be difficult to think of anything else, but talking about our wedding gets me excited, and I find it's a welcome distraction.

Chapter Fifteen - The Bureau

We arrive in Washington D.C. and take a taxi to Chris's apartment building.

We walk inside the lobby with our bags and Chris presses the elevator up button. He says, "Once my dad's inheritance came through, I upgraded my living arrangements. I like this place much better than the other building." The doors open and we step inside. He presses the elevator button for floor five. "For tonight, how about we enjoy each other's company on what might be the last night of anonymity."

"That sounds good. What did you have in mind?" I tease.

"Why don't you read it and find out." He points to his temple and winks.

"I don't think I need to read your mind."

The elevator doors open, halting our conversation. We exit and walk down the hall a little way then stop at his door. He quickly unlocks and opens it for me.

"Go ahead," he says, motioning inside the room.

I walk in, set down my bag, and take in the surroundings. Chris has a fairly nice view of the city and an open spacious apartment furnished with decent furniture. Nothing too extravagant, though.

Chris comes up behind me grabs me around my waist, pulling my body to his in a hug. His mouth descends to the side of my neck where he applies gentle kisses. "I'm so happy to be with you right now." He kisses my ear.

"Me too." I turn around in his arms and wrap my arms around his neck. He kisses my forehead, then my mouth.

My whole body zings to life and I kiss him back.

Chris's phone rings.

He groans and pulls his head away from mine. "Why does this always happen?" He drops his arms, walks to his bag and removes his phone. He looks at the screen. "It's the office. They know I'm on vacation. You know what? I'm not going to answer it." He silences the ringer and sets the phone down. Then he comes back to me. "Let's order us some food and stay in tonight."

I snuggle closer to him and say, "I like the sound of that." I tilt my chin up and look him in the eye. He lowers his mouth to mine and cups the back of my head with his hands. His lips are warm and inviting yet caring. My stomach growls.

"Yeah, yeah," Chris says, and drops his hold again. "Food. What would you like?"

I grab the handle of my suitcase and walk toward the bathroom, "I'm going to change into something more comfortable. Order whatever you want."

"Clothing or food," he calls behind me.

I look over my shoulder and give him a sly smile. He smiles back—like I saw in the vision last night. I enter the bathroom and shut the door. I rummage through my suitcase for clothing options. I don't want to come across as suggestive, but I also kind of want a little attention tonight. I mean, I *am* his fiancé now.

A pair of yoga pants and cute T-shirt wins out. I don't mind the way the clothes hug my body, and I'm hoping Chris won't mind either. After removing my other shirt and untangling it from my necklace, I pull the clean shirt over my head. The tag itches my throat and I realize the shirt is backward. Just before twisting it around, I see the tag and notice for the first time there's a penguin on it.

My mind zips into flashback mode to when Chris first

told me about the penguin and the pebble. I smile brightly and look in the mirror. He planned to propose to me in that way for a long time. He set it up in my mind so I'd fall for all the cues. I don't even think there was a pebble on the sand at all. He probably had it in his pocket. Sleight of hand.

My smile falls as I remember how hard it was to bring him back after the diamond insertion. He almost didn't live. I fight back tears and find it hard to breathe. I keep seeing his vacant stare and bloody chest in my mind's eye. My heart pounds in my chest as I relive the scary memory and I use my healing power to suppress the way my body is reacting. Am I having an anxiety attack? Is this what post traumatic stress feels like?

I tell myself over and over that he's okay. He's a Diamond Bearer now. He can harness the greater healing power. I take a deep cleansing breath and let it out slowly. I don't know what will happen between us tonight, but I don't want to look to the future. Instead, I do my normal future safety scan to make sure I'll be alive tomorrow. I close my eyes and focus. The unmistakable black fog of obsidian halts my ability. We must be about to expose the obsidian again tonight.

Instead of being afraid, I get excited. If we are around obsidian, it means no one can interrupt us. No bi-locating or mind-reading or anything. Just him and I, alone. My body tingles at the thought. I rummage through my bag and pull out the obsidian container. I'll bring it out with me to show I want to be completely alone with him. Crimson is just going to have to look the other way. I kind of like this rebellious side of me.

I turn to leave the bathroom, then stop when I hear knocking, but not on the bathroom door. Someone is knocking on Chris's apartment door.

Chris? I speak to his mind.

It's Max Corvus. Stay hidden, Calli.

Max Corvus? Focusing my Hunter's hearing, I listen as Chris mutters a curse word before unlocking his door. Suddenly Chris's connection ends.

I was wrong. The obsidian in our future isn't from me—it's from Max.

I'm not affected yet, though. I wonder if I should call for Crimson? What would I tell her? I don't know if she'd help anyway.

I need topazes, and quick. I perform a mental inventory of which charged topaz I currently have and then panic. I don't have anything charged except for the Runner's topaz on my necklace and the pager topazes from Clara. I dig through my pants pocket that I just took off and remove the contents. I set the small container with Clara's pagers on the counter, followed with three depleted topaz. *Why haven't I recharged these?* I know I'm supposed to always keep topazes charged with Runner, Healer, and Mind-Control powers. At what point did I go lax on this? I grab the roll of medical tape from my bag and strap the three stones to my chest just below my collar bone. I take the pager topazes out of the container and strap them on as well.

I don't know if Chris has a Runner's topaz on his body or any other charged stones. Hopefully these stones will have enough time to collect some power. While scrambling, I listen to their conversation for any indication they might come into the room and find me.

Chris says a little louder than normal, "Well, hey, Max. How the heck are you?"

"Good, good. Alive. I tried to call you."

"Oh, sorry. I thought it was the office. Weren't you in Europe?"

"I was. I figured I'd drop by your place if you weren't going to answer your phone. Can I come in?"

"Who are your friends?" Chris asks.

"They're my bodyguards. They can wait out here in the hall, though. I think I'm fairly safe with you."

"Only fairly?"

I hear the door close. Chris says, "Do you want something to drink?"

"No."

"So, where have you been, Max?"

"All over the place."

"I see you're still wearing obsidian."

"Oh, this old thing. It's more of a good luck charm. I have much more effective protection now. I'm sure you've seen my posts on my blog."

"Not recently, no. Did you put something up within the last week?"

"No."

"So, how long have you been back here? Isn't there a warrant out for your arrest for the New Year's Eve bookstore shooting?"

"That's all cleared up. My friends at the Bureau fixed everything before they brought me home."

"What do you mean?"

"My blog posts found a buyer. They paid handsomely for my info. Part of my price was to get my name cleared. Another price was to help me set up a broadcasting base here and provide me with a team of helpers."

Chris says, "Sounds like you have it all figured out. Are you here to give me my cut?"

"Not quite. I have a question for you. Why did you just fly to Bermuda and back this weekend?"

How does Max know about that?

"Uh, I was on vacation."

"Doing what?"

"That's kind of personal, don't you think? And how did you know where I was?"

"Because my team monitors flight manifests for known Diamond people. Calli Courtnae just arrived on a private flight from Bermuda. When this was pointed out to me, I checked the full manifest and found your name too. It was a small flight, but you already know that. Surely you were aware she was on the plane too. Unless she was invisible. So, Chris, let me ask again. Why did you fly from Bermuda with Calli Courtnae?"

Chris doesn't answer.

I listen to my gut and open the bathroom door. My powers rush out of my body, leaving me vulnerable. I meet Chris's worried eyes and throw him a half smile.

Max steps back and raises both hands in front of his body. "Whoa! Chris! What's going on here?"

"She wants to go to the Feds tomorrow to discuss some stuff."

Max points at Chris and then at me. "You're taking her in tomorrow? What if she escapes tonight?"

I step forward. "I'm here at my own request, Max."

Max shakes his head slightly, blinks a few times, then whips out his phone and turns on the camera. "Is anyone else here?" He moves the phone around his body, scanning the room.

"No," I say. "You're not going to shoot me again are you?"

"Do I need to?" Max backs up to the door, opens it and says, "Guards! Seize them!"

I glance at Chris who looks like I feel. I'm second-guessing the idea of going to the government.

Chris steps back from the approaching guard. "Max, this isn't necessary. We're going in tomorrow."

Max pulls a gun from his jacket and aims it at Chris.

I extend both my wrists in front of me to show I'm not resisting. I turn to Chris and say, "Don't fight it. We'll just go to the Feds tonight.

A guard slaps a cuff on one of my hands, pulls it behind my body and grabs my other arm. I cooperate, knowing if I don't, I might be shot by some power-confusing substance.

Chris relaxes his stance and is cuffed at the same time as me.

Max leans toward Chris, "I know you probably don't need obsidian cuffs, but I'm not going to take a chance with anyone." Max looks at me and points to my necklace. "Remove her necklace," he orders the guard behind me.

Chris says, "Aren't you going to read us our rights? Or do you even have that authority?"

After the necklace is untied and taken off my neck, Max orders, "Let's go. Keep your guns at the ready."

We began walking as a group out into the hallway, toward the elevator. Max is positioned behind us, gun in hand, pointed at Chris. Both our guards have their guns pressed into our backs.

"You didn't answer my question, Max," Chris presses. "What are we being arrested for?"

"I'm not arresting you. I'm taking you in for questioning."

"Since when do you need cuffs and guns for that? I'm going to file a complaint against you. You'll lose your job."

"I hardly think so."

We stop at the elevator and wait for it to arrive.

Chris adds, "I'm going over your head and getting you fired."

The elevator car arrives and the doors open.

"Good luck with that, Harding." Max shoves Chris

into the empty elevator. Chris's guard stumbles to keep up. Max puts his hand up to stop my guard from directing me into the elevator. "We'll wait," Max says. He turns to Chris's guard. "Take him down and put him in your vehicle. If he tries anything, kill him. We'll be down in a minute."

Oh no! I check the taped-on topaz to see if they've absorbed any powers at all before I became disabled by obsidian. Nothing. They're empty.

"Yes sir," the thuggish brute says.

The elevator doors slide shut. Chris's anguished eyes are the last to disappear.

Max turns to me. "What happened to Marketa that night?"

"She's dead."

"*What?* Did you kill her?"

"No. But she tried to kill me."

"Who killed her?"

"How did you two meet?"

"Who killed her?"

"Max, did you know Marketa had a diamond in her body?"

"What? You're making that up. Why won't you tell me who killed her?"

"Tell me how you met her and I'll tell you what you want to know."

"You'll tell me soon enough. I have someone who can get the information out of you."

"You're not taking us to the government, are you."

He chuckles sadistically. "No, Calli, I'm not."

If only Brand was here. We would have known trouble was on its way. I'm really wishing we'd told someone—anyone—of our plans to involve the government. No one knows where we are or what's happening to us. My only hope is that Crimson realizes I'm incapacitated by obsidian. Then I remember Maetha saying our future held obsidian. They probably figure we're using it again and they aren't alarmed by our diamonds going dark.

Max moves closer to me. "You know, Calli, I saw you that day at General Harding's building. You and someone else were in the room. Then, somehow, they went invisible." He laughs a bit and begins walking a circle around me and my guard. "I've driven myself crazy over everything that happened that day. I know what I saw, but no one would believe me. Well, now the whole world is listening. They want to know what I know."

"Good for you."

"Yes. It is. You know, I'll tell you how I met Marketa. She recognized you in the video footage of the Tennessee robbery I posted on my blog. She contacted me and told me she was hired to be your protector at college. She fed me information about you and told me you'd come looking for me if I followed her instructions. She was right. Now it's your turn to tell me who killed her."

"Of course she was right, Max. She was working both sides. She made everything possible. She used you for her own agenda. I think you're still being used by someone else."

"Oh, and you would know."

"Yeah. Marketa was killed by another Diamond Bearer for being a traitor."

"So, Jonas Flemming killed her?"

"I didn't say that."

"Exactly how many of these diamonds are floating around?"

I shrug my shoulders.

He presses further. "Where's your invisible boyfriend, Brand Safferson? And where's Jonas? Is he in Bermuda?

Huh?"

I fire back at him. "Who set you up with the whole invisible bubble system to hide your building?"

He's clearly caught off guard. He steps back a little and scrunches his eyebrows. "I don't know what you're talking about."

"You know, Max, for being so scared of people with powers or diamonds, you seem to be oblivious to the danger you put yourself in when you side with Spellcasters."

"Spell-whaters?"

"Which makes me wonder what interest does a Spellcaster have with diamonds?"

Max wags his finger at me. "There wasn't any 'magic' involved with the perimeter. It was simply a drug that confuses people so they forget what they're looking for. Magic doesn't exist." He scoffs and grunts as if he's heard the most ridiculous thing in the world.

"Yet you believe diamonds can contain powers."

"That's different." He crosses his arms and looks up at the elevator arrows.

"Uh, okay." I roll my eyes. "Did Marketa have any friends helping her?"

He taps his foot. "Where's that blasted elevator?"

My wishful-thinking mind concocts a scenario of the elevator opening, revealing Chris with the guard's gun. In slow motion, he subdues Max and the other guard and sends them down in the elevator. Then we go back to Chris's apartment and enjoy the evening. Wouldn't that be great?

The elevator chime sounds, pulling me back to reality, then the doors open, revealing an empty space. No rescuer coming for me.

"Go." The guard behind me pushes me forward.

I imagine myself ramming my body into Max, then the guard, then running to . . . somewhere. I know better, though. I'd be shot in a heartbeat. I don't have Runners' reflexes if obsidian is present. Where is Max's obsidian anyway? I decide to probe in that direction.

The elevator doors close and we begin our descent.

I say, "I can't believe you're still relying on obsidian to mute my powers. You know we've found ways out around that."

"I'm aware. But, it still works in a pinch."

"Are you aware the Chinese developed a new material that works better than obsidian?"

"I heard something like that," he says.

"Interesting you only heard about it, but you were not given the same weapon from your Spellcaster."

The guard behind me says, "She doesn't shut up, does she."

I wiggle my wrists to see if I might be able to get out of the cuffs.

Max leans in close as we near the ground floor. "I know what you're trying to do and it's not going to work." He grabs my hands to stop me from moving them. I feel his fingers touch my engagement ring. "Well, well, what do we have here? Miss Diamond Girl is engaged? To whom?"

"Take off my cuffs and I'll tell you."

"Yeah, right."

The doors open to an empty foyer. No rescue team. *Why can't I get one of those unexpected rescues, like in the movies?* I'm the only one who can save myself now. The best way would be to not get shot, and keep Max moderately happy.

The guard grabs my upper arm and directs me though the foyer to the door. Through the windows I see a man standing outside a parked car, waiting. Max holds the building door open. I notice sweat beads on his forehead as

I walk by, his eyes dart this way and that.

He must be nervous, or scared. So am I.

The guard walks me to the back door of the car the driver has opened. To my right is another car identical to this one. I see Chris in the back seat. His head moves right and left, trying to get a better view of me around the driver. His lips are moving, but I can't read them.

"Get in," the guard orders.

I climb in, with difficulty because of my hands cuffed behind my back. The guard places his hand on my head and prevents me from hitting the door frame. I've never been arrested before, but I imagine this is what it would feel like. Max gets in the back seat from the other side and the guard takes the front passenger seat.

Max says to the guard, "Call base and tell them we're on our way with a diamond." Max pulls out a long knife with an obsidian blade from a side pocket on the outside of his leg. The blade is at least eight inches long. Judging from the size of the blade, I'd say this is why we lost our powers before getting the obsidian cuffs.

I say, looking at the blade, "My powers are already removed by the cuffs. More obsidian won't remove more powers."

"Oh, I think this will remove more powers." He makes slicing motions in the air indicating his intentions to cut out my diamond.

No! How did I let myself get into this situation? I need to think clearly. I need to keep my head on, literally. I calm myself and say, "But Max, if you touch my diamond, you will die."

He puts the blade right up to my neck, leans close to my face and says, "Not if you're dead first."

"Sir," the guard interrupts. "She wants to talk to you." He holds the phone toward Max.

Max moves away from me. My heart is beating so fast I feel like it's going to explode. I take a deep breath and try again to calm myself.

"Yes," Max says into the phone. Even though I don't have access to my Hunters hearing ability, I can still hear the voice simply because the volume it set so high.

"Do not kill her there. Do you hear me?" the female voice says with a strong accent, one like Amenemhet's.

"But we don't need her, just her heart."

"If you kill her, you'll bring on the wrath of the goddess. Besides, we need Calli for her knowledge. That prize is larger than the diamond or the goddess."

Max scrunches his eyes shut.

"Take her to the Bureau."

"Not base?" he asks.

"The Bureau. I'll send Bushman over to interrogate her. When we get what we need, you can do what you want."

"Copy that."

Max hands the phone to the guard in the front. "Call the other car and tell them we're heading to the Bureau, not base." Max then pulls a black cloth bag from a compartment between the front seats. He grasps the opening and says to me, "Can't have you seeing where we're going." Then he slips the bag over my head, blocking my vision.

I'm left wondering who the woman is and how she knows about Crimson? What knowledge in my head is she talking about? Is she part of Vorherrschaft? Or is she a Diamond Bearer? I thought we'd uncovered all the dissenters. Why is she referring to Crimson as a goddess?

I also think about what kind of methods the interrogator will use. What will happen to Chris? We need to get the obsidian cuffs off him soon so he can heal his heart.

I've got to get a grip. Presently, Chris and I are in Washington D.C. which is where we need to be to talk with the Disaster Planning people. That is the goal. Maybe this will still all work out in the end. However, no one knows what we plan to do. Jonas and Maetha knew we were headed to D.C., but that's all. Chris and I could be killed in a matter of minutes and no one would know any better.

My heart races beneath my ribs as terror freezes my lungs. I gasp for air. My wrists hurt from the tight cuffs and the unnatural angle of my arms. My hands burn hot. Why?

Max exclaims, "What's happening? Where's that light coming from?"

"What is it sir?" I hear the guard's voice.

"I don't know!" Max yells. "What are you doing, Calli?"

I can't see anything because of the black bag, but my hands feel like they're on fire.

"What's in your hand?" Max demands.

"Nothing," I say.

"Show me."

"I can't. They're cuffed."

"Should I pull over, sir?" the driver asks with a shaky voice.

"No. Keep driving." Max grabs my shoulders and pulls my body forward.

I remember how I felt when I shocked Chris's heart, how my hands burned. Technically, I shouldn't be able to use any powers with the obsidian cuffs and with Max's huge blade in the vicinity. Yet, clearly something is happening. Internally, I feel like a pressure gauge is climbing toward the red zone of the dial. I can visualize in my mind the electricity in my body, along with Max's because he still has a hold of my shoulders. Somehow the healing power of the Sanguine Diamond has activated, allowing me to feel him. I direct my building energy toward Max into one big jolt and feel a zapping pain on my ring finger. I hear a strange yelping and then the weight of what I can only assume is Max falls on my lap.

"Sir! Sir, are you all right?" The guard cries out. "What did you do to him?"

I don't know. My hands begin to cool down.

The car swerves left and right then comes to a halt. The driver's door opens.

"What are you doing?" the guard shouts.

Car horns blare as they speed by. The driver says, "No one said she could electrocute people. I'm outta here."

I hear commotion and movement in the front of the car. In the meantime, I wiggle my legs and knees, trying to get Max off them. It sounds like the guard moved to the driver seat. I hear the car door slam shut. He mutters to himself unintelligibly.

My body experiences an obvious energy drain like what happened after I shocked Chris's heart. I need to get out of these cuffs somehow. I ask the guard, "Hey, is Max dead?"

The guard doesn't answer. He puts the car in gear and begins driving. More car horns are heard.

"I won't hurt you, sir, if you'll take the bag off my head." I start to feel dizzy.

No answer. My mind begins to spin kind of like when Brand pulls me back when he repeats. This isn't quite the same whirling sensation, however. No, this is the "I'm about to pass out" feeling. "If Max is still alive, he won't be for long. He probably can't breathe at his present angle. You should help him."

Nothing.

I wrack my brain for something to say that will get the

guard to listen. The phone rings in the front seat.

"What?" the guard frantically asks.

"What happened to Roizen?" The voice on the other end fills the car. The guard must have hit the speakerphone button.

"He bailed after she electrocuted Max!"

"What?"

"You heard me. Why didn't you stop to help?"

"Too much traffic."

I think to myself how it must have looked to have the interior of the car filled with the blue-green light accompanied with the bolt of electricity. No way would the other car stop after seeing that. I wonder if Chris saw it. He'd recognize the light from when we healed my shoulder, but I imagine he'd also be confused, wondering how I got away from obsidian so I could use the power. Then again, maybe Chris has a black bag over his head too.

The guard responds to the other car, "Are you watching for the goddess?"

What did he say? Hope builds in my chest at the possibility Crimson's nearby. Maybe she's been watching the whole time. Then dark clouds of anger dampen my spirit. She wasn't going to help save Chris on the beach. She expected him to die. I have no reason to believe she would help him now either, other than to retrieve the diamond from him so it doesn't fall into the wrong hands.

"We haven't seen her or the other invisible guy."

"Copy that. I'm almost there." The guard ends the call. He doesn't say anything to me, not that I expected him to.

This situation is all my fault. I suggested to Chris we go to the government. I led us into this mess. I convinced him against his better judgment and now he could die. Even if they don't kill him outright, if they keep him in the obsidian cuffs for too long, his heart will.

Why did I think nothing bad would happen to us? Why was I so naïve as to think we'd be fine? Have I let this power of being an indestructible Diamond Bearer go to my head? I can be controlled and stopped. I can be killed all too easily especially if I'm unconscious, which I'm about to be. No, I let my anger and emotions take control. I was so upset over Chris nearly dying and no help offered that I acted irrationally. And I dragged him into my irrationality.

How many times have I heard Maetha or Crimson tell us we need to control our anger and not let it control us? All it took was the possibility of the incredibly huge loss of someone I dearly love to get me to act against Crimson's will—something I didn't ever see myself doing.

The driver sharply turns the car right and I fall against the door, unable to hold my body upright any longer. As images swirl through my mind, my hearing muffles like I'm underwater. The last thing I think about is Chris on one knee, asking me to be his better half.

I'm so sorry, Chris.

Thank You!

Thanks for reading my books! I hope you'll take the time to leave a review on Amazon or Barnes&Noble or where you purchased *The Diamond Bearers' Rising*. I'd really appreciate it.

Also, drop on over to my website and let me know what you thought of the series by using the Contact Me form. While you're visiting my site, sign up for my newsletter to be kept updated on the progress of Book 7 in The Unaltered series, and to receive exclusive freebies and news. Thanks again for reading my books. --Lorena

Books by Lorena Angell

The Unaltered Series

A Diamond in My Pocket, Book 1
A Diamond in My Heart, Book 2
The Diamond of Freedom, Book 3
The Diamond Bearers' Destiny, Book 4
The Diamond Bearer's Secret, Book 5
The Diamond Bearers' Rising, Book 6
Books 7-10 coming soon!

The Lost Crown Series

Royal Refugee
Royal Resistance
Royal Redemption

ABOUT THE AUTHOR

Lorena Angell is the internationally bestselling author of the YA fantasy series, *The Unaltered.* Inspired by an interview from J.K. Rowling, Lorena began to write and published her first book in 2011. Since then, she's earned over 4,200 reviews (average of 4.5 stars), has been a #1 bestseller in over 11 countries and wants nothing more than to write more books for her readers.

Connect with Lorena Angell at:

www.LorenaAngell.com

Twitter: @LorenaAngell1

Facebook: The Unaltered Diamond Series

Instagram: the.unaltered.series

Made in the USA
Monee, IL
04 August 2020

37603039R00177